SUNNYSIDE

SUNNYSIDE

DONNA CANTOR

AVON BOOKS NEW YORK

This is a work of fiction. Names, characters, places and incidents either are the product of the author's imagination or are used fictitiously. Any resemblance to actual events, locales, organizations, or persons, living or dead, is entirely coincidental and beyond the intent of either the author or the publisher.

AVON BOOKS, INC.
1350 Avenue of the Americas
New York, New York 10019

Copyright © 1999 by Donna Cantor
Interior design by Kellan Peck
Published by arrangement with the author
Visit our website at **http://www.AvonBooks.com**
ISBN: 0-380-79571-X

Library of Congress Cataloging in Publication Data:
Cantor, Donna.
    Sunnyside / Donna Cantor.
    p.   cm.
    I. Title.
PS3553.A5474S85   1999   98-45224
813'.54—dc21   CIP

First Avon Books Trade Paperback Printing: February 1999

AVON TRADEMARK REG. U.S. PAT. OFF. AND IN OTHER COUNTRIES, MARCA REGISTRADA, HECHO EN U.S.A.

Printed in the U.S.A.

OPM   10 9 8 7 6 5 4 3 2 1

For Jeff who has always backed me up,
both on the A-drive and throughout life's twists and turns.
And for Michael, Jason, and Nicole with love.

Acknowledgments

I would like to thank Lucia Macro, Yedida Soloff, Christine Zika, and Kate Hengerer for their time, advice, and suggestions. I wish there were a way to thank the late Sue Bartczak for her patience and encouragement. *You are not forgotten.*

SUNNYSIDE

One

Agnes Conlin is dead and I can't believe it. I mean hey, these things do happen, after all she was seventy-nine years old and people don't live forever. Still, I just never thought of her as an old lady. But here she is, body arranged just so in the casket, rosary dripping through those broad fingers like a tutti frutti Italian ice.

Her daughter, Trudy Emmet, had her dressed in this thick, red and black checked woolen suit. Like a jerk I'm looking at her and thinking, Poor Mrs. Conlin, she's going to sweat plenty in that outfit.

I've seen my neighbor thousands of times but she never looked as captivating as she does tonight. Her hair has been swept back and swirled high like orange cotton candy. Her face, that nice crinkly, smiley face, has actually discovered a cool elegance. I'm talking elegance bordering on sophistication. Gone is the scratchy cigarette laugh. Gone is the friendly shove in the small of my unsuspecting back. And more than likely she's not on her way to bingo.

I am an amateur at these wakes, an observer more than a participant, not belonging to the Catholic Church, or any other church for that matter. I can remember my mother informing me at the age of five that our family was Jewish. At the time it meant I was forbidden to say "cross my heart and hope to die." But Sunday school dropout and all, a pinch of religious instruction must have stuck with me because I do remember not to kneel when viewing Mrs. Conlin. It's on this minor technicality going back a few thousand years, something like that. So I stroll over, give her my best serious, soulful look, and make my way back to the blue velvet folding chairs where most of the people from our building and surrounding neighborhood are gathered to pay their respects.

"Oh yeah. I'm really gonna miss her," Rose Petruzzi says in an exaggerated hush in order to maintain proper decorum in the Edward X. Healy Funeral Parlor. "Always a smile she had. Never bothered nobody. And always good for a laugh," she tells Trudy.

"You know, my mother lived with us for twenty-two years," Trudy says, "since Tommy was seven. I don't know what the hell I'm gonna do without her. She was a pisser, let me tell you. One time, Rose, I swear to you she put all of Tommy's drawers in a paper bag and made him bring 'em down to the incinerator room. Told him it was garbage. 'Take it out for Nana Agnes,' she says to him. Well, Tommy, maybe he was eight at the time. He knows nothing. He starts dumping the stuff out. He sees his drawers drop out of the bag, runs up the stairs and starts hollering, 'Nana, what's the matter with you? Those are my drawers.' My mother tells him, 'They were thrown all over the floor. It's gotta be garbage!' Well, this kid went to school that day with no drawers on underneath. Meanwhile, I had to run down to Woolworth's and buy him seven new pair. God, I'm gonna miss her."

Now, I'm happy to say Tommy doesn't walk into the funeral parlor at this point. I know I wouldn't want people staring at my backside at a time like this.

The first hour passes quickly. The first shift of mourners trickle out the door. My mother had already walked back to our building with some neighbors. My father is working nights now, driving for a neighborhood car service. So these days he is completely exempt from respects paying. Mom had tried her best to get me to go home with her, but my friends and I had decided to have a few drinks right next door at Buckley's. Hey, a night out is a night out, right?

Then Tommy walks in and steals some of the attention away from the corpse. He's dressed in a black Italian cut suit, a white-on-white fitted shirt, and a black and white paisley tie anchored with a gold tie bar. Had my mother stayed around, she would have whispered "Yankee doodle dandy" in my ear. He looks way too good for a time like this, but he seems unaware of the glances directed toward him. He does a quick kneel and cross, strokes his grandmother's hair, mumbles something and heads toward his mother. He apologizes for being late and gives her a kiss and squeeze.

"Let me ask you something," she says to him. "Why didn't you come down in uniform? Nana always thought how handsome you look dressed as a police officer."

"Give me a break, huh? Nana wouldn't have cared if I showed up naked. Anyhow, I'm plainclothes these days, remember?" This remark brings the drawers story back up again. And everyone starts laughing, Tommy especially.

"So, where's my little brother at?" he murmurs to Trudy when the laughter dies down.

"Matty's out helping Raymond with the van. He'll be here in a few minutes."

"My ass."

"Watch your mouth. Nana not three feet away from you. Dead. God rest her soul." Trudy crosses herself again.

"She said worse in her day. And where the hell is Teresa Ann and that Wall Street husband of hers? She couldn't make the twenty minute drive from Manhattan to be with you tonight? She better be at the mass, that's all I gotta say."

"Cut it out," he's told. He cuts it out but his lips pull into a one-cornered frown. I hadn't seen him for ages, not since high school, and that was nearly ten years ago. He had always been real easy on the eyes. Tall, at least six-two, thin. Straight dark brown hair pushed back off his face. And hidden behind those gray-tinted wire frames are deep-set navy-blue eyes that look thoughtful but reveal nothing. His nose is long, too long, actually, but at least it angles up optimistically at the tip. And his mouth appears to be able to twist into any shape at a given moment.

Look at me, drooling in the Edward X. Healy Funeral Parlor. Oh Mrs. Conlin, forgive me. I've been in a slump for a while and not just in the guy department. My whole life is on ice, one frozen monotony waiting impatiently for the spring thaw. I'm still living at home. I can do my job on automatic pilot. I shouldn't be complaining, though. At least I have my health.

We start our saunter out of Healy's at close to eleven o'clock. I go back to whisper one last goodbye to Mrs. Conlin, and then wouldn't you know it, tears start running down my cheeks. I can't help it. I'm sobbing a little, too. I'm sobbing a lot. I remember the crooked waddle I'll never see again, her thousand decibel shout from the upstairs window, the six boxes of Girl Scout cookies she ordered one year just to put me over the top for the Hasbro Snowcone Maker. And another door to my childhood slams shut forever. Gone.

Lucky for me Ellen Clabber and Rose Petruzzi's daughter, Louise, my two best girlfriends, are outside already. I'd never hear the end of this, crying for the dead at one of these wakes.

"You knew my grandmother well, did you?"

It's Tommy's voice behind me. I cannot run and hide, although it is tempting.

"It's me, Joanna Barron from the building, 4B." That's right, be cool. Give only name and apartment number in case he's taking prisoners. I'm still all damp and teary. Embarrassing.

He produces a pressed white handkerchief from his breast pocket. I thought everyone had switched to tissues twenty years ago.

"Yeah, you looked real familiar. I just couldn't place the face. Been a long time, huh? You still live—yeah I guess you do," he answers his own question. "I moved to Woodhaven after I got on the force. Come on," he puts a large, steady hand on my still trembling shoulder. "We're heading over to Buckley's for a few, catch up on old times. Do you some good."

Smooth. This one's an operator. "I'm sorry for making such a scene. You must feel bad enough without me adding to it. I really should learn to control myself better."

"No, you don't want to do that. That's the one thing you don't want to do. Then you'd be just like everyone else here, deader than the deceased. Take it from me."

"I see." I dry my tears and regain some composure. "Are you always so free with your advice?" What nerve. Who was he, telling me how to act?

"I see Miss Barron of 4B has a bit of a temper there. That's all right. I love a good fight. Anyways, I didn't mean no offense. I save up my advice for real special occasions. You know, like weddings and funerals."

I dab my eyes for what I hope is one last time. Okay, maybe he's just trying to be nice. "Your grandmother was so caring and kind, and she was wickedly funny. I really liked her a lot. I can't believe she's gone."

"Gone? Her? You gotta be kidding. She's living her second life in my head. I've told her to bug off at least three times today. Excuse me a sec. Hang tight. I'll be right back."

He goes to kiss his mother goodbye, and we walk together out Healy's and into Buckley's, barely stepping out onto Queens Boulevard.

At a wobbly, narrow table sits Ellen, her occasional live-in Ralph, Louise and her husband Hector, me, Tommy, and his little brother Matty. *He* had the good sense to show up one minute before closing.

Buckley's is one of those neighborhood bars that are supposedly near extinction. It is dark, thank goodness, because I can picture my two brown eyes, red-rimmed from crying, mascara smudged attractively across my cheeks. All eight of us are seated at a table intended for six. Matty, a short, stocky, pit bull of a man, immediately

starts flirting with the waitress. She calls him Matty
honey. Apparently he is a regular here.

In the back of my head I hear my mother chiming in,
"Of course, Joanna. Those people all drink. You know
that." Go to sleep, Mom. You have work tomorrow. Everyone's ordering scotch, except for Matty, who requests
a Heineken. I hate scotch. I hate beer. The pressure is
on. What do I want? What do I want? "A strawberry
daiquiri, please."

My girlfriends are laughing. The men just smile. The
waitress, Patti, a girl of twenty-one with canary yellow
hair, hot pink lips, black boots over white leggings, is my
Beverage Adviser. "Hon, we can make it for you but it
won't be frozen. We don't—"

"It's okay. That's how I like them."

Ellen, in her usual crass way, says, "You think you're
in the fucking Bahamas or what? Sunnyside, Jo. Queens
Boulevard." Thank you, Ellen. She's never one to let po-
liteness get in the way of her true feelings. Profanity still
turns my cheeks red and from time to time I get a twenty-
year-old aftertaste of Ivory soap.

The conversation turns to neighborhood gossip and
catch-up. Ellen works the register in the drugstore off Fortieth Street. Her older and married boyfriend Ralph works
for the telephone company. He's a dark, paunchy man,
reserved compared to Ellen. Ellen's voice, although not
exceedingly loud, can carry. It's called presence, I think.
She has loads of presence, built low to the ground on a
wide frame, a 40DD who one time, it must have been in
the ninth grade, dragged her older brother Gerald by the
feet down the hall and into the incinerator room for some
stupid reason. I remember now. He accidentally chipped
her bowling ball when his baseball bat struck it instead
of the mouse he was trying to pulverize. I once told Ralph
this story, let him know what he's up against. He promised me he'd do his best to stay away from any of her
sporting equipment.

Louise and Hector, Ellen and Ralph, all live now in
Rose Petruzzi's old four-family house downaways on

Thirty-ninth Street. Hector installs windows and Louise does accounts payable for C.J.'s Auto Body, right next door to her house. Hector works for cash off the books. Louise works for health benefits. She says together they have one great job.

Matty, I see almost every day. He drives a delivery van for Schwab's, the uniform manufacturer where my mom works, half a block from our building. Matty is always in and out of our lobby, a toothpick jammed in his mouth. He still lives at home, much to his regret and his mother's relief.

"How's that fancy office job of yours going?" Ellen addresses not me but the entire table and all of Buckley's with good-natured sarcasm. "I'm only sorry I didn't go to LaGuardia College and learn word processing so I could make a fortune in Manhattan in what's the name of that advertising place?"

"Reeves and Barnett. And it's a market research agency, not an advertising agency. And I'm making such a fortune I still can't afford to move out." I could afford a place with a roommate, but my friends are already spoken for. A stranger? I have reservations. A stranger might butt in more than Mom. A stranger might outsnore the TV louder than Dad. Still, I keep searching the classifieds.

A second round of drinks arrives. Hector and Louise's cigarette stubs form ash mountains in the too small ashtray.

"It still cracks me up, you being a cop, Tommy," Hector says. "Man, of all people, I never would have expected you to end up on the right side of the law. Not in a million. You and me were always into trouble. Trouble in school, trouble on the block. Them were the days."

"Yeah, my times on the street with you gave me a lot of experience with the criminal element," he says with a grin. "Don't you find it funny that you're installing windows for a living? We sure as shit broke enough of them."

Hector laughs.

"Why don't you come by no more?" Louise asks him. "You haven't stopped by in months. And listen you, hos-

pital or no hospital, don't you go thinking we ever for-
gave you for missing our wedding."

"What can I say? I'm working nights, weekends. Same
as always."

"You? All work and no play?" Ellen asks.

"No comment."

"Anyone serious?" she persists.

"My work is the serious. The rest better be fun in
the sun."

Two fruity drinks and I'm numb to the legs. Our
group looks like a meeting of Penguins Anonymous,
dressed as we are in black and white, standard wake attire. The walls in Buckley's are paneled a dull, dark
brown. The only two spots of vivid color come from my
glass and the waitress's lipstick.

Tommy stands up after a while and insists on paying
the tab. Matty, who abandoned our table two Heinekens
ago, sits with Barmaid Patti, bar stool to bar stool, oblivi-
ous to his surroundings. Tommy breaks him out of his
reverie with a friendly goodbye jab.

Matty smirks. "Hey Tommy, you doing any buy-busts
in the 'hood any time soon? Wish you'd give me some
warning when you're going undercover, huh bro? Man, I
don't want to be locked up. Especially by you. You'll be
tucking me in at Rikers."

The muscles in Tommy's jaw tighten and the dark line
of his brows sink behind the wire frames like the horizon
slipping behind gray clouds. "Why don't you just shut
up for once in your life?" are his parting words.

I start walking down the block with my friends, and
Tommy says, "Wait. I'll drive you. My car's right across
the street."

Ellen gives me a shove. "Go for it!"

I'd like to believe that nobody heard this.

Tommy stretches, rubs his eyes beneath his glasses.
Somewhere his face has lost its glossy coating of playful
cool. The car starts after some hesitation. It's a blue Celica
GT with a standard transmission. Manual dexterity. I'm

always impressed with any kind of fine motor coordination.

It is a soggy night, warmer than usual for March. The stores on Queens Boulevard are all closed and gated. The elevated tracks of the number 7 IRT loom above us, a metal and concrete brontosaurus that connects Flushing to Manhattan. We turn down Thirty-ninth Street, passing rows of six-story brown brick apartment buildings. Ugly, run-down piles of dirt, bricks, and soot-encrusted windows. But maybe I'm being a bit harsh. After all, it's not a slum. Don't go feeling sorry for me. I do not live in a slum. There are no burnt-out buildings here, no drug addicts hanging out at the corner, nothing like that.

What do we have? The usual assortment of stores. Let's see, we have plenty of fast food, a supermarket, check-cashing place, liquor store, candy store, bar, Laundromat, pharmacy, five and dime, bank, Argentine bakery, OTB, Korean restaurant, Greek grocery, that topless place, to name just a few. I mean if someone scrubbed it down some with a wire brush this could be Main Street U.S.A.

Double-wide strollers bumping down pockmarked sidewalks. Groups of kids playing freeze tag. Old men huddled together on street corners, fighting the old wars over and over again. The Green Line bus doing its slalom around the double-parked cars on Queens Boulevard. Families of pigeons cooing from above the covering of the elevated tracks. The twist and clank of quarters being fed to a hungry parking meter. Parents shouting to kids from dusty windowsills. Those are the sights and sounds of my home. And smells? Sabaret hot dogs and grilled beef on sticks. The scent of vinyl and plastic rushing out from open factory doors. Pizza. Bus exhaust. Home.

Over on Thirty-ninth Street warehouses and factories rise up from the sidewalks. Sunnyside ventures out to meet its ambitious friend, Long Island City, which offers storage, light manufacturing, residential and office space before a winking Manhattan skyline. Behind us is Sunnyside proper. The apartment buildings are prettier here, cleaner. They are living their second lives happily as co-ops. Two-family row houses tag along the co-ops like little kids.

My building is on Fortieth Street in one of those dingy, brown, six-story rent-stabilized piles of brick and soot. From my bedroom window, if I stick my head out far enough west, I can see the two gray sisters, the Chrysler Building and the Empire State Building. See, I have a view.

"Come on, I'll take you up. It's late."

"No," I say. "It's not necessary." I'm independent. But he's out of the car already, the blue Celica double-parked. We ride up on the elevator. After two daiquiris that oily, metallic smell sickens me. That's not all. Roz Lefkowitz is sautéing garlic in 4E. Garlic at one A.M. Go figure people.

"Thanks for coming down tonight. It was real nice seeing you again." He leans over to kiss my cheek, but he doesn't stop there. His mouth leaves a trail of soft, tiny kisses across my face to my lips and I'm not pushing him away. I can't believe I'm making out in the hallway like a thirteen-year-old. And my heart is banging away inside me. Then he stops and holds me close for an extra long minute.

"Tommy, what are we doing?"

He looks serious for a second but he brightens immediately when he sees me take notice. "Just wanted a taste of your daiquiri, Sunshine. Not bad. Come here again." His easy charm makes a quick return.

"No, I don't think so." I yank myself away from him.

"Ah come on, don't you be getting that fiery look again. You really can't shoot me for trying."

I fumble around my pocketbook for the key and he takes my hand. "Tell you what I'm gonna do. Because I'm such a great guy, I'm willing to overlook that quick temper of yours. And I'm willing to call you, if that meets with your approval."

I'm smiling now, grinning like the village idiot, probably. "Yes, I can't see any harm in a phone call." I try to sound casual but fail, naturally, because I want him to call me. I want to be held again, close to that hard chest. We'll have fun in the sun. That's all the man wants. Fun in the sun. I want more than fun in the sun. I want someone to be there when it's cloudy too. I know for sure he's going to be nothing but trouble, but call, call.

I sleep a useless five hours until my alarm sounds at seven-thirty. I awake in a room that had been furnished when I was nine, half in Mediterranean and half in white French provincial. My father had once put in a three year stint as a furniture salesman. He got a good price on it too, since they were leftover floor samples. According to last Sunday's Home Design section of the *New York Times*, eclectic is all the rage these days.

The only major change since childhood is the vacancy in the twin bed next to mine, my older sister Arlene's bed. She moved up to a queen when she married Gary Sussman, CPA, three years ago.

In her own self-absorbed way, Arlene actually did me quite a favor, took all the pressure off. She graduated from Binghamton with a B.S. in accounting and the coveted MRS from Gary. All she has to do now is produce an adorable grandchild and my mother is assured a box seat in Jewish heaven.

"She married a pro-fes-sion-al," my mother tells me from time to time. "Your sister is a smart girl, and you can be just as smart, Joanna. Aim high like Arlene. Try to improve yourself. And whatever you do, don't follow in my footsteps."

Eight o'clock. If I'm out the door in twenty minutes I can still make work by nine. I bang on the bathroom door.

"Daddy, I'm late."

"I just got home. I'll be out in a minute." I wait for the flush, the drizzle of water and the howl of the pipes as the air rushes back in them.

"How was work?" I ask on my way in.

"Good. I hear they're electing me for president of Rainbow Cars. You better get moving. You're running late. Your mother left early today. Want some coffee?"

"No time."

"You got a new suit on? I like it. Good color for you."
This pleases me. Daddy had once worked for a textile
manufacturer. The man knows fabric. I'm wearing a peach
cotton blend with a white lacy blouse. I think the peach
color makes my brown eyes look more tawny and my
hair more auburn and less chestnut. Other than its ordinary color, I like my hair. It's past my shoulders and
curly. It can be air-dried. In my twenty-seven years I've
never had to develop blow-drying skills.

It does sound a trifle conceited to describe oneself as
decent looking, but I am decent looking. Not stunning,
decent. I'm five-five, thin, fairly flat chested, a B with
room to spare. I have one of those heart-shaped faces that
flashes girl-next-door rather than exotic, alluring beauty.
I want to return as an exotic, alluring beauty. You can
keep the Ivory girl. As far as I can see, guys only take
her on fishing trips.

My father gulps down his last cup of instant before a
few hours of morning television and the resulting sleep
on the sofa. Our TV has replaced my mother's chatty com-
panionship during the work week. It's not until Saturday
that they have to communicate at all. It's always a familiar
refrain. "Sol, do me a favor. My sister Hannah needs . . .
Sol, can you take my sister Ruthie to Dr. Kappel?"

My father works car service five nights and chauffeurs
his sisters-in-law two afternoons. And he cannot deny my
mother because he knows she deserved better than this.
She was halfway through her bachelor's in English when
she met my dad.

"He wasn't bald then," she tells me. "He had a nice
head of blond curly hair. Ringlets like yours but blond.
You should have seen him, Joanna, when he was in the
Army. Oh, your daddy was a dreamboat. During his tour
right after Korea I quit school and got a job sewing in
Schwab's Uniform. It was only temporary and we needed
money to set up an apartment. When Daddy got back I
was supposed to finish my degree and teach. I'm a born
teacher. You know that, Joanna. Well, your father was not

trained for anything in particular but he had a nice way about him. He started in a men's shoe store but the salary was peanuts. Not enough for the rent so I kept my job at Schwab's. What else could I do? I didn't know office work because my high school diploma was Academic not Commercial. It was lucky for me I took the six week Singer Sewing course one summer. Never did I dream that from that six week course I'd be sewing for thirty-two years. Let this be a lesson to you. Don't get me wrong. Your father is a wonderful man."

That's enough of Sol and May Barron. Dad's snoring over one of those Good Morning shows and I'm out the door, as punctual as the telephone bill.

Two

The IRT Flushing line hauls me to and from Reeves and Barnett, located at Forty-second and Madison, in about twenty minutes, no kidding. If there is any one saving grace about living on the Long Island City–Sunnyside border it's that I can be in and out of midtown in incredible time. For this reason alone some of our seedy, old apartment buildings are being co-oped and bought by attaché-carrying junior executives who reason that an easy commute is not only meant for poor slobs. Respectable eighty-thousand-a-year MBAs want a short hop into Manhattan too. 'Tis unfortunate, though, that they have to inhabit the same cramped space as working-class third generation Irish, Italians, Germans, and first generation Koreans, Indians, Turks, and Colombians. I'm sure they cannot find a decent four-star restaurant for miles. Pity. Do I lack proper respect for these young successful managers? Quite all right. They don't exactly look up to us secretarial types either.

Reeves and Barnett is such a pleasant change from dull, dingy home. Yes, yes, it does sound trivial, but I'm in love with the surroundings. I love the bouncy, mauve carpet under my feet, the bright fluorescents beaming overhead, and the streakless partitions that compartmentalize us by our function and station in the hierarchy.

Clerks, secretaries, research assistants, project leaders, assistant V.P.'s, vice presidents, head honchos. At Reeves and Barnett everyone knows his place and his worth. No delusions of grandeur are tolerated or encouraged by either Ms. Claudia Reeves or by Ms. Dahlia Barnett.

Rumor has it these two middle-aged lesbians began their agency twenty-two years ago by swiping one little old Rolodex from the research department of Ogilvy & Mather. But this is strictly hearsay. Either way, they now employ 120 people and contract work out to seven other agencies as well. Let's be nice and give them the benefit of the doubt.

I sit in a Plexiglas cubicle at the foot of Ms. Dahlia Barnett's office. I handle correspondence only—no field reports, no bids, no questionnaires. I screen Ms. Dahlia Barnett's calls. I serve coffee to Ms. Dahlia Barnett. I am paid to absorb and regurgitate the philosophies of this one person, my boss. It has taught me something invaluable about myself, and I am forever grateful to this firm.

I have learned the meaning of the word ambivalence. One day Dahlia said, "Joanna, your ambivalence is showing." Look, at least I was smart enough not to check my slip, but as soon as she walked out I just had to check the dictionary, couldn't make this one out in context. Well, she was right. I am both attracted to and repelled by the field of marketing. I have just a lukewarm response to product, price, positioning, and that fourth forgotten P that Ms. Barnett tries to instill in me every day. Was it prudence, promotion, or patience? Whatever. As my time in the firm increases I find myself beginning to feign a tiny interest in the whims and buying habits of the American public by demographics.

No, I do not want to go to night school for ten years to help R.J. Reynolds-Nabisco capture the critical one percent share of market necessary to launch a new brand of cigarettes.

On second thought, maybe you shouldn't loan me the textbooks, Ms. Barnett. Here I always thought my family was middle class. You've shown me we're not all that high up on the pyramid. We're lower-lower middle class, or is it upper-upper working class? I forget. All I know is we lower types are too busy meeting our basic needs to self-actualize. Does that make us inferior? According to the books, we're lower life-forms, soulless little amoeba just waiting around for the right product to come on the market so we can evolve into a more sophisticated lifeform.

I do care a little about launching a campaign, but I do not care about Procter and Gamble's remarkable influence on consumer marketing in the twentieth century. Keep your green books, your red books, your database of industry contacts. I am more content working my amateur ego massage, my organization and human relations skills on this well-dressed gay workaholic. I do not want that MBA just yet, Ms. Barnett. I don't know what it is I want just yet and it irks me that at the age of twenty-seven I still don't know what to do with my life. There are four-year-olds out there who know they want to be teachers or doctors or mail carriers. I envy them. They have goals.

Another saving grace about Reeves and Barnett is Vivien Oliver, my friend and mentor. Vivien is from Guyana. Vivien is a he. Vivien has the gentlest voice and speaks with the most proper of accents. His face is the color of wet Rockaway shore.

Vivien is in his early forties, bearded, with a soldier's posture. He has a wife and two young sons. He tells me he has lived in New York for five years now. But when he dreams, he is always in Guyana. Each night we all travel back with him to Guyana—Dahlia and me—his neighbors, his children's friends. Vivien used to have my job. She once admitted to me that he was hired on the basis of his accent. After all, he sounds so cultured over the phone, so European. "Unlike you, Joanna," she must want to say. It's a shame I had to promote him, she implies.

Vivien is currently a field supervisor at one of our sites in downtown Brooklyn. Reeves and Barnett paid for his graduate school, which he attended at night. He is

standing by my desk. He comes into the main office every
other week or so and he always stops by and says hello.
"Come on, Joanna. What are you waiting for? Ms. Barnett
will pay one hundred percent for a grade of B and above.
Do you always want to be bringing the coffee?"

"No, Vivien."

"I started out like you, but nearer to the bottom. I was
an American cliché, a poor immigrant with large dreams.
I don't know why you aren't more willing to work your
way up. You're an American by birth. You have to want
more. All Americans want more."

"I don't know if market research is for me," I tell
him. "And you had a head start. You already had your
undergraduate degree. It would take me years. . . ."

He unconsciously strokes his dark beard. "Where are
you going, Joanna? Yes, it would take years, but they'd
take you more seriously here. And more importantly,
you'd take yourself more seriously."

"I don't know if this is what I want. Sometimes the
people here sicken me, present company excluded. I hate
the way they categorize people by income and purchases.
Basically, they're a bunch of snobs."

"Are you the only American who doesn't know how
to play the game? They say in order to make an omelet,
the cook must crack some eggs. There is going to be a
seminar over at the Marriott Marquis next month. Why
don't you mention it to Ms. Barnett? Show her you're
interested."

"Viven, you're becoming very pushy."

"Five years in New York will do that. Promise me
you'll ask."

"Okay, okay. Maybe you're right. I guess it couldn't
hurt, especially if the company will pay for it."

My work, my secretarial profession, is scorned these
days by women who have leaped through the managerial
doors broken down in the not too distant past by former
secretaries. Tell me though, at what else can you dress
up, sit down, be efficient, lunch and gossip for an hour,

sit down again, organize, philosophize, and go home with
a paycheck? I do not knock you successful-dressing,
thirty-second, let's do drinks, let's network types—so
don't knock me. Besides, while you ladies are preparing
your clever little presentations and missing your lunch,
Dahlia takes me out on her corporate card once a month
to any restaurant of her choosing. I know who she favors
and who she savagely mocks behind your hundred percent worsted wool backs.

Can it be five o'clock already, Dahlia? Yes, you have
a good weekend too. Opening the house in the Hamp-
tons? Yes, I'd love to one weekend. No, I've never been.

My own weekend does not sound as promising as my
boss's. Rather than opening a summer home on Long Island on Saturday, the Barron family will be washing their
mattress covers in the basement of their building. By the
way, Vivien mentioned to me something about a week-
long market research seminar given next month over at
the Marriott Marquis. Vivien? Yes, he is charming and
very European, although Guyana is in South America, if
you can believe it. He said that over the years, they were
ruled by the French and the British and the Portuguese.
Maybe even the Dutch, I don't remember. Yes, the end
result is a cultured accent. I know, I know, the clients love
to hear that on the phone. The seminar? Sure thing, I'll
get you the details by next week.

Sunday unfolds into a warm, beautiful day.

"Ellen Clabber called while you were showering.
Coming over in fifteen minutes. I said okay." My mother
speaks in stenographic bursts when she's preoccupied.

My jeans get tugged up, a lightweight sweater is
thrown on. I rope my hair into a ponytail. Soon we're
walking up Queens Boulevard for a White Castle lunch.
We—Ellen, Louise, Louise's three-year-old son Frankie,
and myself. Hector and Ralph were busy changing the oil
in their cars, another telltale sign of spring. I can't imagine
being too busy for little steamed, square, oniony hamburgers served in a real facsimile of a castle. I smell tar

being applied to leaky rooftops. Spring, the season of roof repair. Overweight pigeons strut fearlessly beneath the elevated tracks, sending feathers and droppings from above. Yes, spring has definitely found Sunnyside.

I adore Frankie. He's the brattiest three-year-old I've ever known. He wipes ketchup on the sleeve of my sweater. He hurls his Coke at the next table. Louise is about ready to strangle him.

"Frankie, we're going home."

"No way."

"Let's go. You're being bad."

"No way."

"I'm getting the wooden spoon."

"It's home."

"He needs a good beating," Louise explains to me and Ellen. "My mother-in-law is spoiling him rotten. While I'm at work, this woman is doing it her way, the Cuban way. Everything love, love."

"Louise," I say. "She's trying to do her best. You can't expect her to do everything your way."

"I expect her to do something my way. (Frankie, sit down.) Am I speaking Greek to you? Get your coulie on the chair. *Now.*"

He sits. I cringe. My eyes meet Ellen's. She doesn't send me the signal, the signal that she thinks Louise is losing it, losing it quickly.

"You're acting bitchier than usual. You getting laid enough?" Ellen asks with genuine concern.

"No. Hector's been working a lot of overtime."

Frankie is sharing my fries. Oh, is he cute. His little body is skinny and deep tan. And his hair is a soft, curly light brown like his mother's before she heaped on the bleach and the mousse. Louise presses a three-inch spike heel into my ankle. "Don't spoil him, Jo. He's got his own fries."

Frankie smiles at Louise. "I love you, Mommy."

Louise leans over and kisses the top of his head. "You're my main man, Franks."

How many White Castle hamburgers can a human

being eat? Ellen Clabber can eat twelve. She has a whippet's narrow, pointy face and sandy-colored short hair. If it wasn't for the 40DD chest, she could pass for a guy. Ms. Tough Broad. Softball has begun and she's pitching this year for Buckley's Bar and Grill. I've watched her play. Her short, wide legs are as strong as twin jackhammers pounding the pavement on size 10½E shoes. The muscles in her arms bulge and her hands are broad, topped with thick, long fingers.

Louise ordered four burgers for herself but finishes only three, followed by two sticks of spearmint gum. "I don't know why you drag us here, Ellen. I'm getting cramps already." She clutches a belt loop on her tight acid-washed jeans. A Virginia Slims is lit, moussed and bleached hair is tossed behind her bony shoulder blades. Gold-jacketed cubic zirconium earrings jingle in her ears. Sunglasses, airbrushed fingernails. She's not pretty, but guys are drawn to her like kids to red lollipops. *Bitch*, she proclaims to the world.

"You're probably getting your period," Ellen tells her.

I had ordered only two burgers and I do finish them. They're quite tasty but I feel them sitting against my ribs already. I was really in the mood for something light, perhaps a pasta salad with vinaigrette. Ms. Wimp, that's me.

"Look at this one, two midget hamburgers." Ellen points to me. "No wonder you're so skinny."

"Fast food is not the best thing in the world for your body." Well, it's not.

Louise says, "Screw that. Nothing's good for you no more. Smoking, drinking, eating. Now with AIDS, you can't even screw around in peace."

Ellen answers, "I don't listen to none of that health shit no more. Drives me nuts. By the way, did Tommy McClellan call you?"

I blush. Twenty-seven years old and still blushing, a curse I tell you. "Why is your face all red? You got the hots for him, don't you? Admit it."

"Get lost. He's just a fast-talking cop."

Ellen goes on. "I don't see you doing any better. Not
for a long time. Not since your sister set you up with that
Jewish pharmacy guy, what's-his-face?"

"Howie."

"Howie, yeah, Howie. He was nice. Whatever happened to him?"

"He married another Jewish pharmacist." My lack of
higher education bothered him. He wanted an achiever.
Louise clip-clops on her spikes to rescue an elderly couple
from Frankie. White Castle has become a regular senior
citizen's center. These pathetic old people order one tiny
hamburger and a cup of coffee and get a lunch out for
around a dollar, a Social Security bargain.

We follow Louise. She's waving us on to meet Frankie's newfound companions. Oh, what do you know, it's
my aunt Adele and uncle Jack. Aunt Adele is my father's
eldest and most lovable sister. She lives with Uncle Jack
in our building too, that is between shock treatments. In
fact they were the ones who got my parents into the
building thirty-two years ago. We love them anyway.

I kiss them and try not to focus on their skimpy meal.
They are dressed up as if they are on their way to a
matinee. My uncle has on an ancient black suit and an
extra-wide tie to match his extra-wide smile. Aunt Adele
wears a tan jumper under a string of blue, clunky beads.
Wisps of steel-gray hair spring out from under her blue
crocheted cap. I know their routine, a White Castle lunch
and a subway ride. Where are they headed? The Sheraton
Center in the City. Aunt Adele and Uncle Jack spend their
afternoons in the hotel lobby observing people check in
and check out. On good days they can spot a celebrity
or two.

I wish Aunt Adele and Uncle Jack luck in the city.
They tell me to send regards to my sister Arlene tomor-
row. The whole family must know when we visit Arlene.
She is, after all, the pride of the Barrons.

Yes, the Barrons are at it again. My family and I have
journeys to make and exciting people to see during our
weekends. We do the relative hop more often than not.

This particular Sunday we're committed to Sister Arlene and her husband Gary. As my mother keeps telling me, "Arlene has done well for herself. Follow her example. Look at that house she has. Can you imagine? A house with a three-car garage. It should only happen to you. Maybe she knows somebody. Should I ask her?"

Doing well, according to Mom, means following these basic guidelines. Listed in her order of importance, they are:

1. EARN A CREDENTIAL.
2. MARRY A MAN WITH POTENTIAL.
3. IMPROVE YOURSELF.
4. SURROUND YOURSELF WITH CULTURE.

My sister has met all the criteria for doing well under the May Barron Doing Well Guidelines, with the possible exception of Rule #4. Although her old Barry Manilow collection might be considered high culture in her circle. Arlene has even surpassed my mother's great expectations. She is currently the Consumer Queen of the new up-and-coming South Jersey suburb of Kent. Through the G.I. plan (Generous In-laws), Gary and Arlene have recently purchased a stunning brand new, cathedral-ceilinged, four-bedroom Center Hall Colonial which is currently being overdecorated and overaccessorized by the very same Queen Arlene.

Through research and observation, and following the strict teachings of their decorator, Arlene has learned the brand name and function of every consumer item necessary to a Kent household. It's known as keeping up with the Shapiros. Arlene doesn't buy blinds, she invests in Levolors. She doesn't buy a refrigerator, she orders top of the line Sub-Zero. Yes, freezer below thank you. Green carpet? No. Mint Karastan? Yes. Do not panel the basement. Tongue and groove the modular entertainment room. Arlene chants daily: Thomas-ville, Hen-re-don, Mikassa. Dis-count, dis-count, the chorus echoes.

Before Arlene moved to Kent, we were blissfully ignorant of just what could be done in and around a home. We've learned that one can (a) go completely modern in the family room, (b) pickle the kitchen cabinets, (c) barnside the entrance hall. Delegate. Coordinate. Delegate the responsibility to a reliable decorator who will coordinate the living space.

Now we are sitting in Arlene's family room. It is not another living room, I am told, because it has a television, and not just any television but a fifty-two-inch, top-of-the-line Sony. The living room is for formal entertaining, for sitting and chatting. Adults only. Hands off the Lladro please. My dad has the fifty-two-inch Sony tuned to a Mets exhibition game on cable. He sits in a corner, blind to his surroundings. With the crowd and announcer hum, he could just as well be in Port St. Lucie.

Gary is out in the backyard overseeing the landscaper, who is planting $7,000 worth of trees and shrubbery into their one-eighth an acre plot that was once part of a farm. In Kent, the developers rightly assumed that former lower-middle-class apartment-dwelling Jews and Italians from Brooklyn and Queens would know instinctively what to do with an oversized house, but would not have idea one what to do with a generous parcel of land.

As it is, the place looks as if the houses were flown in from a Hollywood set and hot-glued to the ground. They are all so new, so perfect, so untouched by human history. And where are the people? Where are the noisy kids playing box-ball on the sidewalk? Where's the ice cream man who can maneuver his truck around the hockey players without taking the sideview mirror off the double-parked Cavalier? Where is the baby carriage being pushed by the woman with the pink rollers growing out of her head? I cannot hear the squeal of wire shopping carts being pulled over chipped curbs by old men and women who never saw the need to drive. Tell me, is there life in Kent that exists beyond the bubble of the car and the mall?

Arlene, my mother, and myself are in each other's company. We sit in moderate contentment on a modular

plum corduroy pub-backed sofa facing walls that had
been grass-papered, and certainly not painted. My sneakers are adorning a rectangular white and plum laminated
coffee table. Arlene frowns once in a while at the imitation
Reeboks gracing her furniture but she says nothing. We're
in the family room and the community bylaws state
clearly that feet are permitted.

We sit. We talk. Topics drift in and pull out, tides
of continuing conversation dating back to childhood and
washing up in some remote future.

"Arlene, honey, what's with your job?" my mother
asks. Arlene's successes give her such a shot of maternal
pride.

"Don't get me started, " Arlene replies. My head
snaps to attention. I like hearing about trouble in Arlene's
paradise. "One of the most arrogant brokers you'd ever
want to meet barges into my office—my office, mind
you—and starts questioning me about disability for his
pregnant secretary. His se-cre-ta-ry for God's sake! Can
you believe this? I tell him I'm the comptroller, not some
nothing in benefits. He tells me she became pregnant before joining the firm and we should not have to shell out
one cent. I'm slaving over a regression analysis on the
P.C. and he's talking about some stupid secretary."

"Maybe she's not so stupid."

"That's not what I meant and you know it. Don't be
so damn sensitive."

I look up at Arlene. Her best feature is her tiny, up-
turned nose, courtesy of my parent's Sweet Sixteen gift of
plastic surgery. She is short, like both of my parents, but
not dumpy. There is a real dumpiness potential, though.
Her hair is chestnut-brown like mine, but it is straight,
cut short, cut serious. Her eyes are also brown but nar-
rower than my own. But it is her walk that really distin-
guishes her in a crowd. She is constantly hunched
forward, ready to pounce on anything that comes her
way.

"Girls, girls." Mother speaks. "I have some good news

to share. Your cousin Sharon is expecting in September. Aunt Ruthie is thrilled, as you can well imagine.

"Wow, that's nice," I sing. It will be great having a baby around at family functions. I'd rather listen to a crying baby than my snooty sister any day.

"Where does she think she's going to put a baby in a one-bedroom condo?"

"The same place I put you, Arlene, before we paid off the super for the two-bedroom. The baby will sleep in their room for a while. Where else?"

"I'm sorry, that's just not my way of doing things." We then hear about Arlene's grand scheme. "First you establish a career and put aside some money. Then you complete a proper home environment. The child should have his own room, a backyard to run around in, a playroom to entertain his friends. When the environment is conducive, only then should people even consider bringing children into their lives."

My mother laughs. "Oh, Arlene. If Daddy and I had felt that way, you and Joanna wouldn't be sitting here right now."

Not wishing to illuminate us any further, Arlene stretches, stands up and starts adjusting her family room knickknacks. "I hear you're seeing Tommy McClellan," she accuses.

"You hear wrong." I glance over at the short, chubby guilty one on my right. My mother is staring up at the high-hatted, sand-painted ceiling. "I am not seeing him. I'm going to see him on Saturday night."

"It's only my opinion, Joanna, but if I were you I wouldn't see him. Not Saturday, not any time. And by the way, Gary's brother Sandy is back from Dallas. He asked about you. He asked if you were seeing anyone. I gave him your number. He's doing very well for himself now. He'd doing computer consulting."

"You could have asked me first, you know."

"Don't be a fool. Tommy McClellan will be trouble for you. I know. He's very wild, if you catch my drift."

"What do you know? What could you know about
him?"

"He's my age. Twenty-nine. We graduated at the
same time."

"Yes, he went to plain, old, ordinary Bryant High
School like me, and you went to Stuyvesant, the school
for math and science geniuses in Manhattan. I fail to see
any connection."

"I can remember him getting high in our hallways."

"You lived with Aunt Naomi and Uncle Marc during
high school. Did you see him lighting up all the way from
the City?"

"There's no talking to you, is there?"

"Not when you don't know what you're talking
about."

"I love your slacks, Arlene," Mother Kissinger says.

"Lizzie Claiborne. She gives a good fit in the seat."
My sister pinches her ample seat to demonstrate. If she
comes any closer I'm going to kick her.

"By the way, I have been invited by my boss to a
week long marketing seminar at the Marriott Marquis
next month." I wanted to impress Arlene with something, anything.

"It's about time you gave some consideration to your
career. Do you have what to wear?"

"No. They'll just have to accept me in my straw hat
and overalls."

My mother laughs. "You're very funny, Joanna. Just
like your father."

"No, it's not funny," Arlene says. "Some people
don't appreciate concern. Do you carry a briefcase?" she
asks me.

"Why would I need a briefcase? I don't carry my
work home."

"You need a good quality leather briefcase for people
to take you seriously."

"And what would I put in this good quality leather
briefcase?"

"Paper, pens. You will be taking notes, I assume."

"I can carry paper and pens in my bag."
"You just don't get it."
"Oh, I get it all right. I have to pretend to be you."
I'll ask Vivien about the briefcase. He would know. And he wouldn't act so self-righteous about it either.

My brother-in-law Gary the Fair, overseer of the North 40, reenters through the sliding glass doors. I like Gary. We all like him. I give him credit for silently putting up with Arlene's search for perfection at a discount. "Whaddya say we order in some deli?"
"Ga-ry," she whines, "we had that last night." My sister's kitchen has imported granite counters from Milan, but to my knowledge she has never prepared a meal on them. She knows only how to import food. Like everything else in Kent, the counters are for show.
My dad announces he's alive too. "Arlene, how do you shut this thing off?"
Another Sunday's entertainment with the relatives winds down to the finish. On the ride home, my parents are oozing with pride.
"Did you get a load of that TV set?" my father asks. "Big bucks."
"Did you get a load of that gardener in the back?"
"That TV set is bigger than our bathroom."
"Joanna, why don't you go out with Sandy? He's a nice-looking boy. He could be Gary's twin. Nice, just like Gary."
I sigh as the car leaves Kent, New Jersey. I can't say for sure, but I don't think this is what I am searching for. Lucky us, next Sunday we're scheduled for an afternoon of comedy-drama with Aunt Naomi and Uncle Marc, unless of course my friends drag me out to White Castle.

Three

I'm feeling very clever this evening. Tommy and I are going dancing. He's picking me up around eight. The way I see it, though, he'll probably stop in to see his family before he comes down to get me. If I keep my eye to the window I can catch a glimpse of what he's wearing so I don't look like a complete misfit. Ah-ha! See, I'm right. A navy-blue suit. Navy and white-striped shirt. White collar. Maroon tie. Navy suspenders. Suspenders? Tommy McClellan? Well fancy that. Maybe he wants to climb up a rung or two on the old socioeconomic fashion ladder.

Good, I'll wear the lightweight cranberry knit with the big lace collar and my faux pearl bracelet. Ms. Barnett, Dahlia when she's in a good mood, had instilled in me the existence of a positive fixed correlation between a display of pearls and membership in an upper socioeconomic stratum. I pray that this correlation is as high for survey participants wearing imitation as well as cultured pearls. I tuck my diaphragm into my pocketbook just in the event, although I doubt it will make it out of its case. I've had it eight years, but it's almost like new.

Elevator doors, footsteps, doorbell, adrenaline rush. As usual, May and Sol Barron are my official greeters. It's sad, twenty-seven years old and my dates still have to get past Mom and Dad. My parents are in their typical Saturday night date clothes too. Dad's wearing a pair of tan chinos that was recently carbon-dated and determined to be from the Iron Age. Mom is wearing a nine-dollar pink sleeveless duster. Middle-aged dumpy women wear dusters when they don't feel like squeezing into the strict confines of a terry-cloth bathrobe.

From my bedroom I can hear them all talking about the police force. That makes sense. They can't grill him about his family because they already know them. My mother and his brother both work at Schwab's, but a conversation about Matty's fine points would be very brief. They could talk about his mother. She is decent enough but I'm sure she doesn't read the *New York Times* on Sunday. This constitutes worthy, intellectual behavior for my mother. If you don't read this newspaper, you are an ignoramus. My father, she admits, is the one exception needed to prove the rule. I guess I am only half a moron in her eyes, because I make it my business to wade through Arts and Entertainment, Travel & Leisure, and the Book Review. I find it critical at Reeves and Barnett to at least appear well-read. As long as I can flaunt my superficial knowledge of the latest shows, resorts, and books, I am able to keep up with Dahlia's trend-attuned killer research staff.

"Hey Tommy," I say as I make my grand entrance from the foyer.

"Hey Sunshine. You sure look pretty."

"Have a nice time," my mother echoes into the hallway. And I wonder if she means it.

The super's apartment is off the lobby, directly opposite the elevator. Mr. and Mrs. Gurtz live rent-free but have handled all tenant complaints since the owner and absentee landlord, Mr. Santini, bought the building twenty years ago. Whereas Mr. Gurtz is the fixer, Mrs. Gurtz is our building monitor. Day or night, Mrs. Gurtz sticks her head out of her apartment door every time the elevator rumbles open. She never sleeps, although she never appears fully awake either. She knows everything about Mr. Santini's building and its inhabitants. A pair of gray Valium eyes stare out from under a huge, lopsided, blond Afro wig. The space directly in front of her apartment stinks of grease, cat litter, and Jean Naté.

"Hey there, hot stuff," Tommy grins. "You still dry humping Santini down in the laundry room?"

Door slam.

His Celica is parked in front of the fire hydrant, part of his benefit package, he tells me. He lights a cigarette. "Mind?"

"No, didn't know you smoked."

"Not enough. I'm trying to increase, still on the same pack since Thursday."

I check the brand, an occupational fetish. Newport, menthol box. I would bet he didn't know that Newport's billboard ads are strategically placed to reach the urban black consumer. Lorillard, you sly devil, how did you steal this one away from the Marlboro Man?

We take the Long Island Expressway to the Clearview and end up in Bayside. I'm very good at reading the signs above the highways just in the event I'm being kidnapped. We exit and end up on Bell Boulevard. Oh no, we're getting off Bell Boulevard. We're dancing at Fort Totten? No, my mistake. A huge catering hall dazzles its lights into Little Neck Bay, BAY MANOR, the sign flashes.

He gets a Dewar's on the rocks and I order a piña colada. This makes him smile and nearly convinces me never to order an alcoholic beverage again. We put our dinner orders in also, stuffed shrimp for me and prime rib well-done for him. And when all that ordering is out of the way we get up to dance. We dance fast. We dance slow and easy. This man can move, no two ways about it.

When our food comes, we sit down reluctantly.

"So, what do you do during nine to five in the big city?"

"I work for a market research firm called Reeves and Barnett."

"Mmmm. Sounds impressive."

"It's not, not my end of it anyway. Actually, I shuffle a stack of papers from one side of the desk to the other.

Once in a while I get a paper cut. And you, Mr. Policeman? Tell me about your job."

"Nah, Sweetie, not tonight. Got the day off and I don't
want to think about it. But let me tell you something, I
bet we got a lot in common."

"How's that?"

"I shuffle a shitload of papers too. I'm drowning in
paperwork, just like you."

We dance some more. The music pulsates louder now.
I can feel percussion in my chest. A man bumps into us
and apologizes. Tommy leads me outside along the dock
and we watch the black ripples tease the rocky shore. It
would be a great setting for a kiss, much better than the
stinking hallway. But he doesn't kiss me. Instead, he leans
against the stone wall and looks out at the water. He talks
to the bay, he talks more to the bay than he does to me.

"When I was a kid my father promised me we'd live
here someday. He'd buy us a house on the water, right
smack between the Throgs Neck and the Whitestone
Bridge. That way we'd always know what the traffic was
like. Oh yeah, and every summer we'd be renting a spot
down by Breezy Point. He had a lot of dreams, my father.
Big dreams—but what the hell did I know? I was a kid.
Now I know I'm never going to live in a house by the
water. Shit, even a two-family in Sunnyside cost $200,000,
and they're attached on six sides. Way out of my range,
but it don't matter. I guess I'm born to rent. But it sure
would be nice to own one of them boats someday. I'd
steer her under them two bridges and just keep on going."

"You know, I can picture you in a speedboat."

"Nah, I'm getting tired of going fast, been speeding
for way too long. I want to slow down, real easy. A small
sailboat, that's what I've been dreaming about, not the
kind that you need a crew of eight. What do you dream
about, Jo? What do you want for yourself?"

"I don't dream, really. I take it one day at a time."

"That's real smart. You won't ever be disappointed."

"And as far as wanting something, all I want is to
know what to do with the rest of my life."

He grins. "Is that all?"

His hand folds into mine and we walk farther along the dock. We walk until I shiver, and Tommy notices. "Come on," he says, "let's go back and grab some dessert."

We drink cappuccino and share a piece of chocolate cheesecake. He kisses a crumb off my face. His skin smells delicious, a blend of soap and tobacco. It's a reassuring smell, a comforting smell. My dad used to smell soapy and smoky. That was before my mother flushed his last carton of Winstons and backed up every toilet from 4B down to LB.

We dance some more, nearly one in the morning it is. I imagine we'll be leaving soon. Yes, he does drive me home. His. He rents a three-room basement apartment in Woodhaven. Park Lane South is his street, right off of Woodhaven Boulevard. He's the side door on the third two-family semi from the corner. If I'm not out of there in ten minutes, be a dear and call the police. On second thought, call the National Guard.

"Come in for a second, Sunshine," he says. "I'm thirsty."

He leads me down a side entrance, about ten narrow steps to the basement. A black ten-speed is parked on the landing. I didn't figure him to be a bike rider but he tells me he rides every night after work. He says if you go fast enough you can wipe out the whole day. He has a surprisingly large eat-in kitchen, a small living room, bathroom, and a closed door. I assume this closed door opens to a bedroom but I'm not about to request the fifty cent tour.

I use his bathroom. It's spotless, unlike Howie's bachelor bathroom where I could hold conversations with the stains after a few visits. I trickle my pee very quietly in case he's listening. I slip my diaphragm in just in case and I brush my hair and wash my face so I look pretty.

"Want a drink?" he asks when I join him in the kitchen.

"Do you have rum?"

"Jesus, Mary, and Joseph! You people, all you know is booze, booze, and more booze. I was thinking of tea. I always have a cup before— You like tea?"

"Yes, that sounds good." I'm quite relieved he's not an alcoholic. My mother's predate briefing disclosed that his father was an alcoholic who had taken off years ago, leaving Trudy to raise three small children.

Tommy gets busy. He loosens his tie, gets out two cups and saucers, boils water, and reaches for a box of Red Rose tea bags. This brand I'm not certain about. I think they've locked up the sixty-five-and-over market in the Northeast. I take mine plain. He drinks his like a sick child, three teaspoons of sugar and plenty of milk.

We sit in his kitchen and sip our tea. He has a small apartment-size refrigerator, white metallic cabinets, and a stainless steel range. His table and chairs looked vaguely familiar. Four varnished oak chairs studded with red vinyl cushions surround a heavy white rectangular wrought-iron table. What touches me, though, is the sight of an iron that had cooled its heel on the scratched butcher-block counter top. It pleases me a little to picture him pressing his shirt before he came to get me.

From the kitchen I glance out into the living room. A worn brown tweed love seat faces a portable TV. His coffee table is not a table but a huge blue and white Styrofoam ice chest. That must be very convenient in the summer months. A four-shelf plywood bookcase houses an old stereo, a telephone book, some manuals, and last Sunday's *News*. What really grabs my attention, though, is a salmon-cushioned blond wood 1950s "I Love Lucy" telephone table. He keeps an assortment of liquor on the tabletop, but that is not what holds my interest. I know this table. I haven't seen it for years, but I know it.

"That table used to be in our lobby. How did you end up with it?"

"It was a housewarming gift from my brother."

"Matty stole the lobby furniture! My God, didn't that upset you?"

"Hell no. I tell you, it was the nicest thing anyone ever done for me."

I shake my head in disbelief. A picture of Arlene and her decorator analyzing Tommy's uncoordinated but functional furnishings enters my mind. We finish our tea, a not uncomfortable silence. I clear the table for him and throw him a so-what's-next look. I know what is next, actually, but I want to see just how all this will proceed. For the record, I know what comes next, and I want very much what comes next.

"Come, Sunshine," he says softly, and reaches for my hand. "I'll show you the rest of my underground palace." He opens the door to his bedroom and switches on a bright overhead light. Rather than a modern, unkempt bachelor platform mating mattress, what stands before me is a solid, ornate, carved, mahogany, Victorian bedroom set. Two carefree trumpeting cherubs adorn the head-board. A simple white cotton Antoinette bedspread lay neatly across a double bed. There's this wonderful scent of old lemon-polished wood and camphor. . . .

"It's beautiful, Tommy."

"Just got it. It was my grandmother's."

I spot two objects on his dresser that convince me that perhaps I don't belong here. The first is a three-inch wooden crucifix that most likely also belonged to Nana Agnes. The second and far more objectionable is a dull, heavy-looking revolver which is sprawled out across his bureau with the carefree innocence of a pocket comb. He must have seen my eyes fixate on the gun so he opens the drawer and rests it on a stack of sweaters. "Okay?"

I nod.

"I better take this off too." He removes his suit jacket and pulls out another gun from the waistband of his pants.

"Were you expecting trouble from me?"

"No trouble, Sunshine—regulation when I'm in the city limits."

We sit on Nana Agnes's bed and kiss, nothing heavy. I could get up now, end it. I could. But I don't want to.

"Mind if I shut the light, Jo? My eyes are killing me."
It's not just a line. His eyes do look a little bloodshot.
"No, shut it."

It's nice to be kissed by Tommy McClellan in a dark
Victorian bedroom. It's nice to watch him remove his tie
and his shirt and follow the path his clothes take as they
sail gracefully across the bare floor. My dress, Tommy
shows me, can travel a similar path. His body is mean-
lean and pulled tight with developed muscle that show
only when flexed. He feels me shake when he holds me
close, and he asks softly, "You're not . . . ?"

"No, of course not," I assure him with a voice loaded
with false sophistication. I'm only four or five times
removed.

"Easy there," he drawls into the night. "Don't be
scared now, Jo. It's just me, Tommy from upstairs. Remember, I've been on top of you all my life." And in this
cool darkness I feel his mouth press on my lips, on the
curve of my neck, my breasts, my belly. It doesn't stop
there. In this cool darkness my mouth wanders along the
symmetry of his body too. I become brave in the shadows.

"Jo, we gotta be careful." He leans over and yanks
open the top drawer of his night table.

"It's already taken care of, but I guess it can't hurt to
be extra safe."

"You Jewish girls think of everything, huh?"

And I feel him enter gently, his mouth never ceasing
an investigation of my ears, my eyelids, my throat. We
rock gently and smoothly until we reach a peaceful pla-
teau and we linger there for a long time. Then we quicken
and quicken again, an upward spiral of pleasure. I feel
his arms clutch me tighter and tighter against his chest
and then a succession of fiery hot bursts warm my insides,
followed by a long bittersweet blossom of relief that leads
to almost nothing, nothing at all, just our heartbeats slow-
ing down to rest. I sleep a peaceful, dreamless sleep, all
my fears crushed in raw tenderness.

*   *   *

"Jo." He nudges me. "Wake up, Sunshine. It's four in the morning. I gotta drive you home."

I dress in a hurry. I've got to get home before sunrise or my parents may have to admit something to themselves. He switches the light on and throws on a pair of gray sweat pants and a T-shirt. He straps a shoulder holster on and covers it with a sweatshirt. I notice a white, bumpy scar low on the left side of his rib cage. I say nothing.

"Occupational injury," he explains. "Hey, you ever get yourself caught in one of them automatic staple guns? It's real wicked. You ever get wounded by your paperwork?"

He runs the red lights cautiously and gets me home in fifteen minutes. Our car ride is blessedly silent. He has the brains not to ask me Howie the pharmacist's three stupid postsex questions: 1. How was I? 2. How was it for you? 3. Did you?

I try to convince myself I am not an easy girl. I've only been with one other man two years ago, and that was a major disappointment to say the least. For Howie, my body was comprised of only two autonomous parts, and never did he stray from either. And he was noisy too, used to shout and moan, and thrash about like a fish pulled from the pier. Awful it was, but I really didn't know. Now I know.

Rationalization, Joanna. You just slept with a man on a first date. Of course the wake does not count as a date. Absolutely not. Where are your standards? I ask myself. But I just wanted to be held close and loved for a while. Is loneliness a crime in this state? He's using you. No, can't you tell he's lonely too? Believe that, fool. All he wants is fun in the sun. Those were his very words.

"Come on," he says, slamming the gears into park. "We'll take the stairs. I don't want to see my pal Mrs. Gurtz again."

We run up five flights without stopping. I'm ready for an oxygen tent, but he's all right. "I'll get you in shape. Got a bike?"

"Yeah, Arlene left me hers. It's not as fancy as yours."

"Don't matter. One day we'll go riding. Hey, I'm working an eight-to-four next Saturday but I could get you at night if you're willing."

"Yes, oh yes."

He bends down to kiss my cheek. "Sweet dreams."

To say that I am not looking forward to our trek into Manhattan to visit my mother's dearest sisters on four hours of sleep is an understatement. But I will go. It's our family's favorite form of entertainment—visiting the relatives. Other families go ice-skating or fishing. The Barron family visits.

Manhattan will always be the City to us outerborough residents. The City is very different from the other four boroughs. It's fast and trendy. People dress better. You don't see many people walking around in plaid housecoats, white socks, and open-toed slippers in Manhattan. As a kid, my sister and I had to dress up when we visited our family in Manhattan. We were going to the City, after all.

I am comfortable in the City only between nine and five weekdays. When the number 7 Flushing line deposits me in Queens at five-thirty, I breathe an inaudible sigh of relief. I can be myself.

My aunt Naomi and my uncle Marc live in an enormous Manhattan apartment complex on East Twentieth Street off the FDR Drive. Their development is called Peter Cooper Village. Widowed Aunt Ruthie, the baby sister, lives a few blocks away in a related but slightly older complex called Stuyvesant Town. It comes to one essential difference. Peter Cooper is wired for air-conditioning and Stuyvesant Town is not. Starting in May, expect Aunt Ruthie to be just a teensy bit crankier than Aunt Naomi. We have a little time before May.

My mother and I, in the tradition of the Marines, land first. My father rides around and around the East Side searching for a parking spot. He'll catch up with us in half an hour or so.

It is immediately evident even at a first glimpse that these three women are sisters. Some people even take

them for triplets. They are all close in height (short) and
weight (chubby). They all have wide faces, are short, and
at this stage dyed, light brown hair and good skin. Aunt
Naomi's nose does point slightly to the left, Aunt Ruthie's
to the right, and my mother's remains stuck in neutral.
Happily, I do not resemble them. I am told that my father's father had been tall and thin, and if I ever meet up
with him in an afterlife, I owe him big-time.

It is wrong, however, to lump the three sisters together. Do not think for a moment that these women are
indistinguishable. Aunt Naomi had captured her Marc, a
tenured NYU professor of sociology. My aunt Ruthie, or
Baby Ruth, as my father calls her privately, found and
subsequently lost my uncle Mort, a now deceased book
editor. Let us note that the two Manhattan sisters did
complete four years of college. They had established
their credentials.

As a result of these educational and financial differences between the Manhattan sisters and the Queens sister, my mother envies the lifestyle of her two siblings,
and idolizes the women. And they do not discourage this
behavior, they nurture it, feed, fertilize, and water it. My
father, whose low self-esteem is further eroded by Uncle
Marc's random idea tossing, is meek and even apologetic
in their presence.

In addition, my parents owe Naomi and Marc a non-
repayable debt, which can bring out the sibling idolatry
in anyone. My sister Arlene had lived with Aunt Naomi
and Uncle Marc all through high school in order that she
could associate with a better class of people, my mother's
phrase. Yes, I too was offered the same social-expanding
opportunity, but I declined. It just wasn't right for me.

We sit, this Sunday, in Aunt Naomi's large living
room and listen to Uncle Marc's ever-running political
and social commentary. "These right-to-lifers are at it
again it seems. It's merely an extension of Dirk Hyme's
theory of alienation. Alienation is alienation, after all.
Once could be as alienated to one's body as easily as
alienated to the structure at large."

My father looks out the window about now, pre-
tending to check on the car. He hovers around the window, letting the rest of us get a better view of center stage.
Naomi, the loyal wife, points to Marc and says, "I wish
I had one-eighth of his knowledge."

Baby Ruth pipes in, "My Mort in his day read more
books than anyone alive. God rest."

My mother is busy absorbing the scene in its entirety,
the abundant art on display, the neat rows of teak book-
shelves, her sisters' tailored clothing. Oh, the pleasant afternoons they must spend at the museums, the stores, the
theater. She's too busy focusing on the backdrop to hear
much of the dialogue.

Uncle Marc's comments fall on impaired ears. The Barron family hears you, Uncle Marc; we don't understand
you and you count on that. You're just busy letting us
know how educationally inferior we are. We wish we had
Arlene here, our family's intellectual representative, to go
one-on-one with you, but she's at a mall somewhere having her bedspread dyed to coordinate with the balloon
shades.

"Sol, dear," Aunt Ruthie calls to the window, "would
you be able to drive me to Valley Stream next Saturday?
Sharon, she's expecting, you know, needs me to help pick
out a layette, and Marc will be busy working on his papers. I know it's an imposition. . . ."

"Don't be silly, Ruthie. We're family," my mother answers. "Right, Sol?"

"Of course. No problem."

I guess it's okay not to know diddly about alienation
when one is willing to drive Aunt Ruthie to Valley
Stream.

"Come everyone, let's eat. I'm experimenting today,"
Aunt Naomi warns. "Ruthie, tell them. Tell them. They
should know."

"Naomi and I have decided to become vegetarians."

"You what? Why?" my mother asks.

Aunt Ruthie goes on. "The two of us saw Dr. Kappel
on Thursday morning for our checkups. We both had

blood tests, and the results were not good. Cholesterol. Ours is too high and we have the bad kind, the kind that can kill you."

"Dr. Kappel told you to stop eating meat and chicken? And fish too?"

"No," Naomi explains. "This is our own idea, just to be safe. He put us on a diet that limits animal protein, but Ruthie and I agree that drastic measures must be taken. After all, cholesterol is dangerous. It could kill us. We are not going to let that happen. And you, May, you should get your blood tested every three months too, as a prevention. Nothing more. It's prophylactic."

I smile. My mother shrugs. I know she's thinking that her union medical plan might not cover all the blood tests. "So what can you eat?"

"Beans," Aunt Ruthie answers. "Beans are very good. Brown rice. Not so much dairy. Salads, pasta, oat bran, and oatmeal, but no egg yolks. Egg yolks are killers. They tell you on the news. We are never going to eat egg yolks again."

"Aunt Naomi, what about your famous triple-layer chocolate decadence cake? It's my favorite."

"Jo, darling, for you I'll make it on an occasion. Enjoy it, in moderation, mind you, but be careful with it. You understand. This cholesterol runs in the family. Aunt Ruthie and I are terrified."

Uncle Marc passes down a bowl of mock egg salad. It's made from the whites so it is not dangerous. "We're just trying to save all of you," Aunt Ruthie says. "One day you'll thank us."

"The relationship between the farmer and the food supply could be likened to the relationship of the worker in a factory, in that the end result of the labor is neither realized nor experienced," Uncle Marc tells us.

My mother, I am sure, is wondering if he's knocking factory workers. She is very sensitive about this. Sewing, my mother tells me, is artistic work. She's a hand-embroiderer, after all, not someone who sits at a machine. And not just an embroiderer, a supervisor of embroiderers, a teacher, an embroidery teacher. Please don't get her started, Uncle Marc.

And all the while my mind is on Tommy McClellan. Will he call again? Was I funny and sunny enough for him? Do I really want to get involved with a man who won't say two words about his work? And why? Doesn't he trust me? Does he think I'll take out a full-page ad in the *Criminal Gazette?*

"Sol," a voice penetrates through my head, "what do you think of the mock egg salad?"

"Delicious. Naomi, it's delicious. It's a pleasure to come here. May is lucky to have such wonderful sisters, people who care for her." He can't help but think of his own sister, Crazy Aunt Adele. She would be incapable of preparing mock egg salad even on a good day. In fact, I don't think she could put together traditional egg salad if her life depended on it.

"We're having fresh fruit for dessert."

Be still my heart.

And when I'm back in my room, this rash spreads across me, an annoying, irritating, Peter Cooper rash, and it's bothering me more than usual today. On most Sundays I can ignore it, but today it's worse than ever, so there, Uncle Marc. You have successfully removed Tommy McClellan out of my mind for a while in order for me to deal with a Barron inferiority complex. You made me feel so Sunnyside today, so rough and uncultured. Primitive, that's us. And you love it. It makes you feel so special.

See, Uncle Marc, I'm pulling down the H book of the *World Encyclopedia* in order to get some relief. I'll find out just who this Dirk Hyme guy is, the one that you infected us with this afternoon. Guess what? He's not even in the book. I check Dirk Hyne, Dirk Hyme, Dirk Heine, Dirk Hine. Forget it. This guy hasn't even made it into the *World Encyclopedia.* Obviously, he's small-time. I'm feeling better already.

Four

Monday through Friday lumbers along like an over-heated, overstuffed bus. I want it to be Saturday immediately. Move, move, move. I have no patience to hear Dahlia Barnett's too detailed explanation of how logo recognition is tested amongst eighteen- to forty-nine-year-old female credit card holders.

This marketing business is really giving me the chills lately.

That week-long seminar that Vivien had me attend was more intimidating than the lines at Motor Vehicles, even with a good quality leather briefcase dangling at my side.

I was the only one there who wasn't in charge of some important project. The group leader had all thirty of us introduce ourselves and summarize our business backgrounds. My summary was very brief. I didn't say much after that.

Like I said to Vivien, all marketing really is, is just a devious method of lumping people into small, defenseless target groups, in order to capture their disposable income and further increase some oversized company's share of market. I don't see how it's legal either, but all of this is in the textbook Dahlia's having me read, now that she thinks I'm getting serious about the firm. The knowledge

Dahlia and the seminar leader impress upon me stays
with me, takes me over like a fatal disease. I cannot enter
a person's kitchen or bathroom without checking over
their supermarket purchases. Wicked, just wicked. Vivien
says it's a means to an end. I say it doesn't make it right.
He says he wants to move his family to a two-family
house in Canarsie, Brooklyn. He'd like to bring his mother
to the States. Vivien has his eyes on the field manager's
spot. I have my eyes on this stupid briefcase that cost me
a nice chunk of my paycheck.

On Thursday night I looked at a studio over in Kew
Gardens. It was about a hundred a month over what I
wanted to spend and as small as my cubicle at work. The
last tenant had knocked holes in the walls, and when I
mentioned it to the super he pretended not to understand
any English. All he kept saying was, "Apartment near
train. Apartment near train." Thanks, but no thanks.

When Saturday finally makes its long awaited entrance this humid spring morning, it is a rude one. Mr.
and Mrs. Lee, operators of the run-down candy store over
the side entrance of our building, have decided to get
smart after all these years. I guess they weren't earning
enough selling coffee, newspapers, and sandwiches, so
this month they brought in a lottery machine. Now the
Lee's Golden Sun Candy Store is always packed. Each
Saturday from the street below, the din of voices rises to
my window from early morning and throughout the day.
The jackpot, my uncle Jack calls up to me as he stands
on line, is up to $23 million. No one has won for days. A
crowd winds around the corner like a famished snake.
And they wait and wait, toothless old men and women,
young parents with crying infants buckled into their carriers, middle-aged men and women with their weary eyes
on retirement. It's their only hope of escaping from the
crush of day-to-day struggle.

Tommy called me after he finished up his shift and
asked if I wouldn't mind if we stay in at his place. He
was broke, he told me, almost flat out broke. Matty had
cracked up the Schwab van on the way to the Long Island

City post office Friday morning. It had to get fixed over the weekend or his brother would be out of a job.

My mother had already filled me in on the details Friday night. Since my date with Tommy, I get a concise summary of his brother's irresponsible and sometimes illegal activities at Schwab's. It's my mother's none too subtle way of telling me to watch out, they're related. And don't forget the father.

"How's your brother?" my mother asks when he arrives. "He looked all shook up after he came back."

"Yeah, he chipped his front tooth, scraped up his chin, but he'll live. Let me tell you something. His supervisor gave him the keys to the van. What's his name? You know, the fat son-in-law?"

"Jerry Lieder."

"That's the one. He really ain't all that bright, is he?"

"Well," my mother says in her wise-owl voice, "he's the son-in-law. He has the son-in-law job. A little work. A lot of pay."

"That's what I thought. Mrs. Barron, one of his friends from the place told me Matty still had the swizzle stick from Buckley's stuck in his mouth, and this idiot lets him drive."

"What does your mother have to say?" my father asks from his corner of the sofa.

"Please," Tommy lowers his voice, "this is our little secret. She thinks Matty fell." He wriggles the narrow tip of his long nose. "You get your apartment painted?"

"Oh no. Mrs. Gurtz had her husband come in here just last year, we're not due for another painting. *I* am painting," she says. "I always give the bathroom a fresh coat. Something cheerful. You know, just to perk up the house. Let me show you."

Oh, I don't believe this. She's leading him by the wrist, past our six-ton, avocado-green scalloped draperies, past the gold and avocado cut-velvet sofa, past a fraying gold club chair, and flings open the bathroom door to unveil her latest endeavor in peach melba semigloss.

He nods his head. "Uh-huh, I see what you mean,

really livens the place up. Sunshine, you didn't tell me
your mother was an artist."

She's not the only one, Tommy. "She is one talented
lady," I say, giving my mother an extra plug. "My mother
was put in charge of all the new embroiderers. Right now
she's teaching two Indian sisters how to stitch the anchor
and stars on an admiral's shoulder boards. It's really an
art."

"Yes," my mother says with some pride. "My two
new pupils, Narinda and Bupinda."

"You know," he says, "Matty had mentioned that
Schwab's is a real equal opportunity employer."

After we get into his car, he imparts with some surprise, "Jeeze, I didn't know Schwab had a mixed bag
working for him. I mean I knew he had a whole bunch of
spics without green cards, but I thought it ended there." I
see him peek at me to gauge my reaction.

"No, he lets anyone work there. Blacks, Greeks, Spanish, Egyptians, Italians, Jamaicans, Indians. I'm telling
you, he even has one stupid Irish guy who doesn't know
enough to stay home when he's drunk. But then we all
know how trashy those people are."

"Them people are the worst," he says with a grin.

His apartment is pleasantly cool, considering how
sticky the afternoon had been, and he attributes it to living
in a cellar. I sit down on the love seat and rest my legs
on the Styrofoam ice chest. He switches on the baseball
game, stifles a yawn and says, "Mmmm, this is the life."
And it is. Comfortable, very comfortable. He kisses me
slowly all over my face and neck. His mouth is warm but
I shiver. He pulls me on top of him and we grind into
each other, clothes and all.

"Tommy?"

"What?"

"We're dry humping, just like Mr. Santini and Mrs.
Gurtz."

"Yeah, sweetie, I guess we are." He goes back to kissing my neck.

"I can't do anything else but this tonight."

"Oh, is your friend in town? Louise or Ellen? Come on out, girls! You hiding in there? Nah, they'd never fit, Ellen especially." He laughs. "What makes you think I was going to try anything more? You Jewish girls, youse are the horniest things going. Everything sex, sex, sex!"

"Very funny. Where's this dinner you promised me? I don't smell anything cooking. If you got me here under false pretenses the joke's on you because all you're getting tonight is conversation."

"I let the cook off tonight. Since I'm a kid I always hated talking in front of the help. Let's order in some Chinese, whaddya say?"

"Okay. I like Chinese food. It's tastier than donkey chow."

"You got that right. Irish cookbooks are real skinny."

Over our egg rolls and lo mein we take one giant step, yes you may, from joking to talking. I trace my short, exciting career path from word-processing clerk all the way to executive secretary in a market research firm. He listens with rapt attention, as if I am disclosing crucial information. I half expect him to pull out a pad and get it all down in writing. He even waits a few seconds to make sure not to interrupt me. I could get used to this.

"Tell me," he says, "you were such a smart girl. I remember you and your sister running home from school just to get a jump on your homework. The two of youse never made it outside till four-thirty. Why didn't you go off to college like your sister?" My mother must have put him up to this.

"I was an okay student but nothing special. No one was about to hand me a scholarship, and since my parents both worked, we just topped the limit for financial aid. And they wouldn't let me be burdened with a loan. Oh no, my parents insisted on paying for Arlene's four years at Binghamton, and they would have done the same for me. But I couldn't do that to them. Arlene's four years really wiped them out. Lucky for her she was up in Binghamton. She didn't have to hear the fights and see my mother go to pieces every time a new semester's tuition was due. I just couldn't make them go through that another time. Besides, Arlene really deserved to go. She was always the one with the goals. And me, I never had any goals. Life gets in the way of goals sometimes."

"Betcha Arlene had no trouble asking."

"She never has any trouble asking for anything. She expects it and it sort of comes to her, just like that. They're still paying off her wedding, twelve thousand plus interest. She deserved it, though. They're very proud of her accomplishments, and this wedding was a reward. But she should have at least offered back some of the gift money, I think."

"They wouldn't have taken it from her anyway."

"That's not the half of it," I tell him between noodle dips into the duck sauce. "They're still paying off her trip to England. She spent two weeks there the summer after she got out of grad school. They just couldn't say no to her, because she did everything she was told. And she never really considered the money angle." He's too good a listener, he brought out my confession without the bright light in my face. And I'm talking too much. Really, I don't usually reveal this much.

"Jesus, how do they make ends meet with all them loans? The interest payments must kill 'em."

"Like everyone else, I guess. They work the mirror trick. Charge on Visa, pay on MasterCard. Get a bank loan to pay off the department stores. Mirrors."

"Like the mirror house in Rockaway Playland. Remember that? You didn't know where you began and the mirrors ended. Twisted everything, though. I never liked them mirrors much. And when they crack, sweetie, forget it."

We move on to the beef and broccoli. "Whatever happened to your sister?" I ask him. I picture a blond, pigtailed, freckled girl in her red plaid uniform, white blouse, white knee socks, and black velvet saddle shoes, parochial school chic.

He frowns but his eyes remain a cool, dark, emotionless blue. "Oh, we hardly never see her. She's a real big-shot corporate lawyer. She has nothing to do with us no more. She don't leave Manhattan too much. Teresa Ann, she's our little princess. She gets the brains. She gets to go to Catholic school, the CYO camps. She wins the scholarship to Seton Hall, and between her grades and her ass-kissing she skips right into Princeton Law." He backs away from the table. "Sweetie, I'm dying. Mind if I take my shirt off?"

"No, I don't mind." Not at all. He tosses the blue checked cotton shirt on an unoccupied kitchen chair. I avoid staring at the bumpy scar tissue that tops the belt loop of his jeans. I look anywhere but at the scar, but he notices.

"I was shot, right where the vest ended. Looks worse than it is."

"What happened?"

"A robbery collar that went sour on me. Happened a few years ago when I was still on patrol. Let me tell you, it was more trouble than it was worth. Paid hell for it too. A stupid no win situation, you know, damned if you do, dead if you don't."

"What do you mean?"

"I discharged my weapon. Law don't hold with that no more. I mean you're given a gun but they really don't like you using it, not when the situation ain't so clear. And not when the perp's sixteen and colored. While I'm mending in the hospital, the D.A. does some digging. I'm cleared after the grand jury finally put their heads together and realize my ass was on the line and I wasn't out there for target practice. Good thing for me my partner's face was as dark as the kid's. I even got a citation, but just to make sure I'd never do that again, they shipped me out of my precinct for a while. Great, I think. Maybe they'll stick me in Forest Hills or Douglaston, where I can really get a good rest. But no such luck. They throw me in fucking Williamsburg, Brooklyn. Community Affairs. I get to play neighborhood referee between the Hasids and the coloreds."

"Did he die?"

"Are you kidding? Every night I'd get down on my

knees and pray to God that this scumbag would make it. Believe me, if he kicked off, I'd still be out in Williamsburg."

"Why did you become a cop?"

"Real simple. I look great in blue."

Obviously, I am not the first to ask him this question. I don't smile, I just look. He shrugs, obligated to go on. "Sweetie, you're the only girl I ever took out who wants conversation from me. I don't know, I was sick of being another fuck-up in a long line of fuck-ups. I felt sorry for my mother, really. My father disappeared one day, you know the old story, went downstairs for a pack of cigarettes and forgot to come back. He was drunk half the time anyway so it wasn't too much of a loss. But you want to know something, it was my grandmother that turned me around. Senior year. Must have been like three in the morning. She caught me sneaking in stoned out of my face and she went nuts. 'Tommy, you're going to end up a shit just like your father if you don't straighten out. My daughter deserves better than to be hurt twice, so why don't you get the hell out of here now, before you got to crawl out?' The old lady always knew how to get me right where I live. 'No, Nana, I'll straighten out, you'll see,' I told her. I mean at that point I would have said anything to get her off my back, but I knew she was right. Only it's too late to do a complete turn-around in school, but I snuck out of Bryant with a diploma. Billy Emmet—you know Billy, my mother's second husband—told me about the police test. I said, all right, what the hell. The pay ain't bad, the benefits are decent, and I did want my mother to be proud of me, at least not ashamed to mention my name in public. Nana was right as usual. My mother definitely had enough grief for a lifetime. So I got one of these blue and orange Arco civil service books and studied till I knew it cold. And you know what? I passed this test first try. And the physical, that was a piece of cake for someone used to running up and down the back stairs at Bryant. And then I got called up." He throws his shirt back on, leaving it unbuttoned.

"Want to take a walk? This food is sticking me."

"Okay. Can I borrow a sweatshirt or something?" The night air had become damp, chilly. I could feel the breeze from the small windows above the room.

"Sure, sweetie. I can't believe you're cold." He gets me a worn, navy-blue sweatshirt. It's as comfortable as he is. "Next time I'm over we're going to bring your sister's bike over. Then we could ride together."

"I haven't ridden in ages." I'm getting sore just thinking about it.

"Oh, it's just like sex, you never forget."

We walk up toward Woodhaven Boulevard. Cars whiz by, their red lights shoot off into the night. "Sorry I couldn't take you out better tonight," he says.

"I don't care about that."

"Yeah, but I do. It bothers the shit out of me. Every goddamn month I try to be good, put something away for a rainy day. I make decent money, with the overtime and all. And still every month it disappears on me. This month it's that fucking Schwab van, three hundred and fifty bucks I'm out till Matty hits at the track. Last month we made the funeral, and I won't even tell you how much that set me and my mother back. And next month it will be something else. It never fails. I'm caught up in this fucking race just to stand still."

"You have to learn the mirror game. Work a little magic with your cards."

"Oh, I know that game all too well. In the end, Mr. Visa and Mr. Discover are the ones holding the cards. Come on, Sunshine, I'll buy you Sunday's paper."

Why don't I offer to buy the papers? Why didn't I buy dinner, for that matter? He's a Sunnyside boy, that's why. Sunnyside boys don't know from women's liberation, not on dates anyhow. I hate to admit it but it all comes down to marketing, right? Know your customer.

We walk back to his block with the Sunday *News* and my mother's *New York Times*. He starts his car, drives me home. Already I'm memorizing the rows of buildings and stores between our two apartments, the distance between us, less than I had thought. "Your job sounds way too dangerous. You know, come to think of it, bus drivers wear blue also."

Behind the gray-tinted lenses his eyes are cool, fixed on the steady rhythm of traffic. "Shit. Now you tell me."

May skids into June rather suddenly. The days turn unbearably warm too fast, turning my family's kitchen and living room into one long pizza oven. To reduce the strain on the fraying electrical system, each family is permitted one single, solitary air conditioner. Our one arctic blast originates from my parents' bedroom with an assist from a monstrous electric floor fan that stands guard at their open door. When Con Edison is in good shape, my bedroom, which is directly opposite theirs, becomes almost balmy. Just before I drift off into a sweaty sleep, a vision appears, a vision of my own thermostat. It is winter. I feel faint from the heat surging through the radiators. It is summer. I catch frostbite from the central air. Darn, we must get that thing adjusted.

It is June and I'm confused. Well, let's say I'm cautiously attracted. I'd rather be a June cliché, an in-love cliché, but I have too many doubts. I love the smell of his skin, his hurried walk, his boisterous laugh, his gentle touch, his quick grin. I love the way he makes love to me. I love the way he listens to me. But—in the history of Joanna Barron there always seems to be a *but* or three—but I can't bring myself to ignore his crassness, his prejudice, his common ways. So, maybe I have let my mother's standards seep in and become my own. So, maybe I have let my mother's good wishes for my future become my own. So, maybe I can do better. And yet . . . And yet, there is something between us more than physical. Something.

And what will the future bring? I ask myself. Time ticks away. Twenty-seven will edge into thirty and careen head first into thirty-five. So, I ask myself, is there a remote possibility of a future with Tommy McClellan or am I wasting precious time?

*   *   *

Eight o'clock Tuesday night, Tommy calls. He's shouting into the phone yet I can hardly hear him. "Jo, can
you drive over for a little while? There's some people I
want you to meet."

"Sounds like a party."

"Nah, just some guys from the station. I'm stealing
their money at poker."

"I don't want to be there with a bunch of guys. I'll
meet them some other—"

"No, come on down. My partner's wife is here too.
You know how to get here?"

Any other person would have taken offense at this
question. The trip involves about two turns. I am not of-
fended. Tommy knows my sense of direction is underde-
veloped. "Yes," I say proudly. "I have completely
memorized the journey."

"Good. Listen up. Double park in front of the house.
You'll never find a spot big enough for your father's car."

"You'll fix it for me if I get a ticket?"

"The hell with the ticket. Get your buns down here.
Forthwith," he yells into the phone. "These humps don't
think you exist. They think I'm full of shit. You gotta
show. My ass is on the line."

"Oh, when you ask me so nicely, how can I refuse?"

I borrow my father's 1979 Buick Electra 225. This car
can accommodate my family plus my mother's two sisters
and their six shopping bags. This is not a car, this is a
relative transport vehicle.

From the curb I can hear a bunch of loud male voices.
I get hesitant. What if I don't make the grade with the
family? I base my insight on a book review of a recent
Wambaugh novel. A police officer and his fellow officers
are as close or closer than his actual family. The screen
door is unlocked. I walk down his steps into Tommy's
kitchen.

The room is as smoky as a Friday night bar. Empty
bottles of Heineken decorate the counter. An overturned
bowl of popcorn is our host's centerpiece this evening.

Under this racket of laughter and table pounding there's ongoing conversation about mutts and collars and plants. Get me out of here.

"Hey, Sunshine! How long you standing there?" Tommy's voice calls out. "I'd like you to meet my partner Eddie Profeta." He points to a tall, beefy man with a thick brown drooping moustache. The moustache smiles at me. "And," Tommy continues, "my other partner in Anti-crime. Officer Paul Bryzinski."

"Hey, Jo."

"And last and in my opinion least is my very old friend, Sergeant George Watkins."

Sergeant Watkins, a huge black man in his late forties, smiles and offers up his hand. I shake it hesitantly. He looks strong enough to remove it.

"Don't mind Jo," Tommy confides loudly to Watkins. "She just ain't used to seeing colored in my apartment."

Sergeant Watkins laughs and shakes his massive head from side to side. "All cops are niggers," he says. "We're the blue niggers."

"Shame on you, George. Don't you ever use that word in front of Jo, please. First, she'll tell you flat out you're some kind of ignorant racist and you're full of prejudice for people that haven't had your opportunities. Then she'll make a horrible-looking face, it's awful. Show everyone that face. No, no, that ain't it but it's a real nice shade of red, sweetie."

"Lisa!" Eddie calls. "Come here. Tommy's eighty-five is here. You better meet her before she walks out."

From the living room I hear the closing of books, the scratchy sound of paper on paper. A pretty, petite, black-haired, olive-skinned girl enters. "Hi," she says warmly. "Want to get out of this dump? Let's go for coffee." I could kiss her. I really could.

We take my dad's car to an all-night Dunkin' Donuts. "Are you and Eddie married long?" I ask.

"Two years this June, but we grew up together."

We order coffee and Bavarian creams. Leave me alone, Aunt Ruthie, I don't want an oat bran muffin. "Does

Eddie talk much about his work, you know, the day-to-
day stuff?"

"Here and there, depends on his day. He's been happier since he hooked up with Anticrime. Sure is better
than the crazy hours he had when he was wearing the
bag, as they say, which means in uniform. He's studying
for the sergeant's exam. Doesn't Tommy tell you
anything?"

"A little bit, but only when I ask. I can't even tell
when he's serious." He does have a serious side. I've seen
it slow to come and quick to leave. I've seen the shadow
of its image deep within his dark blue eyes.

"You can call me. I even made myself a dictionary of
all the terms I had to ask Eddie to explain to me. Did
you hear Eddie call you an eight-five? All that means is
a girlfriend."

"Oh, here I was wondering what I'd have to do to
make a hundred."

I ask for a copy of the dictionary, couldn't hurt. "Are
you worried about him all the time?"

She tosses the thick coat of black hair away from her
face. "No, I try hard not to think so much. I keep busy.
I'm running back and forth to Queens College three nights
a week. I'm almost finished with my bachelor's and then
I'll quit my day job and start going to school full-time.
B.A. in Sociology, and if I'm accepted someplace, a mas-
ter's in Social Work."

Credentials, I think. "Sociology? I have an uncle who's
a full-time sociology professor at NYU. Tell me, have you
ever heard of someone named Dirk Hyne? My uncle mentioned him a few weeks ago."

Lisa Profeta looks pensive for a minute. She takes a
bite out of her Bavarian cream. "Dirk Hyne? Durkheim,
Emile Durkheim, one of the founding fathers of sociology.
Why would anyone care to bring him up in a conversation
outside of the classroom?"

"My uncle really likes to show off for the family. I
think he gets off on making other people feel stupid."

Lisa looks up into my face. She stares but it's not of-

Moe looks at me with disgust. I didn't order the bris-
ket. "Coleslaw comes. What are you drinking?"

"Mmm. I don't know. A Coke with ice."

"And you?" Moe asks Sandy.

"Pastrami on pump. French fries. You'll help me out
on those, Joanna."

"To drink?"

"Dr. Brown's cel-ray."

"We're all out."

"Out? What do you mean, out? I'm waiting two years.
I was on foreign soil. I couldn't get a cel-ray for all the
money in the world."

"So," he shrugs, "take a seltzer, maybe."

"All right. Seltzer it is," Gary says, then turns to me.
"Let me ask you something, Joanna. Are you serious
about this guy?"

"I might be, but I don't know if I want to be."

Sandy nods and rest his chin on his hand.

"Was there anyone special in Texas?"

"Yes. Someone very special. We were engaged. And
then we weren't engaged."

"I'm sorry to hear that. Gary never mentioned
anything."

"I'm looking for a fresh start, a blank page, if you
know what I mean."

"I don't think that's possible. Everyone comes with a
history. Even if you met a six-year-old, chances are she
was dumped by a boy in kindergarten and was locked in
a codependent relationship in preschool."

"Yeah, true enough. Jeez, when did you get so
philosophical?"

"What can I tell you? I'm great when it comes to other
people's lives."

Moe shuffles over with our plates in his two scrawny
arms. The sandwiches are two-handers, bursting with
flavored meats. Our glasses sweat circles onto the poly-
urethane table. I smell my sandwich before I allow my
teeth to come in for a landing. "This is great."

"Yeah. I really missed this."

"Well Dorothy, there's no place like home," I say, eating one of Sandy's thick steak fries.

"You know you're not anything at all like Arlene. She's so . . . what's the word I'm looking for without putting my foot in my mouth?"

"Managerial."

"That's it. Thank you."

"My uncle Jack calls my sister an MFC."

"That doesn't sound too good."

"No, it's not what you're thinking. MFC is Madame Full Charge."

Sandy laughs quietly. "That's a good one."

"I think you and Gary are a lot alike. You're both great guys. Your parents must've done something right."

"Oh sure, give them all the credit."

Later Sandy settles up with Moe and drives me back home.

"Thanks," I say hugging him when I get to my door. And I brush a kiss on the top of his cheekbone.

"Good luck with your situation."

"Oh thanks. Sandy, this meal was a minivacation from all my problems."

"Good," he smiles. "Now, it would have been really perfect if Garber's had my cel-ray tonic."

"I guess I'll be running into you at one of those holiday things in the fall."

"You bet. We'll compare notes."

"And histories."

My mother is sitting in our apartment in front of the TV, sipping iced tea.

"Hey Ma. You're up late tonight."

"So where'd you go?"

"I told you. A deli. A deli in Forest Hills."

"Garber's? On Austin Street?"

"Yes, that's the one."

"It's very good. We met the Sussmans there many years ago. So?"

"What do you mean, so?" Like I don't know.

"Did you have a nice time?"

"Very nice. He's a very nice guy."

"And well-spoken."

"Yes. And well-spoken."

"He's educated too. And he has a good job."

"Yes, it seems so."

She swirls the cubes quickly around the glass. "Will you see him again?"

"I'll probably bump into him at Arlene's house now and then. Won't I?"

"That much I know. Would you go out with him again?"

"As a friend, yes."

"Didn't you like him?"

"Of course I like him. He's a great guy. He's like Gary with a Texas twang."

"What does that mean?"

"I love Gary, Ma. He's like a brother to me. And I like Sandy the same way."

"That's a good start, right? Other things can develop if you let them." She inches off the couch and shuts the television. Her nightgown is wrinkled and it sticks like a bandage to her fleshy legs. "They say a little cooler tomorrow. Schwab's must've reached a hundred and twelve. Those fans do nothing. The office has air-conditioning, naturally. Why should they care if we're melting in the back as long as the work gets out?"

"Why don't you call in sick? Tomorrow's Friday. You'll have a long weekend."

"And do what?"

"And do nothing. Rest."

"Rest? My mind never rests. When you're settled down with the person who's right for you, then I'll first rest."

"Good night, Ma." If I let it, the conversation would go full circle. We'd reach Sandy Sussman once again. And she'd ask me why I couldn't learn to love him. And I wouldn't have a decent answer for her.

Eight

The next night, Friday night, I am asked to keep Aunt Adele company. My uncle Jack has to pay his respects for an old Army buddy in Brooklyn, and Aunt Adele is better kept away from such things. Although her bouts of depression seem to be under control, Uncle Jack doesn't want to risk a repeat. I remember once many years ago my aunt Adele actually believed she was dead. The shock treatments relieved her "delusions of deadness," as Arlene put it. Now Aunt Adele knows she's alive. Though I am sure that this ailment is not as uncommon as you would think. Plenty of people walk around not knowing whether they are dead or alive. Aunt Adele just made a big thing out of it.

I really don't mind keeping my aunt company. In a way, it's no different than babysitting a seven-year-old. Aunt Adele is sitting on a kitchen chair surrounded by a couple of stacks of romance novels. Their covers are old, bent, and yellowed. The handsome men are creased and their ladies are pale and wrinkled. She has read all of them over and over again, but she forgets. She must read them once more. Once more the broad-shouldered, square-jawed hero will realize by page 175 that he is deeply in love with the spoiled, willful, yet exquisite heroine. He will turn out to be abundantly rich and have royal blood flowing through his veins. Of course they will live happily ever after. Aunt Adele will pick up another book. The hero will have a different name. He will be just as square jawed and just as good looking. By page 175 their passion will be kindled and flame up into a deep, burning love. They will marry and inherit a fortune. They will live happily ever after. Aunt Adele will forget all about them in half a day. Their chiseled faces are now blurred and fuzzy. Did she read that one before or was it the book next to it? It doesn't matter, Uncle Jack will tell her. Read it again, Adele.

I only hope Aunt Adele is capable of realizing real romantic heroes might be named Jack. They may have gray, thinning hair and stooped shoulders. Their jaws might be round. They may even wear shiny suits.

"You look so beautiful," Aunt Adele tells me. "Like a lady from long ago. Lady Joanna."

"It's just an old pair of shorts that used to be jeans, Aunt Adele. I guess you like the purple T-shirt."

"Purple is the color for royalty."

"Aren't you a little hot in your cap?" She's in her light blue crocheted cap tonight. No season has been invented for Aunt Adele where a cap wasn't required dress.

"No. The night air gives me a chill. Old bones."

"Want to play cards?"

"Cards? I don't know. Maybe."

There is a knock at her door. Maybe my mother changed her mind. I twist the doorknob and pull back the door and see Tommy standing at the other end of it.

"Hey, come on in. I'm keeping my aunt company for a while."

"I want to talk to you, Jo."

"I can't leave her alone. My uncle should be back soon. I'm the second shift. Come on in."

Yes, Tommy would know my aunt Adele. Everyone did. Her erratic behavior through the halls of our building was legendary.

His eyes are expressionless beneath his glasses. "Yeah, all right," he mumbles.

I watch him take in his surroundings with one grand sweep of his navy-blues. Odd, mismatched pieces of furniture. A solitary table setting. A pinochle deck. The stacks of aged romance novels. Model airplanes. The tweed carpet worn to its padding. Tommy picks up a picture of my uncle Jack in his World War II uniform. He stares at the young face under the too large cap. He puts the picture back on its spot on the lace doily and I hear the hint of a sigh escape from his throat.

"Aunt Adele, is it okay if Tommy sits down with us?"

"Oh sure. Let's have a tea party for Lady Joanna and her young man."

I get up and stick a pot of water on the stove to boil. Tommy picks up one of Aunt Adele's romances and then places it down. "You're some reader there, huh?"

"Reader? Yes. I like to read about love, about the handsome man and the beautiful girl. I tell Jack the stories work better than the pills the doctor gives me. They give me a nice, calm feeling."

Tommy nods his head. "Yeah, I can understand that," he says softly. "You can visit other places, nicer places."

"I don't see your grandma Agnes much these days. Where is she hiding?"

Tommy glances at me in the kitchen and I shake my head. "Oh," he says. "She's around. She's living with me now. Haunts me all the time."

"Tell her Adele says hello."

"I'll do that. She always had—has a kind word about you too."

I stir the sugar and milk into Aunt Adele's tea. Tommy takes his own. I like mine plain. "Can we put grape jelly on the Ritz crackers, Joanna?"

"Oh sure. Can I maybe open a window Aunt Adele?"

"You're hot?"

"Well it is August and we are drinking hot tea."

"Yes, you're right. I didn't think of that. Young people need air. I'll open—"

"Sit still," Tommy says. "I got it." He bangs the center frame of the old casement window with the palm of his hand and wrenches it upward. Everyone in the building has a love-hate relationship with the old windows. We hate them because they're drafty and they always get stuck. We love them because old windows mean the building isn't on its way to being co-oped and our apartments won't be sold out from under us. "I see your uncle coming."

"Aunt Adele, Uncle Jack is coming upstairs."

"He looked so handsome tonight. He wore his gray plaid suit."

I wash the teacups and listen for Uncle Jack's key.

"Hey, thanks a lot, Jo," he says with his wide grin. He extends his hand out to Tommy. "Good to see you again."

"Jack, that's Agnes Conlin's grandson, Tommy."

"I know who it is, Adele. He's helped us on a few occasions that I'd rather forget. Thanks a lot, Jo."

"Oh, we had a little tea party with Ritz crackers and grape jelly."

"A party for our Lady Joanna," my aunt adds, "in her royal purple frock."

We take the stairs down to the lobby and walk into the courtyard in front of our building. It is dark. The semicircle of chairs has been dismantled for the night. Tommy leans his shoulders against the bricks. From where I'm standing, he looks like he is carrying the weight of the entire building on his back. "You got something you maybe want to tell me?"

"Thanks for being so understanding about my aunt. What did my uncle mean about you helping them?"

He shrugs. "Nothing. I did my job. Your aunt had one of her episodes and I happened to be around. I waited with your uncle till the ambulance came. I talked to her, that's all. And another time I walked her home from Queens Boulevard. I saw her wandering around in the rain and I saw her home. It was no big deal. She always been like that, huh?"

"Yeah. I guess so. She seems to be okay for now."

"Your uncle must be a regular saint."

"Yes. He has a lot of patience."

"Jo, what's going on here? You playing head games with me?"

"What are you talking about?"

"Last night. Remember? Eight P.M. Incident involving a gray Volvo with Texas plates. Suspect is an unidentified white male. Early to mid-thirties. Five-eleven, approximately 190 pounds. No distinguishing marks."

"Oh, I don't believe this. Who ratted?"

"Who do you think?"

"Brother Matthew."

"Bingo."

"Do you want to take a walk or something?" I ask.

"I ain't moving from this here spot until you can make me understand what's happening. Maybe I'm crazy but I thought we had some understanding here."

The little porcupine pricks of guilt begin to irritate the back of my neck. "We're not married, you know. We're not engaged. As far as I can understand, we're dating. In this state, that leaves us free to come and go as we please." I regret saying it as soon as it flies out of my mouth.

"Is that some city thing? Because if it is, I'm real ignorant about your Manhattan ways, having grown up on this very spot. Because in my part of town, Sunnyside Queens, if two people are seeing each other, they don't see no one else until they break it off. Does that unspoken rule ring a little bell in your head?"

I stood right beside him not wanting to look at him, not wanting to deal with his questions. "Once upon a time I heard someone in Buckley's mention that work is the serious and everything else better be fun in the sun."

"And how many drinks did the speaker of those words have that night?"

"Oh, he was pretty sober as far as I could tell. Maybe he had one scotch, maybe two the most."

"Not counting the three he had beforehand just to get him through the wake in one piece. And the half a bottle he downed the day before when he got the call from his mother at the hospital and he learned of the death of his number one fan."

"So you're saying you didn't mean what you said?"

"I don't know what the hell I'm saying. Maybe I meant it then, I don't know. That was then. I don't mean it anymore."

A car whizzes by and I lose my concentration for a minute. "Tommy, you don't exactly have a reputation for your long, serious relationships."

"No, I guess I don't."

"So, I took a little vacation from you. I had dinner with a regular civilian, a nice guy. He's the same nice person on Tuesday that he was on Monday. He'll be nice on Wednesday too. To tell you the truth, I'm afraid of you. You scare me."

"What is it? My temper? My gun?"

Oh, his gun. It would be strapped to his ankle tonight, under his jeans. I played mental games with that gun all the time. Where is he hiding the gun? No, it wasn't the gun. It was the job itself. Believe me, that's his baggage. That's his ex-wife and five kids. "No," I say after a while. "Not your temper. Not your gun. It's your inability to communicate. Sometimes you hide under this coating of nastiness for weeks. You don't explain. You cut yourself off from the rest of the world. You're so angry. And you don't hesitate to take it out on anybody who crosses your path."

"What if I could get word out to you when I'm on one of these assignments? Would that help?"

I raise my shoulders. "Well, yeah, that would help. But what about who you turn into?" Sandy will always be Sandy. Tommy could end up being anybody.

"I don't think I'll have to do that again real soon. But you gotta understand, when I'm angry like that, I'm not mad at you. I'm mad at the world. And I'm mad at myself."

"You wanted to hurt me that July fourth at Louise's pool. I could see it in your face."

"I wanted to hurt myself. You just happened to be

there. And I don't want to talk about that. I'm trying real hard to forget it. And I'm hoping you can forget it too."

"The guy Matty saw me with is an old friend of the family. He's Arlene's husband's brother."

"From Texas? Who-wee! He must be the old cowhand from Delancey and Grand!"

"Very funny. He's from Queens. He just lived in Texas for a while."

"Let's see if I got this straight. He's single. Jewish. Musta been to college. Good job. Talks real nice. He can buy you a house right near your sister like you told me about. Three car garage. Modern appliances. Playroom for the kids. Can't say I blame you. He's starting to sound good to me."

"He's a family friend. We went to a deli together, that's all." Wouldn't it be great if I could love Sandy? Life would be easier, neater. My mother would be happy. My sister would climb off my back.

Tommy walks away from the building. He stretches. "I wish you could spend the whole night with me. I'd wake up early, make us some coffee, set you up a bowl of Frosted Flakes. Then we'd go on back to bed for a few hours."

"I can't do that."

"I know you can't, Sunshine, but I can dream. Anyways, I got us an invitation to my sister's on Sunday, if you're not busy."

"Teresa Ann?"

"Yep. I guilted her into a lunch. Finally you'll get to see the class side of the McClellan tribe. We're not all a bunch of lowlifes. You up to it?"

"Yeah. I'd like to see her again. Have you noticed Mr. Santini had Mr. Gurtz paint the courtyard floor red?"

"Yeah, I saw it on the way in. Too ugly for words. The bastard probably siphoned off a pint of blood from each tenant. I should rope it off. It looks too much like a crime scene. Jesus Christ almighty."

"What's the matter?"

"You see that guy driving real slow in that Ford?"

"Yeah."

"It's the third time he's passed by. Shit. He's looking for my brother. I know it. I just know it. Jo, go on upstairs. He's coming out of the car. Go on up."

I do not move. I stand next to him. The man has a protruding belly and a receding hairline. What's left of the hair is shimmering with grease. The street lamp finds every limp strand. It curls on the back of his neck. His eyes root around the dark courtyard.

"Can I help you, pal?" Tommy asks.

"Maybe. Matty McClellan live here?"

"Who?"

"McClellan. Blond kid. Pug face. Built like a brick shithouse."

"Never heard of him. I've lived here all my life. There's no one in there by that name. You know any McClellans in that building?" Tommy asks me.

"No. There used to be a McBride but he moved out." Lying is easy. I should lie more often. I am good at it.

The man glances through the glass doors and spots the rows of dull, smudged brass mailboxes in the lobby. "Just the same. I'll go take a look for myself."

"It's kind of late to be looking for someone, ain't it?"

The man sticks out a stubbled chin. "Yeah, what's it to you?"

"I don't want no trouble in there, that's all."

"Who the fuck are you?"

"I'm a cop, that's who, and a little birdy tells me you better get your ass on out of here."

"You're a cop? That's good by me. That kid owes me three hundred dollars. And it's in my rights to go get it."

"Let me ask you something, who do you work for?"

"Nobody."

"Don't hand me that bullshit. I'm not looking for no trouble."

"Bobby Dellacourt. He's outta Howard Beach."

Tommy shakes his head slowly. "All right. We can do this one of two ways. You can go into that building, ring every friggin' doorbell and maybe you find him and maybe you don't. Obviously the kid don't got the money or he would have met you where he usually meets you at four-thirty in the afternoon. So you're going back empty-handed to Mr. Dellacourt. And that ain't gonna make him too happy. Or you can take these here sixty dollars I got in my wallet. Tell Mr. Dellacourt you beat the kid within an inch of his life, got a partial on the vig tonight and you'll get the rest on Monday at your usual spot. And then you'll look like a real hero."

The man grabs the three twenties Tommy holds out to him. "Why you doing this?"

"Because I'm Santa Claus. And if you ever come within ten feet of this building again, you and that goon with the lead pipe that's hiding in your backseat—don't think I missed him—will be sporting two brand new shiny assholes."

The man starts walking to his car. "Monday," he says to Tommy. "You tell your friend no excuses."

Tommy watches them pull away. When the Ford becomes invisible in the night, he turns to me. "Let's get one thing straight here, Joanna, when I say go upstairs, you get yourself upstairs. You fly upstairs. You understand me?"

I nod.

"You all right?"

I nod again, too weak to speak.

"You're shaking like a leaf. Do you know that? Come on, Lady Jo, your knight in shining armor will escort you on up to your palace."

"Who were they?"

"Good friends of my brother. You know if I wasn't standing here, they would have gone into my mother's apartment. She would have been scared out of her mind. Jesus Christ, if those two wouldn't have killed him, I would have."

"He owes so much money?"

"He owes on what he owes. His vig, his interest, is more than what I pay rent on my apartment. He can't get out from under and that's exactly how them people like it. And he's my cross to bear, Jo, because as long as I'm alive I'm not going to let anything happen to him."

The elevator lets us out on my floor. He kisses me good night and he stops, looks around, and he kisses me good night again. "I'm sorry you had to see that. I'd like to keep all the ugly out of here."

"Are you going home?" I'm very tired all of a sudden.

"I'm going to pay Matty a little visit if he's home, and if he's not home I'll just have to track him down."

"Don't hurt him, Tommy."

"Hurt him? You kidding me? He was Golden Gloves once upon a time. No, once again I got to go hammer it into his thick mick skull that you don't jerk these people around. If you say you're going to be in front of Schwab's at four-thirty in the afternoon, you better be there with a smile on your face and a stack of bills in your hand. You don't go out at lunch, cash your paycheck at Buckley's and put it down on another pony. It just don't work like that. I'll call you tomorrow, sweetie, okay? I'm real sorry about all this. Come on, one more for the road." He holds me tighter and tighter and then I am released to 4B. "Get some sleep, Sunshine."

Sunday is such a special day for the two of us, more special for Tommy because he had to rearrange his schedule to make it happen. He has invited us over to his sister's duplex on Eighty-third and Second, and Teresa Ann just couldn't say no. I'm a lumpy mixture of nerves and curiosity because I haven't seen Teresa Ann since she graduated from St. Bernadette's Catholic High School for Girls. She is my age to the month but we never had much to do with one another. She had her St. Bernie's friends and I was Bryant all the way.

Tommy stops by at twelve-thirty, looking happy and relaxed. No matter what he says, he is very proud of his sister and I know he wants to show her off for me. I notice his T-shirt is in one piece and his jeans have only one hole at the back pocket. I gather that he believes that lunch with Teresa Ann and her husband does not call for formal attire, or even business casual if he owned such clothes. I play it safe with a pink sundress and a short white jacket. A sundress and jacket is the summer answer to I-don't-know-what-to-wear. They are the woman's answer to Dockers and Rockports.

My mother and father are in good spirits as well. Daddy will be driving them to Flushing Meadow Park today. My mother loves to sit on a lawn chair surrounded by grass. She hates our block because it's all hard, ugly concrete—a red slab, she calls it. Unlike the other tenants, she doesn't relish sitting in the courtyard of our building and gossiping with the neighbors. She much prefers a lawn, and since her two sisters don't require Daddy's driving services, May and Sol Barron will be heading to greener pastures.

"I see Matty got his tooth fixed," my mother says to Tommy. "You know, they did a wonderful job. You can't even tell." My mother looks like a visitor from Munchkin-land whenever she stands next to Tommy.

"Uh-huh," Tommy says. "For that money the dentist should have cemented in a whole new set. But we're not finished there yet. Not a chance. My brother, bless him, hasn't been to see a dentist since he was twelve. They X-ray him and they find seven cavities. And your union, Mrs. Barron—"

"May, call me May."

"And your union, May, they don't pay dental. Am I right?"

"Yes, they always talk about this at the meetings but nothing ever comes of it."

"May, I'm gonna be paying for Matty's fillings for the rest of my life. Please don't say nothing to my mother because all these years she's giving him money for the dentist. It just got put into the horse's mouth, if you know what I mean. But I'm on to him. I don't give him the money, I deliver him with the money."

"You're a good brother," my father says. I had forgotten he was in the room.

Tommy shrugs. "Nah, he'd do the same for me. Matty

has a good heart when you come down to it. It's his brains that need a tune-up."

The telephone rings. My mother looks mystified. "Tommy, it's for you, Mrs. Gurtz."

He takes the phone. "Hiya hot stuff! Don't say a word 'cause both you and I know there's a ten day grace period on the rent. My mother has lived in this here building— Not the rent. So what the hell do you want?"

I can hear Mrs. Gurtz's flat, dull tones but I can't make out the words. "What do you do, track me down? This is the second time this month. Can't I get a few hours off?"

Her voice again.

"All right, keep it in your pants. Shit, you owe me, lady." He excuses himself.

My parents are a little impressed now. Tommy's status has risen in their estimation to that of social worker. He could be a rabbi, a solver of domestic problems.

Rabbi McClellan returns twenty minutes later with a deep, red scratch across his cheek. He smiles his big, easy smile. "It's the nice people I get to help. That's what I love about being a cop."

"Look at you!"

"This? It's nothing. Actually, after she ripped my face open, I had a very calming effect on the Wosinskis. You know I used to do this shit all the time when I was on patrol, but never alone. That's the secret to domestics. You need a partner, two to divide and two to conquer. How 'bout *you* come with me next time?"

My mother runs immediately into the bathroom for the cotton and Bactine. May has a live one! She stands up on a kitchen chair to reach his face. "Hold still. You don't want an infection. Not today, not with all those diseases going around."

"Jesus Christ. You're killing me."

My mother shows how tough she is. She holds up the fingers on her right hand. The skin on the underside is shredded into papery bits. "This is my big promotion from the sewing machine to hand-embroidery with aluminum bullion thread. For ten years now I'm sewing with wire. And we clean those shoulder boards with benzine."

Tommy winces. "See Jo, and you think I got a dangerous job."

After we say our goodbyes, I try to persuade Tommy not to drive into Manhattan. The traffic in the City is always heavy. There will be no place to park. Besides, the IRT will get us uptown in no time.

He tells me he hates the trains. They're dirty. The people in them are dirty. Nothing could convince him to take one, no way.

After losing that argument, I move on to the next order of business, the bottle of wine. After all, we are invited to lunch. We cannot show up empty-handed. True, the lower uppers would arrive with flowers, but let's not push things. Wine is my second choice, respectable, upper middle. He hates wine. Wine sucks. All it is is grape juice gone sour. How about a cake? A nice, lower-middle-class cake. He agrees to a cake and he pulls the car alongside King Kullen. No, we are not bringing a supermarket cake. It's not proper. Tommy does not care for the word proper. He says all kinds of rude words when he hears it but in the end he complies reluctantly to stopping by a bakery in the City.

By the time we arrive at Teresa Ann's, we are sweaty and worn-out. The Celica's air conditioner had met its maker along the way, its passing not exactly taken in stride by its owner. I keep my I-told-you-so's to myself but between the traffic and the fifteen dollar fee to park the car, it's an effort. Tommy just looks at me in the L'il Sweet Nuthin's Bake Shop. Eighteen dollars for chocolate layer. His silence is too loud.

Jordan and Teresa Ann's duplex apartment is mighty impressive. They live in a white brick four-story building adorned with overflowing window boxes. Their lobby furniture is nicer than what's in Aunt Naomi's living room. A doorman in a uniform announces our arrival through an intercom.

When they open their door—a heavy, solid, oaken

door, that is—I am taken aback. Teresa Ann looks nothing like a St. Bernie's girl. She handed in her plaid uniform for one of those white linen town-and-country pantsuits. Her blond hair is pulled back into a short black-ribboned ponytail. Pearl studs dot her small ears. Her small freckled nose sails through the air. She has become a Wasp, I think.

Jordan Arbrewster, her husband, must have vaccinated her with his particular strain of Protestantism, Episcopalian, I'd bet. According to Dahlia Barnett, these are the ones with the old money. And we all know that old money spends differently than new money.

"Hello, how are you?" she greets me in a fluty, girlish voice, arm outstretched. "I'm Terry." She does not recognize me, not at all.

Tommy grins at her shortened name. "Hey Little Sister." Then he picks her up, spins her around. "I miss you."

She smiles, but says nothing.

We are led across a white ceramic-tiled floor to a large living room filled with antique chairs and tables, modern paintings, and beige nubby couches. These antiques look even older than Tommy's mahogany bedroom set. The pieces are of a lighter wood and are designed without cherubs and eagle claws. Plain, old but plain. When I admire it, she tells me it's Shaker. This must rank right up there with Henredon and Thomasville.

I get introduced to Jordan, a tall, fair, balding man of at least forty with a large, cleft chin. (I myself have a small cleft in my chin too but not from a dip in the Barron gene pool. My cleft formed in the third grade when the city bus stopped short and my chin didn't.) Large cleft chin wears penny loafers without pennies and without socks. "How are you?" he asks. Ooooh, that *are* can slice. He really can pronounce an R, pronounces it sharper than I've ever heard.

"How ya doin'?" I reply. No, do I really speak like that? Gee, five minutes ago I spoke like the anchor on the seven o'clock news.

Tommy reminds his sister that I lived in her old build-

ing, that she knows me and Arlene. She tugs at her ponytail. "I really don't recall. I apologize, Joanna. It was such
a long time ago."

In half an hour I can tell that Teresa Ann has successfully erased her childhood along the yellow-bricked road
to upward mobility. She and her husband are lawyers—
attorneys, as she puts it—litigation attorneys retained by
the legal department of an international brokerage house.
Tommy told me they're the kind of lawyers who don't
ever get their hands dirty.

"Got a beer, Teresa Ann? My air conditioner in the
Toyota dropped dead on the way over."

"No. I'm sorry, Tom. We have diet soda, sparkling
water, fruit juice, or white wine."

"How 'bout some water that don't sparkle. I like my
water dull."

Jordan laughs a deep, bellowing Santa Claus laugh.
Trudy had mentioned to me with pride that his family was
one of the founders of Richmond, Virginia, way back when.
My mother refers to these kind of people as the real goyim,
the goyim who aren't trash, I suppose. Hmmm, I would bet
this man is not ashamed to play golf in green knickers. He
has his one-hundred-percent wool suits custom-tailored in
Savile Row, and he's more than passingly familiar with
the floor plan of the Vivian Beaumont. Am I getting this
right, Dahlia?

I can't stop noticing just how poorly and coarsely we
speak. For the first time I'm hearing all of Tommy's he
don'ts, she don'ts, the I'll axe you for I'll ask you, and my
own lovely habit of never pronouncing a final g and slurring
every word into one spongy sentence. Immediately I begin
to select and pronounce my words with caution. Not even
for Dahlia Barnett do I do this, not even for Uncle Marc, so
please imagine how intimidating these two are to me.

"What ever happened to your face, Tom?" Teresa
Ann asks.

"I was very recently mauled by a crazy woman down
in L3. She was brawlin' with her husband for a change."
Tommy is not working at acclimating to his surroundings.

That Poppy business really must have taken a lot out of him. I'm a far better chameleon today.

Boy, it sure is hard to believe that Teresa Ann was once part of the McClellan family. Maybe Princeton Law offers crash courses in poise and elocution for their scholarship students. You never know with these schools. It can't all be observation, couldn't possibly be.

"It would be nice to see you drop by once in a while. Your mother can't understand why her most precious princess ain't been out to see her in over a year." Don't mince those words now, Tommy.

"You don't understand. It is difficult for me to return home, in view of the circumstances."

"You're right, I don't. Is it any skin off your ass to spend one Sunday with your mother? Your mother who still carries your first communion picture around in her wallet? Explain it to me, will ya?"

Jordan and I sit motionless in observation.

"Let me bring in the miniature quiches," Teresa Ann announces. "They should be ready by now."

"Oh, I'm comin' with you, Little Sister. You ain't gettin' off so easy. I ain't leaving until I get some answers."

Jordan and I are left to acquaint ourselves. He gives me a tour of their duplex. My eyes rise to view the elaborate moldings suspended between wall and fifteen-foot ceiling. Prewar, I tell myself.

Then I am drawn to an antique Viennese open-faced tobacco cabinet suspended high upon the dining room wall. Inside, he shows me, are his family's collection of silver spoons dating back to 1703. His parents presented them to him on the occasion of his engagement, as he is the eldest son. Each spoon is engraved with the couple's name, date of marriage, and family crest. I don't hide my awe. Okay, I'm impressed. How nice to be one of those people with meaningful, historical ancestors, people that really belong in America.

I think of the gray, creased photos of my Russian great-grandparents. What a shabby-looking bunch of sourpusses they were. I tell him that my family's coat of

arms were probably crossed ladles over a pot of steaming
matzoh ball soup. Jordan bellows a steady Ho Ho Ho.
Control yourself, Jordan, it's way too early for Christmas.

"Joanna, there really is no difference. The Arbrewsters
were just victims of an earlier pogrom." That's an unusual
way of looking at it. He asks me about my job. Reeves
and Barnett. Yes, he's heard of them. A secretary? Yes,
he's heard of them too.

From the kitchen we hear the battling McClellans.

"I'll never forgive Mother for marrying Billy Emmet.
He has to be the most crass, ill-bred person I've ever encountered, always speaking of his private parts, his Johnson. My God, Tom, it's intolerable. He makes my flesh
crawl."

"That man and his Johnson put you through school.
Ya think Ma coulda managed on her own?"

"I went through on scholarships, so what do you
know?"

"Them scholarships didn't cover everything. Who
paid for your books and your clothes and all those whaddya call them, fees? Who paid for your fees? Did that
drop from the sky? No, Teresa Ann. Billy paid. Just like
he pays for his four kids on Long Island. And what does
he get for his trouble?"

"You and Matthew are as bad as he is. You all belong
in the gutter. You don't know how to elevate yourselves.
Education is wasted on you."

"You were the one that got the private school education. Ma and Nana working bingo every other week and
doing whatever else the church wanted just to keep you
in a uniform. Don't hold that over my head. Matty and I
got nothin'. You got it all, Teresa Ann. You were Ma's
special princess. We were just boys, sure as shit to turn
out like you know who. And ya know somethin'? She
was probably right. But I don't care about the school. The
hell with the school. I care about Ma. And I think deep
down you care about Ma too. So make it your business
to get yourself over there. Let her parade you down the
goddamn halls and let her receive visitors in the lobby.

Let her show off the one good thing that came out of waitin' tables for twenty years."

Teresa Ann doesn't answer. She rises and brings in a tray of miniature quiches and a crudite platter with horseradish dip. Look, I am in my element now. I know these foods from my lunches out with the big boss herself. You see, no Ritz crackers here. No jelly. No Cheez Whiz either. I can function with the lower uppers. Watch me, Dahlia. You too, Vivien. If you can do it, I can do it.

Jordan switches on his CD player. "Do you care for chamber music? I find it very soothing."

"Perfect for dining," I answer with correct pronunce and enunciation.

Tommy eyes me quizzically and bends his mouth into a wiry frown. I disappoint him, I think. Traitor, that frown is saying. Traitor to your class. Traitor to your neighborhood.

"Remember who taught ya how to dance, Teresa Ann?"

"Yes, that I remember. You always were a great dancer, Tom."

"St. Bernadette's held a Christmas dance every year in their gym. Teresa Ann comes home all excited freshman year. Seems the boys from Bishop Kearney's are invited and she gotta learn to dance in a big hurry. Jordy, I showed her some moves that must have had those Kearney boys blue for a week. Christ, them nuns sure knew how to throw a party."

"Jordan, I need your help in the kitchen." He follows his wife's white linen figure.

I turn to Tommy and whisper, "Stop it already. You're embarrassing her. Try to be decent."

"For my mother's sake, I'm trying to get her to be decent. My sister forgets where she comes from. It's like I don't have a sister no more. I want her back. I miss her. I miss laughing with her. I miss telling her stuff. I want to have a sister again. Is that askin' too much? I lost my grandmother. My father lost us, and that's plenty for me. So long as I'm breathing, this one ain't gettin' away. By the way, Jo, don't eat the lettuce. It's all wilted."

"It's radicchio."

"Don't talk dirty at the table."

I lean over and rest my head against his chest. He strokes my cheek. Teresa Ann is lost for good but he'll never give up on her. He'll torture her for the rest of her life.

Our luncheon conversation proceeds more smoothly than that lovely revelation over the hors d'oeuvres. I compliment Teresa Ann on her poached salmon infused in sorrel sauce, and this pleases Tommy a great deal because it identifies the food on his plate.

As we finish dessert, Jordan volunteers. "We'll pay Terry's folks a visit soon. Let's see, we've got the Vineyard next week. I'm traveling in September. Terry's out of town in October. I promised my folks Thanksgiving. Goodness, we're up to December already. That's the pitfalls of a two-career marriage. I guess it's Christmas. Christmas with the McClellans. Truly, I enjoy their company. What a colorful bunch. Good people. Good people."

Teresa Ann rolls her eyes upward but Jordan had her nailed. They would come. She wouldn't make her husband look foolish. At the door she kisses Tommy on the cheek ever so lightly, a fairy princess kiss. He tries to hug her but she steps back, slips away untouched.

"It was very nice meeting you," she tells me.

I thank the host and hostess and we leave the central air-conditioning.

Tommy is silent on the ride home and I don't break the silence. I let my thoughts keep me company. I compare Teresa Ann with my own sister, Queen Arlene. Both are financially successful. Both have married well. Both live in beautiful surroundings. But while a great part of Arlene's existence revolves around improving and upgrading her childhood surroundings, Teresa Ann lives to rub them out.

Tommy drives his car past my exit and heads toward his place. "Come on in. I want to talk to you." We sit on the shabby love seat. Our legs sprawl across the ice chest.

"I'm real sorry about today," he tells me. "Notice I'm always dragging you down?"

I lean over to kiss him. He has such a look of sadness about him since we left his sister's place, and he had arrived at my door so happy. "Some people give and some people take. Teresa Ann's a taker. Arlene's a taker. They never think of anyone but themselves. And you're not about to change it."

"Don't you go comparing Arlene to Teresa Ann. At least your sister visits. At least she admits she's got a family."

"Yes, that she does—but she goes all out to show us how far she's come."

"She really sticks it to you, don't she? Oh, the hell with all of them. It's you I'm pissed at, Jo. Right now it's just you."

"I'm sorry about the cake. I had no idea it would cost that much."

"No, it's not the cake. Don't remind me about that. I'm pissed at you for something far more important than that overpriced piece of shit we had to bring for dessert because it was proper. No, sweetie, you made me break a promise to myself, a promise I made when I was not even seven years old. Think back to the summer when you were five."

"What are you talking about?"

"Jo, when I was seven and you were five, there was a total eclipse of the sun—"

"Gee, I didn't know you were into that astrology stuff. What now? Are you gonna ask me my sign?"

"No, I'm gonna smother you with this here pillow because you keep interrupting me. Listen up, will you? That was the summer my father skipped out. Man, I was one mad little kid. My father left, Ma went off to work. Nana moved in, took care of all of us. Every kid for weeks had it drummed into them not to look up at the sky when it got dark. You'd go blind if you stared up at that sky. Better to forget the whole thing and stay in that afternoon, you know, till it passed over. My grandmother, she had

her hands full that summer. Matty was just a baby, Teresa
Ann was your age. Nana really had a lot on her mind.
She didn't notice that I snuck out when the sky turned
dark. Jo, I was so pissed at God for letting my father run
out on us, I stared up at that dark sky. I stared and stared,
didn't even blink once. I dared God, stuck out my tongue
and dared him to make me blind. And He didn't. And I
felt my heart turn strong and hard and black as that afternoon sun. See, no one could get to me now, not even
God."

I open my mouth to say something, but he puts a
finger to my lips.

He continues. "Wouldn't you know it, though? While
I'm staring up at the sky, your fat-mouth sister Arlene is
on the fire escape with one of them homemade viewers
that let you see the eclipse without blinding yourself. She
sees me downstairs and she starts screaming, "Mrs. Conlin—Tommy's looking up at the eclipse!" Christ, Nana
comes running down with the baby and Teresa Ann. Jo,
she beat my ass so sore I couldn't walk. Then she dragged
me over to the luncheonette and I caught another beating
off Ma. And then, the two geniuses put their heads together. Jesus, Mary, and Joseph, it's a miracle. This kid
looked up at an eclipse and he can still see. My grandmother starts publishing Thank you St. Jude prayers in
the *Sunnyside News*. This didn't last too long, though. I go
into second grade that September and I can't see nothing
on that blackboard. Teacher sends a note home to get my
eyes looked at. Seems God took me up on my dare after
all. I'm going blind all right, but it's real, real slow. Both
of my retinas are doing a slow burn. Every year my eyes
will get a little worse, the doctor told my mother, but I
won't be completely blind till I'm old, and that's if a bullet
don't catch me first. Now, ain't that a kick in the pants?"

"No, it's terrible—"

"Wait, let me finish. It's not the shit with my eyes that
bothers me. They were good enough to get me on the
force. And hell, they haven't gotten all that worse since
that summer. It's that hard, black, burned-out heart I was

left with, the heart that lets nothing in and nothing out.
I swore as a kid, swore I would never love no one so
much again. I would never trust no one so much again,
never cry, and never ever need nobody again. But you
screwed up my promise, didn't you, Sunshine? You had
to see some good in me, didn't you? Just like Nana, you
saw a little good that was worth some trouble. But you
didn't know I wasn't supposed to care. And—And Jesus,
I can't always hold it back with you and I'm real scared,
Jo. Real scared to get involved." The corners of his eyes
shine wet. A solitary tear slides down over the scratch on
his cheek. He buries his face in my hair, so ashamed of
this lonely tear.

"I care for you too. I care a lot. You're always putting
everyone's situation over and above your own. Not everyone does that, you know." My tears flow more readily,
not restrained by any ancient vows. And I find myself
starting to love him a little bit, but I stop myself with a
quick yank of an invisible leash, because my head knows
better. Caring even a little bit for Tommy McClellan
would be hard work. It would be overtime on no sleep.
That ugly world out there keeps busting down our door
and crashing our party. No, that would not work, not
at all.

He wipes his eyes and dries my wet face. "Christ,
we're a friggin' pair today," he says with a half smile.

"Can I be with just Tommy for a little while? Can we
take Matty and Teresa Ann and Arlene and Aunt Adele,
my boss and my mother, and lock them in an attic
somewhere?"

"I'm so sorry, Sunshine. I wish I could make it better
for you. I wish I could give you—"

I smother his words with my mouth. I don't want to
hear my sister's name. I don't want to hear his sister's
name. He scoops me up in his arms and carries me to his
bedroom. He kicks his door shut and finally we are all
alone. Oh, I get so lost in him and I feel him lose himself
in me. If only we could live in that one room, I know we
would be so safe. Safe, just me and Tommy sharing a

pillow below the trumpets of Agnes Conlin's mahogany angels.

That evening we drive back to Sunnyside. At seven o'clock the courtyard is filled with people on lawn chairs, arranged in a wide semicircle, an expectant audience at a show that never begins. A hot breeze swirls ice cream wrappers and newspapers around and around the blood-red floor. Children play freeze tag on the sidewalk. (The Johnny pump is base.) It's all part of our summer ritual, a legacy passed down from tenant to tenant.

We greet our neighbors with the standard, "Hey, how ya doin'?" I kiss Aunt Adele and Uncle Jack, recently returned from the lobby of the Sheraton Center. Guess what? They saw the mayor today. My aunt and uncle are today's courtyard celebrities.

Tommy gently lifts Aunt Adele's bony hand and presses his lips to it. "Madame, you are looking beyond well today."

"Oh, such fancy talk for an old lady." Aunt Adele's face brightens. She straightens her backbone until it's attached to the chair. She pats a wisp of steely hair that had sprung from under her knit cap.

"A beautiful lady is never too old for a compliment, right Jack?"

"Absolutely. Watch out, though, I'm a jealous husband." He winks. "I might have to challenge you to a duel on Queens Boulevard."

Roz Lefkowitz puts her knitting down on her lap. "Get a load of them," she says to the assembled. "They're all nuts here, all touched in the head. It must be the heat."

I am told my parents went for Chinese and would be back soon.

"Come on upstairs. I gotta tell my mother about our visit with the princess."

I'm hesitant. I do not like to walk in on people without any warning. I'm told not to worry. They're all decent.

Trudy is wearing an apron over a bra and a pair of shorts. Billy and Matty are bare-chested but are also wearing shorts. Matty, complete with toothpick, has a short, thick gold crucifix embedded in his hairy, thick chest. Tommy tugs at the chain and asks his brother if he's on his way to an Italian wedding. They sit in the living room, television on but ignored. Billy and Matty are spread out across the floor surrounded by a heaped ashtray, the Sunday *News* sports section and a *Figs* racing report. Apparently they're doing a little secondary research for an upcoming race.

"Jo," his mother calls out. "Don't wait in the foyer, sweetheart. Come in. Excuse the mess. Oh, your dress is darling. Tommy, what happened to your face?"

Billy answers. "Trudy, I keep telling you about them Jewish girls. Nymphs, all of 'em. She couldn't get enough of your son."

I blush, big surprise. "This one time it wasn't me."

"A domestic altercation over at the Wosinski's that your super wanted me to attend to."

Matty looks up from the newspaper. "Them Polacks are animals."

Billy swats Matty's head with a rolled-up *Figs*. "Go to hell. My mother's a Polack."

"Well that don't surprise me any." Trudy winks.

I tell Trudy all about Teresa Ann's beautiful apartment. Yes, she has her own thermostat right in her hallway. And ceramic tile. And a doorman. She has a dishwasher and a microwave. I go on and on. Trudy is so pleased. Her little girl has made it to the top.

"The hell with that, she can't cook to save her life," Tommy adds. "What was that she served us, baked salmon in squirrel gravy? I never tasted nothing like that in this kitchen, and that's the God's honest truth. Them cooking genes skipped right on over her."

"Want a drink, Jo? Tommy, get Jo a drink."

"What do you want, sweetie? A fuzzy navel, or what's that other drink you ordered last week, a frozen sombrero?" He laughs a steady heh-heh-heh.

"Water, plain water, thank you."

"And that's another thing," Tommy says as he returns

from the kitchen. "Teresa Ann don't have regular water. She got herself sparkling water."

"What the hell does she do, fart in it?" Billy asks. I laugh, but just a little.

"Billy, for God's sake," Trudy begs.

I admire Matty's capped tooth. He still looks as strong and broad-chested as a pit bull, but at least today his mouth looks civilized. Well, except for the toothpick.

"That was some fall my baby had." Trudy still doesn't know about the accident with the Schwab van.

"Yeah," Billy adds under his breath, "right off the bar stool."

"Youse all can mark it on your calendars, the princess and her prince are coming home for Christmas," Tommy tells his mother. "Up until then, they're real busy. But they'll squeeze us in for the holidays."

She is so happy now. "Oh, I'm going to invite Jordan's parents too. I told you, they're very fine people, Jo."

"Loaded," Billy says. "They made them a wedding out at their house in Ardsley. You wouldn't believe this, they had valet parking right out in their yard. And this yard of theirs must stretch four blocks around the house. I thought their house was a catering hall, I swear to you. They popped up tents outside. They hired some violin band, brought in food. The food wasn't much, though. We all went out for pizza afterwards."

Trudy tells me it would have been perfect except they had a judge doing the ceremony, not a priest or even a minister.

"Believe it," Tommy says. "A judge. Some political hack does the service. I says to her, why not Pete the mailman or me for Chrissake? At least we're civil service. We passed a goddamn friggin' test! Then I tell her she ain't gonna be married for life. No judge can make that life sentence stick. They'll get off light, get off in three-to-eight and come in on a repeat. She don't listen. She thought I was kidding around."

Then he looks at his mother. Absentmindedly, he strokes the top curl on her teased and bleached blond head. "Ma, I'm working a midnight. We're getting into the vacation season. Mind if I catch a nap here?"

"Go in my room. Switch on the air conditioner."

He asks his brother to walk me downstairs but I decline. Its amazing, but I can handle that one flight all by myself. Tommy and I kiss a quick goodbye. As I leave I hear Billy warn Tommy, "Look out for the wet spot on your mother's side."

And Teresa Ann gave up on all this just to move up a few notches on the marketing pyramid.

My parents have returned from their Chinese supper.

"Did you have a good time?" my mother asks. She's preoccupied, hunched over a stack of brochures on the kitchen table. Her reading glasses have slid almost to the tip of her nose and every so often she taps the bridge automatically like the return key of an electric typewriter.

"Yes, a wonderful day."

"So did we. It was some kind of fair day at the park. There were all different booths set up. Look what your father and I picked up." She slides a handful of pamphlets across the table. They were all about Florida, the Sunshine state.

"You and Daddy going on vacation?" Good. They could use a vacation. My mother is always so tired. It takes her ten minutes to get up from a chair. My father escapes into his own world to avoid my mother's constant disappointment.

"No. We're going to live in Florida when we retire."

Well, this is one on me. I ask her how they would be able to swing that.

"It's all here in these booklets. We can buy a new two-bedroom condo in South Florida for $45,000 with only ten percent down. All we'll need is $4,500 and in four and a half years I'll be sixty-two and Daddy sixty-three, eligible for Social Security. Plus I'll have my union pension. We'll be able to make the payments. I'm sure of it."

My father is asleep on the couch. He can neither confirm nor deny.

"That sounds great, but where are you going to come up with $4,500? Aren't you still paying off Arlene's college loan and the loan Daddy took to make her wedding, and the one to pay for her nose job? And don't forget your Visa and MasterCard. Mom, I think you better worry about cleaning up your debts before you start thinking about buying a condo in Florida."

My mother waves a chubby hand. "I'm positive your father cleaned up those bills years ago. We're saving now. And even after all those debts were paid off, we've still managed to save three thousand dollars. In four and a half years I'm sure we'll be able to put away another fifteen hundred for the house. You'll see. Your mother is going to live out her days in Florida, right next door to your aunt Naomi and aunt Ruthie. The three sisters have already discussed this. Fait accompli, as the French say."

I suggest she ask Arlene to start paying them back, and my mother does her usual ricochet off the ceiling. She was entitled to an education. I was offered the same opportunity. I remind my mother that Arlene's earning good money now. She wouldn't mind. No, the case is closed.

"Joanna, I'd like to have a mother-to-daughter chat with you," she says in her most serious tone.

Whoa, here it comes. It was only a matter of time. I was long overdue for a lecture. Silently, I curse Ellen for shacking up with Ralph. She was my quick ticket out of here. We would have been roommates, and she deserted me for a married man with one arm.

"Joanna, you know I only have your best interests at heart. . . ." It always begins that way.

I complete her thought, "But you should break off with Tommy McClellan. He isn't refined. He isn't Jewish. His father was a drunk. His brother is irresponsible. His mother's husband has no class. Am I getting this right?"

"You take me for a snob. Who am I to be snobbish? I want you to know something. I know that boy from the time he was a baby. Trudy was pregnant with him the same time I was carrying Arlene. We'd sit in the courtyard some afternoons. She's a lovely woman, not an intellectual, mind you, but lovely. She and her mother did a wonderful job of raising the three children. Tommy, you wouldn't know this of course, looks just like his father. That man never gave her a minute's peace. He used to run around, come home drunk. He'd be missing for two, three weeks at a time. From day one he was no good but oh how that Trudy loved him, worshiped him. She must look at Tommy and get frightened. That's how much they resemble each other."

"What are you trying to tell me?"

"It's what I'm trying to ask you. What do you have in common with this boy? You come from a happy home. You're a smart girl. You read books. You've been to college—"

"I have a certificate in word processing and stenography. I hardly call that a college education. And I don't read books, I read book reviews. And I read them mainly to please you."

"Nobody stopped you from getting your credentials." Uh-oh, May Barron's needles are out. "It's not too late either. You are college material. But tell me, Joanna, what do you two talk about? Politics? Music? Somehow, I doubt this. He would be a perfect husband for your friend Ellen. She should only kick out that married schlepper and take up with Tommy."

"You have it all figured out, don't you? Now you tell me something, what do you and Daddy talk about? Art? Politics? Music? No, none of those things. Since I've been born maybe you discussed these things once or twice, but so what? You're happy."

My mother pulls her chair closer to mine. She lowers her voice, not to disturb the snorer. "You think I'm happy? I'm not happy. I'm unhappy. I'm depressed, Joanna, only I don't let it show. I'm a great actress. Don't you think I'd like to get out, see a show, hear a concert, go to a ballet, visit a museum? Not only don't we have the money, even if we had the money, your father would not be interested in those things. Your father—and I love him dearly, don't get me wrong—is not interested in anything that involves culture. Give him a television set and a soft couch and he's thrilled to death." She points to the bald, snoring mass on the sofa. A trail of spare change lies beneath him, spilled out on the worn avocado-green carpet. "This is what happens, Joanna, when you marry for looks and charm."

"But you love Daddy."

"Yes, of course I love him. He has a heart of gold. But after thirty-two years, love isn't enough. You start looking for things like financial security, an easier life. Look at Aunt Naomi and Aunt Ruthie. They don't have to work. They join organizations. They go to luncheons, take in matinees. They have an easy life. What kind of life do you want for yourself, Joanna? Do you want to live forever in this building and have to put your kids to sleep in their snowsuits because Mr. Santini is cutting back on the heating oil? You want to struggle all your life and end up in a place like this with a man who is content to watch TV all day long? Look at your sister. Look at Tommy's sister, for that matter. They earned their credentials. They married professionals. They lead comfortable, interesting lives. Don't follow in your mother's footsteps. Use your head, Joanna, and don't ruin your life the way I did mine. It's not too late for you. Give Sandy a chance. You said yourself he's a nice person." Finished.

Actually, I got off easy. Usually, once she begins Life According to May Barron, she can go on till dawn. But I cannot leave without saying anything. This would be correctly interpreted as rudeness. And besides, she managed to hit a few of my tender spots, so I start building a defense.

"First of all, I am not as interested in art and politics as you are. Maybe one day they will interest me but I don't really care for them now. I would rather spend an hour with my friends than an hour in some stuffy museum. Second of all, you're intimating that Tommy is going to become an alcoholic. And third of all you imply

he's not a professional, and he is. He has the citations to prove it." Not bad, all this and she didn't interrupt once.

"Don't jump on your high horse, miss. I didn't say those things. He's a good-natured boy. He looks out for his brother. He treats his mother better than the other two. A real sense of family, he has. He's the nicest boy in the world, Joanna. I like him very much but open your eyes. He's as common as dirt, uneducated. And Gut-in-himmel a mouth like a backed-up toilet. Can you admit this at least? I'm not completely crazy." She stands up and hovers over me, waiting, waiting.

"Those are surface things. They have nothing to do with what's inside. He's a very gentle, caring person." And you know, Mom, you're getting ahead of yourself here as usual. Aren't you? Tommy and I are dating. That's all, dating. We're not exactly eloping out the fifth story window."

"You know if you had gone to live with Aunt Naomi and Uncle Marc you would have encountered a better class of people." Ow, jabbed with the sharpest needle in her pack.

"Yes, using your definition of the word class, I'd have met a better class of people, but not necessarily better people." Ah, here I go getting preachy and self-righteous. It's very annoying even to my ears.

She sits back down. "Just forget I ever said anything. Go take your shower. Go. I guess you'll learn the hard way just like I did. Mark my words, you'll end up in this lousy building the rest of your life. And just like me, you'll only have yourself to blame."

I am dismissed. My mother slips her reading glasses back on. She boards for Florida.

Nine

Monday morning Reeves and Barnett is inundated with beer people, as Dahlia Barnett refers to them when they're not in earshot. Hordes of them headed east from Milwaukee, filling every focus room we have with men between the ages of twenty-one to thirty-five. I don't know where to put myself first. Ms. Reeves is popping little white pills to calm her nerves, and her words are starting to slur. Ms. Barnett is overcompensating, in order to get everything accomplished. The groups are running late. Men are spilling out into the reception room, waiting impatiently for their interviews to begin. Dahlia has me up front directing traffic so we look efficient to our client.

"Hey lady, I gotta get back to work."

"It'll only be a few minutes. We're running a little behind schedule."

"Why is it only ten bucks this time? I got twenty for the deodorant session."

"I don't know. Maybe the interview took longer."

A room frees up. "Come, step this way." I lead twenty men down the hall to one of our focus rooms, which today is filled with separate booths to gather individual response. Then Dahlia's voice comes over the intercom for me to return up front. What does the woman want me to do, fly?

"Yes?"

"There is a man here who would like to speak to you."

"They all want to speak to me. They're all late getting back to work. The money isn't good enough. They want—"

"Joanna, this individual asked for you by name. Stephanie put him in the office. Please don't be long."

I open the door to my cubicle. I stand and wait a half a second for the face to register. "Tommy? I can't believe it. What are you doing here?" He sits on top of my desk, the faded softness of his jeans brushing up against my stacks of files. His presence fills up my space entirely, and I hover awkwardly in the doorway. "I was called into One P.P. this morning, so while I was in the city I thought I'd drop by. Jeez, I thought you'd be a little happier to see me. You have lunch, yet?"

"You had to go into headquarters, One Police Plaza, for what?" This did not sound good. This did not sound good at all.

"For nothing, for bullshit. Jesus, look at this place." He runs his hand over my desk. "Nice stuff you got here, that's real wood, you know. The only desks we got in the precinct are made out of metal. So now that I'm here, introduce me to that guy you're always quoting, the one with the girl's name, what's his face, Francine?"

"Vivien. His name is Vivien. He's at our site in downtown Brooklyn today. Why?"

"I don't know. Just wanted to check him out. See what I'm up against."

"It's nothing like that. I told you a hundred times. He's married. He has two kids. He gives me career advice, that's all. And how did you know where my building was?" It's odd, seeing him here. I realize that Tommy and work don't seem to mesh very well.

"I knew the name of your company. It wasn't too hard for me to get the address. I've tracked people down with a lot less than that. You hungry, Sunshine?"

"I don't know if I can get out. We're very busy, as you can see. This client is an important one."

"That's too bad. My fault. A thousand apologies. I shoulda rang for an appointment, right?"

"Don't be like that. You happened to have picked the one day that we're swamped."

He stands up and I usher him out, past Stephanie the receptionist. "I'll call you when I get home," I say. Now, I feel guilty. Why aren't I happier to see him? I'm only seeing the guy.

"Wait a minute. Joanna? Is your friend a beer drinker?" Ms. Barnett projects across the room.

"Why, you must be Ms. Barnett." Tommy smiles. "Joanna here is always talking a mouthful about you. She tells me you can guess a person's income just by sizing up his watch. It's too bad I left the Rolex on my dresser. No, not the Rolex. What am I saying? That's too showy. That's new money, right? Let me tell you, Ms. Barnett, my money's so old, I'm still carrying pocket change around from the Last Supper. The Tag Heuer, that's the one I left home. By the way, I'm Tommy McClellan," he announces with an extended hand.

"Nice to meet you. Our Joanna doesn't let on too much about her personal life. If you don't mind me asking, do you happen to be a beer drinker, Mr. McClellan?"

"I've been known to hoist a few now and then, strictly in social situations, that is."

"Good. And are you between the ages of twenty-one and thirty-five?"

"Affirmative."

"Would you care to participate in our survey? It will only take fifteen minutes of your time. And there is a ten dollar incentive."

"So youse are looking for beer drinkers, are you? My brother just so happens to be double-parked downstairs. No one knows his beer like my brother, Matty. Ten bucks, you say. Maybe the two of us . . . Hang tight, I'll be right back."

"Great," Dahlia says. "The more the merrier." And

when the door shuts behind him, she raises her eyebrows and chuckles quietly.

I stand helplessly in the reception area. The invisible concrete barrier, separating home and work, is being sledgehammered to bits right before my eyes. There is nothing I can do about it either. The elevator tolls, announcing the arrival of the Brothers McClellan. "Hey Matty."

"Jo. Oh shit, get a load of this place. Tommy, you ever seen carpets like this? These rugs must be four inches thick."

"Her boss is gonna think you're some goddamn hick from Alabama."

"So which way is the beer, Jo?"

"You'll be going in soon. Just stand here on this line."

"I can't be too long, you know. I gotta make the Long Island City post office by two-thirty or my ass is grass."

"What are you worrying about?" Tommy asks. "I'll drive the van. We'll be back in LIC by one-thirty tops. That ten dollar bill will be riding on a horse's back by one forty-five."

"Come on. You're up," I say, pushing them along as fast as I can.

"Don't worry about us, Jo," Matty shouts back at me. "We won't steal nothing big."

"So Joanna, how did you make the acquaintance of those two?" Ms. Barnett asks me when they disappear into the test room.

"Oh, they're just some old friends."

"The tall one is quite a looker, isn't he?"

I feel the beginning of a blush climb up my face. Dahlia was enjoying this too much. "Yes. I really should be getting back to my work."

"Why don't you wait for your old friends to finish? I'm sure you'd like to bid the gentlemen a proper adieu."

I will get even with her. I don't know how. I don't know when. I will make her feel as small.

I wait in the reception area for Matty and Tommy. "How did it go?"

"Lousy," Matty says. "Alls they did was ask me questions."

"Well, what the hell did you expect?" Tommy asks.

"I thought they'd at least let us taste some. You know, compare the brands and all that. I'd be good at that."

"Sorry."

"Where are you going?" I ask Tommy.

"Come here, Matty. Let's be nice and say good-bye to Jo's boss."

"I really don't think that's necessary."

"No problem," Tommy says with his widest grin. Oh, he knows exactly what he's doing. And I will get even with him too.

"Take care there, Ms. Barnett. Don't work my Jo too hard. I don't want her getting tired, now."

Ms. Barnett smiles and shakes her beige-on-beige head. "Thank you gentlemen for helping us out today."

"Hey Ms. Barnett, can I maybe get my name on a list here? Do they ever do them beer taste tests?" Matty asks.

"Why don't I have Joanna add your profile to our database?"

"Listen to that, Tommy. My profile is gonna be in a database."

"If we don't get that van to the post office, your profile is gonna be out of a job. Real nice meeting you there, Ms. Barnett. Catch ya later, Sunshine."

I don't get much work accomplished after they leave. I find myself staring out of Dahlia's window. Midtown Manhattan mocks me from outside the glass. What are you doing here? You can run, Joanna, but you can't hide. Your past will always get in the way. That's what you think. Vivien did it, I glare back. Vivien's friends and relatives are safe in another continent, I am told. Besides, you want what I have. You definitely want the prestige. You know you want the glitter, the shops, the shows. Have you ever been to the Met, Joanna? Have you ever seen a ballet? You don't want to spend the rest of your life looking out at me from across the bridge. I intimidate you big-time, don't I? I like intimidating you. I can make you uncomfortable, can't I? Well, miss, are you strong enough to stand up to me? Tell me, are you willing to pay the price, Joanna? Everything has its price, you know. You've been to Macy's.

"Do you have plans this weekend?" Dahlia interrupts my reverie.

"Nothing special." I would probably be home, fighting with Tommy. He will tell me I treated him like some stranger off the street. He will tell me I was ashamed of him. He will tell me maybe we don't belong together. I, of course, will deny everything. I sigh, "What about you, Ms. Barnett?"

"Ms. Reeves and I will be entertaining a client."

My weekend is not as bad as I had imagined. Tommy never once mentions his visit to my office. I wait for the subject to come shooting up like a submerged beach ball, but it never does. It's almost as if it had never occurred. I don't talk about my work, because I'm afraid of the tension it would create. I hide from his accusations as he crouches behind the wall of his own insecurities. It works for us.

Ten

I lose him again by mid-September. The black ghost has pounced on Tommy and is ready to smother the life out of him. This time I know something isn't kosher when he doesn't call for a couple of days. I know for sure when his partner Eddie Profeta tells me cryptically that Tommy will be out of town for a while.

Once again, irresponsible, look-who's-had-a-few-too-many Matty is laying in wait for me at five-thirty when I get off the number 7 at Fortieth and Bliss.

"Jo, I gotta speak to you."

"I didn't expect to see you at the subway station." What now?

"I knew you office people get off at five. I put two and two together. And I waited here."

He starts walking me home, me in my short navy-blue dress and tan and navy blazer, and him in his inside out cutoff gray sweatshirt and ragged jeans.

"I need your help again." Believe me, he doesn't look like he needs anyone's help. He looks like he could put most of Sunnyside through a cement wall.

"What can I do for you this time?"

"Tommy's in trouble. Serious trouble. My friend Raymond seen him in Corona last night. Swears to me it was him. He could lose his job, from what Raymond seen."

I don't know what to say, how much or how little to divulge. "Maybe what he was doing is part of his job."

"That don't make no sense. They're not going to turn a decorated cop into a street criminal. I mean maybe they'd make him buy, but sell? I really don't think so."

The sidewalk isn't wide enough for the two of us. Matty's short, thick legs and broad shoulders need a sidewalk of their own. "What do you want me to do?"

"We gotta drag him out of there, Jo. He's gonna die there. He's gonna get shot right on the street. He's already been shot once. The priest came and gave him the last rites. He nearly died. Did he ever tell you that? Take it from a born gambler, his odds ain't too good this time. I'd lay half a yard on that."

I caught sight of the Corner Luncheonette. Trudy would be home by now, her shift long over. Jimmy, the owner's son, waves at us through the glass. I smile back at him. It would be nice to escape from the heat in there. Jimmy would have the air conditioner blasting. "You know, Matty, maybe I'll stop in and have a soda. We'll talk some other time. I know this may be hard to believe, but I have my own problems, and your brother is starting to be one of them."

"What?" he says, all flustered. "My brother has his life on the line and you are gonna walk into the Corner and sip soda with the fucking Greeks? This I can't believe. I really thought you cared for him. Guess you had me fooled good."

Matty's short, broad steps quicken into a linebacker's side to side bounce. I hesitate right on the corner of Queens Boulevard. My hand brushes up against the heavy glass door of the Corner and my fingers are about to open and grasp the handle. Then the door swings out and pushes onto me. A little dark-haired boy of six or seven is being led by the arm down Fortieth Street by his mother. The boy's face is stoic. "When you get home, you're gonna catch the beating of your life. Just you wait. How dare you? Who do you think you are? You're nothing but a little brat, a little shitting nothing of a kid."

The boy doesn't plead, doesn't whine, doesn't cry. He

sticks his chin out and walks alongside his mother in slow purposeful steps. I glimpse into his sullen little face and I sigh. I know just what kind of tough guy he'd end up as. I know just what kind of trouble he will bring to some unsuspecting girl. And then the image of another little boy enters my mind, the angry little boy who believed he was tougher than the burning rays of the sun. I would do anything to go back in time to rescue that little boy. If not the man, then the boy. Someone should have saved the boy. "Wait up Matty!" I hear myself call.

Matty freezes solid to the sidewalk. Pit bull through and through, he doesn't pivot, doesn't turn his head, not half an inch. I catch up with him. "What happened to your soda?"

"Matty, the last time you asked me to help him, it sort of made things worse. It blew up right in my face. You know he came over that Fourth of July and he opened up to me. He told me everything he'd been through and everything that was going on inside his head, and then just like this he stopped cold and told me it was police business. He must have thought I was poking around where I didn't belong. And I think he was mad at himself for letting his guard down. There is this possibility I'll be told to go jump off a bridge. So, how about this time you be the concerned citizen, and you go talk to him? I tried once, so let it be your turn. This time you help him."

"Me? Me help him? Ha. That's a laugh. Tommy's not gonna listen to the little brother whose ass he's had to pull out of the fire more times than I'm gonna tell you about. Nah, I don't think so. But maybe you're on to something, Jo. Maybe we can go together."

"What exactly do you have in mind?"

"Well, hows about me, you, and Raymond ride down there tonight? We'll park on a side street so he don't see us. Raymond has a piece—"

"A gun? Raymond has a gun?"

"Shh. All of Fortieth Street don't have to know that."

"No way. I'm not getting involved with this. But I'll call him, okay?"

"What if he leaves the gun home?" Matty slows his pace as our building comes into sight.

"I'm listening. So we go down there, park on a side street, and . . . ?"

"And that's it. If there's no trouble we'll go on home. If there is trouble, me and Raymond are out of the car. I'd take a bullet for him, you know that."

"I don't know. It sounds crazy. We don't belong there. What's the point?"

"The point is insurance, you know, like boxing a number. Smooth out the odds. If nothing happens, no one's the wiser. If he needs help, me and Raymond are there for him. We owe him that much."

"And me? Where do I fit in?"

"We need a car. Raymond's car was took by the repo man last Tuesday night and I spend too much time with the horses to need a car."

"Oh, I don't know. Let me call first. Before we do anything stupid, let me at least give him a call." What if Matty was right? What if Tommy was in danger and no one was there to help him?

"I guess if no one sees us it wouldn't be a big deal. We'd be sitting in a car out of sight. Still, let me go home and give him a call. Just to be on the safe side. I'm sure there's a logical explanation. His job puts him in some crazy situations."

"Is tonight good for you?"

I think. My father's car is usually idle on weeknights. He walks to Rainbow Cars and he drives their cars. "Yeah, it's okay. I don't want to make this too late. We all got work tomorrow. Besides, none of this may be necessary. One phone call might clear everything up."

"Raymond saw him there yesterday past nine o'clock."

"What was Raymond doing in Corona?"

"Nothing bad, really. He was looking to score a little pot, that's all."

I go home and ring his phone. It rings and rings. I try again in ten minutes, in a half an hour. No luck. I think

about what Matty has told me. What's the big deal if
we're hidden away? It's a no lose situation.

I am doing the right thing. Nobody will see us. We
will observe, realize everything is okey-dokey, and then
we'll go home. It will be good for Matty. He'll feel like
he's finally looking out for Tommy, rather than the other
way around. He'll feel he's evening up the score. And
me, of course I wouldn't want to see Tommy get hurt,
but there is this curiosity thing. It's not too different from
the one-way mirror at Reeves and Barnett. I like watching
people unobserved. Who doesn't? Hey you, white collar
male eighteen-to-thirty-five sports enthusiast with income
above thirty-five and below sixty! Don't think I missed
you picking your nose. You can't see me, though. Peeping
Tomasina, am I? No, this is marketing, Mister. We're talking American consumer goods field research here. Dahlia
says we are the force that propels the GNP.

"I need to take the car tonight."
"So where are you going?" Mother May asks.
"Just visiting a friend."
"Who?"
"A girl from work. She lives nearby."
"You don't see enough of each other at work? You
have to see each other at night too?"
I sigh. There's a one bedroom apartment available in
Richmond Hill. It's up five rickety flights and there's this
awful curry smell permeating the place. But suddenly it's
starting to look good. It's starting to smell good. Maybe
I can call the landlord back.
"Yes, I know, I know you're a big girl now. The keys
are on the sofa where they fell out of your father's
pants pocket."

I wait in the lobby for Matty and Raymond. Raymond
is short, dark, and disreputable. He's a schemer, always
figuring out an angle. Tommy is not too keen on
Raymond.
I hand Matty the keys. I am too nervous to drive. And

Matty drives for a living. I let Raymond sit up front, next to Matty. I cower in the back. "Jeez," Matty says at the wheel of my father's Electra, "it's like driving a bus."

"Gas mileage must be lousy," Raymond remarks.

Matty maneuvers through darkened streets. Corona comes upon us way too fast. Raymond points to a corner off Junction Boulevard. "Down there. Near Lefrak City. Hang a right on Fifty-third. That's where I seen him."

"We're just going to look, right?" I ask.

"Yeah, don't worry, Jo. If everything's cool, we'll be home in time to hear them pick the Lotto numbers on Channel 5," Matty assures me.

"Man, I love that Spanish girl," Raymond tells us.

"The chubby one with the long hair?"

"Yeah. She can spin my balls anytime."

"Shut up, Raymond."

"Sorry, Jo."

We pass the corner in question. I am afraid to look out the window.

"There he is," Raymond shouts. "He grew a goatee. Look!"

"Get lost. That's not my brother. That's a spic in shades. See, the guy's wearing black and gold beads. That's Latin King colors. Tommy's no Latin King."

I peek out the window. We are parked off Ninety-fourth Street three cars off the corner, out of sight, facing the avenue. The face is unrecognizable, but the walk, the motions, are unmistakable.

"It's him, Matty."

"You think I don't know my own brother? I'm getting out. I gotta see this for myself."

"No. No."

The car door opens but Raymond and I grab hold and try to pull him inside. "Get in. Are you crazy? If it's not your brother, you don't belong there. And if it is your brother, you'll blow whatever it is he's trying to do."

He slams the door shut. We peer out the window, our car is hidden under a city-planted tree that still clung on to most of its leaves. The avenue is populated by young

people, hanging out on a warm September night. Cars
speed up as the light turns from green to yellow and they
screech to a rubber trail stop at red. A drug buy is in
progress. Cash moves back and forth in quick flitting
hands. "I don't like it," Matty says. "Don't he know he
can lose his pension? Cops got a great pension. I gotta
stop him."

The door opens again. "Shut the friggin' door, Matty,"
Raymond tells him. "You know sometimes I'm dumber
than dirt. I get it now. It's some new undercover thing.
Usually they get cops to buy. This time they're doing
things different."

"I don't like it. I like it when he wore his uniform. I
could recognize him then. I still don't think that's him."

Raymond turns around to me. "Hey, you think he'd
sell to me? I could use a little for Saturday night. Maybe
he'd slip it to me free? Come on, it's like having an uncle
in the carpet business."

"No, Raymond. No. You'd only distract him. He has
to be believable, right? Otherwise it could ruin everything." They are children, two six-year-olds all dressed
up in men's bodies.

"Yeah. Jo's right. Let's just sit here a little while."

We sit and watch some more. People drive by, pur-
chase and leave. A large heavy-muscled Spanish guy
strolls down Fifty-third Avenue with a dog. He is heading
toward Tommy. "That's it. Look at that guy. He's trouble.
I'm getting out."

"Sit down, will you? All the man's doing is walking
his dog."

"It could be a pit bull."

"Start the car, Matty, please. We came and saw what
we had to see. Tommy's undercover, like I told you, and
all is right with the world. Let's go home."

Raymond agrees. "Baby, if I can't score I'm out the
door."

Matty turns the key in the engine. It whines, whines
like my sister Arlene, but it doesn't turn over.

"Try it again. It's a very old car. It's temperamental."

He turns the key once more. Again it complains. "We got ourselves battery problems."

"Oh shit. Jo, you got jumpers in the back?" Raymond asks.

"I guess so." My father would have thought of that, wouldn't he?

"Who can we ask for a jump? How about the friendly dealer on the corner?"

"Matty, you know we can't cross that street. He'll see us for sure. Can you and Raymond push the car backwards? I'll steer. There must be a gas station somewhere in Corona."

I get behind the wheel and I shift into reverse. I am not at my best at reverse. I must turn the back wheels left in order to clear the car behind me. I know to turn the steering wheel all the way to the right but this brings the front tires up on the sidewalk.

"Ease up, Jo. Cut left," Matty tells me. I can barely hear him through the raised windows.

"Left?"

"Yeah," he shouts.

I turn all the way left.

"Stop, Raymond, stop pushing."

Daddy's car taps the car behind me. The other car's alarm goes off. "Oh shit," we say in unison.

The owner of that car, a middle-aged Puerto Rican lady, pokes her head out of her fifth floor window. "You hit my car?"

I look at Matty. "I tapped it. There's no damage."

"Wait, I come down."

The lady comes down in pink cotton pajamas and a bright orange bathrobe. Her hair is up in a steely bun. She touches the spot in question. "A little paint, no? A little paint come off?"

"Will fifty dollars cover it?" I ask. I had fifty dollars in my wallet. That's it.

"Fifty. Si. That will help. The body shop will charge me more. You walk in there it's a hundred dollars. They rob you in there."

"I'm sorry about your car but could I ask a favor of you? Could you give me a jump?"

"A jump? With the cables? Si. Okay. You turn your car around. I don't give up this spot for nobody. No one. Tomorrow is alternate side. It's terrible in the morning."

Raymond gets behind the wheel of my father's car. Matty and I push. The street is narrow. It takes twenty minutes. The lady looks impatient, but she waits on the sidewalk. "I call the police," she says. "I call when this happens. I thought someone is trying to take my radio again. Four radios gone already. Where are they? The police. No matter. I don't need them anyway. *Gracias a Dios.*"

The car turns over and I thank the woman again. "Time for a new car," she calls into the night. "Toyota make a good car."

We hear the police car screeching across the avenue. People scatter into the night. I don't see Tommy anymore. "Let's get out of here," Raymond says.

"She woulda took twenty dollars easy, Jo," Matty tells me. "Body shop my pearly white pucker."

After we drop Raymond off at his building, and we are safe on Fortieth Street, Matty says to me, "Not for nothing, Jo. I still don't think it was him. Maybe you should go visit him, just to make sure."

I call in sick the next day. I leave my parents in blissful ignorance, dressing as if I'm going to put in a day at Reeves and Barnett. I'm extra cheerful early in the morning, sitting down to a cup of coffee with my mother before she heads out to Schwab's.

"Aren't you up early today?" she remarks.

"I have some work to catch up on. I'll get in before nine, you know, before it gets busy."

"You're ambitious, Joanna. You'll go far there. But you'll need a credential, a degree. Why don't you sign up at night?"

"Now where have I heard that before?"

My mother manages half a smile. "So, am I wrong?"

"We'll see." She couldn't know it is the furthest thing from my mind. I've lived twenty-seven years without direction, what's another day? After the door bangs shut I leave a message on Dahlia's voice mail. Yes, I have a stomach virus. It's not a pretty sight. I was praying it was a twenty-four-hour bug and that I'd be back to the ever-probing world of market research tomorrow. Something like that with a sprinkling of tact.

A chilly drizzle drops on the residents of Queens. My purse-size, top-of-the-line taupe Totes umbrella—thank you, Arlene, it's perfect and it goes with everything—and I take the bus into Woodhaven. I do not know if Tommy is there, but I take the chance. If he's out working nights, he very well might be home in the day. A possibility. A chance.

The bus ride is slow. People smell of wet wool and polyester. Umbrellas puddle over damp coats and soggy shoes. The air is close. The windows are fogged over, dripping bus sweat, and I nearly miss my stop.

I walk the couple of blocks to Tommy's apartment very slowly. I stand at Tommy's entrance on the side of the house and ring the bell. I hear nothing. I knock as loud as my knuckles can handle and the door opens slowly. He stares at me in the doorway without expression for what seems like minutes. I stand under my umbrella, in a trance, trying to recognize something familiar in a face that I have come to care about. Close up he looks worse than he did on the Fourth of July. He looks like a savage, a spike-haired, sunken-eyed, goatee-wearing, grizzled savage.

"Can I maybe come in?"

He retreats into the darkness of his underground apartment and I follow him.

"There's no reason for you to be here."

"I'm worried about you. And your brother is too. I came here to see what's with you."

"Thank you for all the concern. I'm fine and dandy. Now go on home, Joanna. I gotta be alone."

I take off my coat and drape it over a kitchen chair. "I'm not going anywhere, Tommy."

"Tommy? Tommy? Who the fuck is Tommy? This is not Tommy. Tommy's gone. Today I'm Dr. Rock, long lost cousin of Nito Santiago, who got sent away last month. Nito invented me for a couple of months off his sentence. So call me Dr. Rock, only I'm not the kind of doctor your mother wanted you to end up with. What you're looking at is a gang-banging drug dealer who has connections all the way up. Get it? I'm dealing drugs in Corona, but you know that already. And maybe next month I'll be sticking up liquor stores in Flushing. I never know just what the department has in store for me because I'm in deep now. Real deep. All jammed up."

"Why can't you get out of this assignment?"

"Because I'm in it until I'm told I'm not in it. That's the way the Job is."

"Matty's friend Raymond saw you."

"And then Raymond and Matty and Jo decide to see for themselves. Did they like what they saw? Tell me, was it worth the price of admission?"

I look away and I sigh. "We hid on a side street. We were under a tree. How did you ever see us?"

"How did I see you? What, are you kidding me? A 1979 Buick Electra 225 rolls down the street and I'm not supposed to notice it? When I'm working, I notice everything. My life depends on it. Anyways, even a blindfolded bat would see the dome light flickering on-off, on-off. Even a deaf dog could hear the three of youse. Get out. Stay in. Get out. Stay in. And I should ignore it, right?"

"You weren't supposed to see us. Matty—"

"Don't Matty me. You let yourself get talked into one of Matty's brilliant schemes? Let me tell you something, Matty is a two-hundred-pound guy with the brains of a four-year-old. They don't make 'em any more irresponsible. Do you know he has a kid? My brother Matty fathered a kid when he was seventeen years old. Seventeen years old he gets a girl pregnant. Do you know what we had to go through? Her father, some wild man with a towel on his head, came to the apartment with a butcher knife. We gotta send a check every month to his kid. And sure as I'm breathing, this little Sayeed is gonna grow up and show up on my doorstep one day looking for a handout. 'Uncle Tommy, I lost all my money on a camel race.' And this here brother of mine now got you chasing his brainstorms. I thought you were smarter than that. Wrong again."

He opens a fresh pack of Newports and pours a glass of Dewar's for himself. "Cheers," he says sullenly.

"You don't have to be so angry. Our intentions were good. We were worried sick about you. And no harm was done."

"No harm was done? Bullshit. I'm working so hard to do my job. I'm working so hard to forget who I am so I can become someone I'm not and then the three of youse appear out of nowhere. At any second I'm expecting Matty or Raymond to jump out of the car, blow my cover, and get me killed. I don't know where to look first."

"I'm sorry."

He refills his glass. "Sorry? You're sorry? You just don't get it, do you? This isn't some TV show that you bring your friends down to watch. This is my reality now. And you, my brother, and that crazy Raymond fucked it up for me."

I sit down at the old salmon-cushioned telephone table. I can remember an easier time, a long ago time, when my legs dangled far above our lobby floor and Arlene and I would argue over who would push the elevator buttons. "We didn't do much of anything. I don't know why you're making such a big deal out of this."

"You don't know which end is up, do you? Aside from breaking my concentration, you also managed to back your father's car up on some P.R.'s car, and somehow a sector car appears out of nowhere, putting a complete halt to what I'm doing. So don't go on asking me why I'm pissed. You're not stupid."

I could see his jaw tighten and the muscles around his cheekbones twitch. He lights another cigarette.

I get up and sit down beside him on the tweed love seat and he edges away. "Don't come near me."

"Why not?"

"Because you're not touching no drug dealer, that's why."

"You're not really a drug dealer. Underneath you're really a police officer. Have you forgotten that?"

He leans over and looks at me hard. His stare is black and hollow-eyed. It wouldn't surprise me if he was using too. That thought spins around my head, a carousel gone haywire. Now I am in deep, as well, maybe too deep. "Listen to me and listen to me good," he says. "I am a drug dealer. I look like a drug dealer. I think like a drug dealer. I talk like a drug dealer. Because if I don't, if I slip, even a little, I'm DOA like a drug dealer. So do me a favor, be the good girl I know you are and go home to Mommy and Daddy and your pretty little office with the big-time clients. Forget about that guy you used to know. As far as you know, he's dead. So forget him. Just erase him from your mind. He's gone. He's outta here. He's history. With any luck, they'll let him back next month. And big, bad Dr. Rock will just have to dig him up, dust him off, and make a sacrifice to Santa Maria that he still has a heartbeat."

Of course I start to cry, and this hollow-eyed stranger that sits apart from me looks on, as helpless as I feel.

"What you're doing to me now is not right and it's not fair. You're killing me, Jo. You're killing me worse than a bullet," he says softly. "And what the three of youse did to me yesterday, that went beyond stupid. I ain't forgiving that one so fast. So go on home."

"I want to help you. I can't stand to see you like this."

"Go home, Sunshine. Let me rot here alone in this rathole until they say I can go back to Anticrime. Why don't you call up that nice Jewish cowboy and you and him go rustle up some corned beef?"

"Shut up. You're so full of hate for everyone. How do you stand yourself?"

"Let's get one thing straight, I don't hate no one worse than I hate myself. So get the hell out of here and leave me alone."

"You look terrible. Let me make you an early lunch."

He laughs a hard ugly laugh. "Lunch? Oh now you want to feed me, do you? Doesn't anything I tell you today bother you any? If I told you I was robbing banks and raping women, would you cater a goddamn buffet for me?"

"It's for your job, that's all." I go into his kitchen and spread Skippy peanut butter and Welch's grape jelly on two Wonder bread sandwiches, pour two Cokes, and bring it over to Tommy. He eats the sandwich in three bites and I feed him half of mine. He downs the Coke in great thirsty gulps.

"You haven't been eating or drinking. That's why your eyes look so hollow. What are you doing, starving yourself?" What a relief. At least he wasn't using. I wouldn't have to deal with that this time.

"Funny, I don't like to feed and water the dealers the way you do. Besides, I'm drinking plenty. How the hell do you think I get through this?"

"You know something, this is worse than Poppy."

"Christ, don't ever remind me about that. That haunts me too. Haunts me all the time. I want you to open your eyes and take a good hard look at what I've become. I joined up so I wouldn't turn out this way, and now they're making me turn out this way. They're even paying me to turn out this way. I hate myself now. I can't look in the mirror no more. You know what I've done, Jo? In between watching the Three Stooges take Corona, last night I sold heroin to a pregnant girl. A kid. Fifteen, maybe sixteen. I got paid for that. It was legal. It was for the almighty NYPD so they can set up the big guys. And like I says, this one goes way up, way up to the Colombians, and these days it don't get much higher than that."

"So there you go. It had a purpose."

"You think that makes any difference? That makes it right? That baby will be born a junkie. He'll start life out with a jones. That's on my head. That'll be on my head till the day I die. I can't expect you to understand that. You in that fancy office I saw, with your wall-to-wall carpet and your gourmet lunches in the best restaurants all eaten on the arm with the dyke bosses. How can I expect you to understand shit about what I do? How can I make you see what I've become? What a mistake we are, the two of us. One big fucking mistake. I knew that the minute I showed up at your work. You had embarrassment written all over you. Face it, we live in two different worlds, you and me."

I reach for his hand and he tugs it away. "Don't let me do this to you, Jo. You're way better than this. Wake up, Sunshine. You don't belong here, so go on home. Go home and forget all about me. Call up that nice guy you told me about and make a life for yourself while you still got a fighting chance."

"Why should I leave you here?"

"Because I'm one sorry-ass guy in deep shit trouble. I'm someone who's slipping into cartoon quicksand and I'm about to be swallowed up whole. Cops are told to get in, and then they can't crawl out. It happens more than you know. They get all jammed up. And it's happening to me. I feel it happening, but I can't stop it. But as long as I'm breathing, it ain't gonna happen to you."

"That won't happen to you. You can't let that happen to you. You have too much going for you. People rely on you. Matty and your mother. They depend on you more than you know."

"I'm so damn sick and tired of carrying everybody. I want out. Sometimes I feel like I'm carrying that whole damn building on my back."

"Let me carry you, just once."

"No way. I'm in this alone. I'm flying solo. So let's you and me make a nice, clean break. Let's do it right now, before you sink into the quicksand with me."

"That's it? We're done? I'm dismissed?" We are over, I am told. Only I don't feel over. I feel empty.

"You got it. Done. Over. Finito. Now pick yourself up and go. And don't you say another word to me. Not one word. Don't you dare look at me with your big brown eyes and tell me to take care of myself. Don't remind me to eat my spinach and drink plenty of milk. Don't tell me to take my umbrella 'cause it's raining and wear my goddamn seat belt 'cause I drive too damn fast. Just go. Leave me the hell alone, already. We're through. Get it? We're done. Over and out. So long. It's been a blast. Don't let the door hit you on the way out."

"One summer day you worked up all the courage you had just to tell me you cared for me."

I stunned him for a moment, stunned him good, but he's quick to recover. "I've said lots of things. It don't mean jack shit."

I gather my belongings and ride the bus home. It was not supposed to turn out this way, not at all. I had gone wrong somewhere. But where did I go wrong? I get off the bus ten blocks too early just to walk in the rain. I leave my umbrella down. I welcome the rain, welcome its wet chill. How it merges with my tears. How it saturates my clothes and soaks into the white of my scalp. My outside is washed clean while my insides remain caked with the sour aftertaste of a relationship gone bad. My building stands before me in utter defiance. Oh you're back, it seems to say. Back again.

I get off the elevator on the fifth floor and ring Trudy's bell.

"Jo. Sweetheart. My God, look at you. Let me get you a towel. Got caught in the rain, huh?"

"Yeah." I take the towel and run it over my face. "Does Matty happen to be around?" It is the last place I want to be, but I feel I owe Matty some kind of explanation. It isn't really his fault. Why should I blame him for my misfortune?

"Matty? No. He's not home yet. I think he had some deliveries to make in the city. Come on in. Wait here with me. I just got off work myself. Dry off a little. You want a cup of tea or something?"

"No. Thanks anyway. I'm coming from Tommy's. I'm kind of upset. I'm very upset." I start to cry into Trudy's towel. "Oh Trudy, I don't know what to do."

She shakes her teased blond head and puts her arm around me. "Jo, sweetheart, what's that son of mine done to you?"

"Well, we were all kind of worried about him so I paid him a visit. He's on this horrible undercover assignment. He has to do some things he's not very comfortable with. And he's changed, Trudy. He's turned himself into something awful. He doesn't want to see anyone. He doesn't want to talk to anyone. I don't know anymore. He doesn't ever want to see me again." I catch a sob with the towel.

"Don't take him so to heart. He didn't mean nothing by it. He gets angry sometimes. That's just the way he is. It will blow over. The clouds will pass. You'll see."

"No. I don't think so. He threw me out of his house. He told me we're done."

"That bastard. Just like my ex, may he roast in hellfire wherever he is. You're too good for him. That's the trouble."

"His job is really taking its toll on him. I've never seen him like this. He's so depressed, Trudy. He's so down. I tried to snap him out of it but I only made it worse."

"He'll come around. Give him some time."

"I don't know, Trudy. He's drinking too much. He's not eating."

"You're real good for him. Maybe you're too good for him. Let him rot there with his scotch bottle if that's what he wants. Just let him stew for a while. Maybe when it all blows over, he'll come to his senses."

I look at Trudy in disbelief. "You surprise me. You being his mother and all. Aren't you worried about him?"

"I stopped worrying about him a long time ago. He's a big boy now. He can take care of himself. You're a nice girl from a nice family. I know all too well what my son is about, so don't let him get to you. And if that seems mean or cruel of me to say, well, call me mean and cruel. But it's the truth. I've had a hard life, Jo. But maybe that's forced me to see things all the more clearer."

Her total detachment leaves me queasier than a White

Castle hamburger. I can't understand it either. I know for a fact Tommy has been very good to Trudy, but in spite of it she's hauling this large malignant lump of resentment around for some unknown reason. Ah families, is there a person alive who could comb through their tight and tangled knots? Is there a person alive who'd want to?

"You know, I heard from Teresa Ann today," Trudy tells me, leaning against the arm of the sofa.

"Oh yeah?"

"Yeah. She and Jordan are going to Paris in November. On a three week vacation, right before Thanksgiving."

"That sounds great."

"Paris. I can't believe it. My daughter is going to France. Can you imagine?"

I want to feel happy along with Trudy but I can't. All I can see is Tommy's haunted, parched face. All I can feel is his canyon of hurt and his mountain of guilt. I want to know why it is that all mothers are in awe of the one child who completely rejects them. Why does Trudy love Teresa Ann best? Why does my mother look up to Arlene so? Why?

And then Trudy sees my sadness. "Aw come on. Don't make yourself sick over him, Jo. My boy is as strong as steel. Always has been. Believe me, they don't come tougher."

No, I want to say. He's softened a little. He's vulnerable and it's my own damned fault. I showed him some tenderness and it only made matters worse for him. It has put him in jeopardy. But I say nothing. Let her dream about Teresa Ann. Let her live the Disney fantasy with her own live ice princess.

The door bangs open with toothpicked Matty on the other side. "Hey Ma. What's up, Jo?"

"Matty, I'm gonna get my hair done. Keep Jo company. Your dear brother's done a number on her. I'll be back in an hour or so. Put a low light under the pot at five-thirty if I'm not home. And stir it a little, huh? Don't let it burn like last time."

"Yeah, all right, Ma. Give it a rest." When she leaves the room he says to me: "So, you seen Tommy today like you said you would?"

"Yeah, he's undercover just like we figured. What he's doing is for his job. I know that him selling drugs for the police department sounds crazy, but it's the truth. It's the hard, ugly facts. He's mad at the world in general. And he hates me in particular. As it just so happens, he broke up with me today."

"I'm real sorry to hear that. I think you were real good together. In fact, I've never seen him so happy."

"Apparently, he didn't feel the same way. And he told me that you better not go back there anymore. He saw us yesterday and it broke his concentration and it ruined everything."

Matty lowers his broad body into the cushions of an armchair. "I don't like it. He's gonna get his ass shot off over there."

"Your mother doesn't seem the least bit worried about him."

He raises his shoulders. "Ma? I don't know. No matter what he does for her, she always has it out for him. Don't ask me why, but that's the way it's always been. My grandmother was always in his corner, though. He was her favorite. I tell you, I miss the old lady. She knew how to balance things out. Make them square."

"I really liked your grandmother, Matty. I miss her."

Matty gets up from the chair. "Want a beer, Jo?"

"No thanks. I better be getting downstairs. My mother thinks I went to work today."

"Jeez, I hope they didn't dock you a day's pay on account of me." Matty downs his Heineken until he's sucking on air.

"Nah, don't worry about it. I called in sick."

"Way to go. By the way, Jo, what's up with your mother?"

"My mother?"

"She don't sleep nights? I seen her catching a nap right on the embroidery table. Why is she so tired?"

"I don't know. I'll ask her. Hey, put a low light under that pot."

"Yeah, thanks, Jo. Thanks for trying. I'm real sorry the way this turned out for the two of youse."

My mother is sitting in the gray damp of the apartment without so much as a light. The TV isn't on. There is no comforting smell of dinner on the stove. She doesn't look up from the sofa when I come through the door.

"Hey, Mom."

"Why didn't you call me back?"

"When did you call? Maybe I didn't get the message."

"Eleven o'clock. I called that fancy shmancy voice mail at eleven, much good it did me."

"I'm sorry. We've been busy. What did you want?"

"I wanted you to stop at the grocery and pick up a few things on the way home from the station. I don't feel well. I punched out at noon. So, let them dock me. It won't make a difference in my life one way or another."

"What's the matter? Matty said you've been falling asleep at work."

"Matty?"

"Yeah, I ran into him in the elevator."

"I'm having trouble sleeping, that's all. It caught up with me today. It's hard to embroider when you're seeing double. Imagine, one of the other girls had to thread my needle. That bullion thread is so bright, it's blinding me. Ah Joanna, it's not good when the eyes go. Not in my line of work."

I switch on a light. "When was the last time you had your eyes checked?"

"I don't know. When was it? August, I think. Not too long ago. The doctor didn't find anything wrong with my prescription. He told me to take breaks from what I was doing. He said I should rest me eyes every half hour or so. He doesn't know my floor supervisor very well."

"What do you need from the store? I'll go back out. I can cook tonight."

"Forget it. It's pouring. We'll call in a pizza, already.

I have no appetite and your father will eat anything. I could serve him cooked cockroaches and he wouldn't know the difference. He'd say, 'May, new recipe tonight? It's delicious.' That's how much he knows about food. A real gourmet he is."

"Mom, are you all right? You seem so blue. Is anything worrying you?"

"Oh no, Joanna, nothing is worrying me. I'm living the absolute life of Riley. Me and my twin, Queen Elizabeth."

"Oh, stop it. Our lives are not much different than anyone else's." I hate it when she's feeling sorry for herself. For God's sake, we aren't homeless and eating out of garbage pails.

"You're right. Aunt Naomi and Aunt Ruthie are stoop-shouldered from leaning over a piece of cloth eight hours a day. You're absolutely right. No difference at all."

"You and your sisters. Stop comparing yourself to them. You're better than they are. Think about it. At least you earn your own living. They're so dependent, and they always have been."

"Oh yes, Joanna. I'm liberated. I'm a liberated woman who is chained from eight in the morning until four in the afternoon to an embroidery table, sewing shoulder boards so that some hotshot Navy captain looks good at his next dinner party."

"It's a living. Like you said to me a little while ago, it will see you to your retirement in Florida."

"I just hope I make it. God, I'll be an old hag by then. Your father will have to wheel me around. A hunchback I'll be. A blind hunchback."

I start to laugh and my mother begins to laugh too. "And what topping would the blind hunchback like on her pizza?"

"Top it with gold," she says.

Eleven

October blows its chilly wind around Sunnyside, signaling the fast approach of the holidays. Gifts have to be bought, and somewhere along the way payment has to be made. A one dollar chance at the N.Y. State Lottery looks awfully enticing in October. Ellen, Louise, and I pool our money three times, but each time we come up empty. That means we will have to pay for our gifts the American way, on our charge cards.

My Christmas/Hanukkah list includes the usual goulash of family, friends, and coworkers. The figure $2,000 climbs into my head and doesn't budge: $2,000 . . . $2,000. It's not as intimidating as it sounds, because I have some money saved from my salary and I am expecting a Christmas bonus from Reeves and Barnett. Last year they gave me $750. Maybe this year I'll get a thousand. I'm sure it all depends on the estrogen levels of the two menopausal principals. If their hot flashes are not too severe on judgment day, I may even land $1,200.

Financially speaking, I am sound. Mentally speaking, I am resigned. In three more weeks I will be twenty-eight years old. I have neither a husband or a career. No plans. No goals. I still sleep in a bed in my parents' home.

I try to remind myself now and then that I do have my health. I have a lovely family and great friends. There is food on my plate and clothes on my back. Yes, people are running around out there who have it much worse than I do. And they go on. Hour after hour. Day after day. So who am I to complain?

I tell my mother, Tommy and I are through. She doesn't ask why. She says she's sorry. I tell my friends we just weren't right for each other. We were too different. They tell me that sounds like so much crap. When Trudy catches me on the elevator, she asks me about her son. Have you heard from Tommy? she asks. No, I tell her. We're really over. Once again she tells me I'm better off without him. I shrug. She's probably right.

The first time he worked undercover, back in June, I was sad, lonely, and confused. Just when we were getting to know one another, he locked me out of his confusion, but not out of his life. It is different this time. He is gone. Physically gone. And I have graciously accepted the decision of the black ghost. Once again doubt has overpowered faith. Once again evil has triumphed gloatingly over decency. Darkness has crept forward and sent out its hairy tentacles to ace out the light.

I take to my room after work. I don't want to go out. I don't want to meet anyone. I don't want to hear about their dreams or listen to their problems. I am content to escape into the cosy womb of night soaps and half-hour sitcoms. Under the glare of the small screen on my bureau, I am safe for a little while.

I try to keep my mind as blank as possible. I don't let myself go over again and again words that cannot be altered. I make a promise to myself that I will not allow this to happen again. Already I was fooled once. Twice is twice too many.

I stop myself from calling Sandy Sussman. I stop myself from thinking of him as a friendly, safe haven in the midst of my personal combat zone. No, I don't call Sandy. I will not use someone the way I have been used. Used and discarded.

When my mother pokes her head in to ask me what I want for my birthday, which is on Halloween, I reply without a moment's hesitation. *A life. I want a life.* Is that too much to ask?

"Your sister is coming on Wednesday, after work. We'll get a cake from Carvel. Wednesday is better than Tuesday. The doorbell doesn't stop on Halloween. Where all these kids come from, God only knows."

I cannot even celebrate my own birthday on the correct day. Everything about me is a compromise. I am resigned. I go to sleep resigned. I go to work resigned. And I come home resigned. My days are consistent.

On Halloween my mother pads to the door on tired feet every time the bell rings. She seems to know every child and parent that shows up at our door. "Oh, you're Rita Stupka's grandson, Jonathan. Yes, say hello to Grandma. You almost had me fooled with that scary monster face."

"Look, Joanna, twins in the carriage. Hansel and Gretel. How adorable. Regards to your mother. I saw her in the dry cleaners the other day. The treatments seem to be working, she told me. Thank God."

"Tiffany, is that you? Yes honey, you do look like Madonna. *Vey is mir.* Does your daddy know you're walking around like that?"

Again and again my mother leaps to her feet with her bags of candy. "Sit down already," I tell her. "Make believe we're not home. Let them go bother someone else. We must have the sucker sign in plain sight."

"Stop it, Joanna. You were a kid too, once upon a time. People gave you and Arlene plenty of candy. Agnes Conlin, may she rest in peace, used to make up a whole plastic pumpkin full of candy. One for you and one for your sister."

"Don't mention that family to me."

"I'm sorry. I wasn't thinking. She was a nice lady. That's all I meant to say."

"It didn't get her anywhere, did it?"

"Sorry I even mentioned it. Oy, there's the bell again."

"Sit down. I got it. Ten o'clock at night. Who sends

a kid out at that hour? People really have their nerve, don't they?''

I approach the door with a scowl and a handful of Nestlé's crunch bars.

"Happy birthday, Sunshine," a person says to me.

I fling the Nestlé crunch bars at this person's face and I close the door. Some birthday. I wouldn't wish it on a dog. I wouldn't wish it on a crotch-sniffing, leg-mounting, drooling kind of dog.

"Come on, Jo. Open up. I want to talk to you."

"Get lost."

"You want me to kick the door in, or you gonna open it?''

"Go, Joanna. Please. See what he wants. You know how long it will take to get Mr. Gurtz to put up a new door?''

"Jo?"

"Go to hell."

"Been there. Done that. Picked up a T-shirt for you. Come on, sweetie. Five minutes. Old times' sake."

"Here, take a sweater," my mother tells me. "Take your keys. Don't let him kick the door in, Joanna."

Five minutes. What a set on him to think I would forgive him in five minutes. Overconfident, fast-talking cop that he is. Did I not have him pegged at the wake? Always go with the first impression. When will I ever learn?

"My mother doesn't want her door damaged," I say in the elevator. "That is the only reason I am talking to you. It is you I'm talking to, right? It gets a little confusing sometimes."

"Care for a Nestlé's crunch bar?" he asks as we reach the lobby. "Thanks again for thinking of me. These are real good."

"Shut up. Just shut up."

"My my, ain't we flying around on the old broomstick tonight?''

"Did you really think I'd open the door, fly into your arms and tell you all was forgiven?''

"Works for me."

"Well it doesn't work for me. I'm going back upstairs. This is a complete waste of time."

"Five minutes. Hey, trick or treat there, Mrs. Gurtz. Got any lollipops for me? I could use a good suck. Jesus Christ. I just can't win. They're all slamming the door in my face tonight."

"I'm not getting in your car," I say when we're outside. "We'll stand right here. Right in front of the building."

"We'll sit in my car. Unless you like egg and shaving cream showers. Maybe in my absence you're getting into the kinky stuff."

I reach all the way back to punch him in the face, but he's quick to intercept the blow, and he's left holding my fist. "Why did you come here?" I pull my hand out of his.

"I came to wish you a happy birthday. I bought—"

"Keep it. Whatever it is, I don't want it."

He jams his hands into the pockets of his sweatshirt. That obnoxious look of smiling amusement finally washes off his face. "And I wanted to tell you how sorry I am for what I said to you last time."

"I see."

"Ah, don't be that way."

"You got no right telling me how to be. You threw me out of your house and pretty much told me to go jump in a lake. And I'm suppose to be nice to you because you're feeling guilty? Maybe that Irish charm worked on your other six hundred girlfriends, but it doesn't do anything for me."

"I said I was sorry. Can't we try again? I can't stop thinking about you. I can't stop thinking about us, and what we were starting to have together. Can't me and you go back to the way it was?"

"No, we certainly can't. For one thing, I don't trust you, not even a little bit."

"What do you mean, trust me?"

"Trust. It's not just a word. It's something you earn."

"That's just what Mrs. Bialik the guidance counselor

at Bryant said after I was caught with a reefer the second
time in two days."

"Well, Mrs. Bialik happened to be right."

"So I'm on a three-day suspension off school property?"

"No. It means I'm not going to set myself up to get
hurt by you again. You fooled me once but this time I
know better. We're done, through, over and out. Just like
you said last time."

"Ah Jo, what I done was wrong and I'm not looking
to excuse it, but maybe you were a little wrong too. You
got yourself involved where you didn't ever belong. I
know you didn't mean to, but you almost threw three
weeks of work into the crapper. I know I kind of lost it
on you that day, but I don't want you involved in that
area of my life. I want to protect you and keep you safe
and far away from all that. Excuse me a minute,
Sunshine. . . . That egg touches my car and I'll put your
ass in the hospital."

"Tommy McClellan. Long time. You know I didn't see
you standing there. How ya doin'?"

"I'm just fine, Raymond. Matty's having a few at
Buckley's. Dollar beers tonight. But we'll catch up some
other time." He turns back to me. "Get in the car, will
you, Jo? I feel like I'm out on public display."

I climb into his car, which is parked in front of the
fire hydrant facing Forty-third Avenue. "I'm just sitting
here. Don't even think of starting the car."

"I missed you, Jo. As soon as that door slammed shut,
I started missing you."

"Yeah? Well you sure took your sweet time letting
me know."

"I needed some time to straighten things away."

"I'm glad for you. Now you'll have all the time in
the world."

"So there's nothing I can do, nothing I can say to make
this right with you? You don't ever want to see me
again?"

I pause a minute. Big talker I am. "I guess we can
be friends."

"Friends? What the hell does that mean? I call you up when I want to throw a football around the schoolyard?"

"No, you call me up when you're ready to treat me as an equal, not like some blessed saint that you only want to show your good side."

He starts the Celica, switches on the wipers and the defroster.

"Just what do you think you're doing?" I ask.

"I'm defrosting my windows, that's all. We musta been breathing too heavy. Jeez, does it ever fail?" He grabs an old towel from the floor and wipes away at the windows. "Tell me, Jo. Just who are these small Japanese cars marketed to? Tell me, in your educated opinion, do I fit into their category? Are they intended for your typical everyday, run-of-the-mill, crack-smoking, dope-dealing cop, or am I the exception?" He shifts the gear into Drive.

"I said I didn't want to go anywhere with you."

"Can't I make you a cup of tea for your birthday? You know, as a friend."

"I know what your cups of tea mean. It's the Irish idea of foreplay."

He starts laughing. "I swear to Christ, one cup of tea and I'll drive you right home."

It is nearly eleven o'clock. A couple of teenagers straggle the streets of Queens seeking out mischief wherever they can find it, but Tommy's block is quiet. A handful of lights shine into the street from the living rooms of the two-family semidetached homes. A cat stands guard in front of Tommy's door.

"Hey Minnew. O'Brien lock you out again? Come on, I got you some cat food." The cat, a sleek gray and white, follows Tommy downstairs to his apartment.

"Who does Minnew belong to?"

"O'Brien, my landlord, when he remembers. To tell you the truth, I like having her around. Keeps the mice in line." He opens a can of cat food into a bowl and puts it down on the kitchen floor. The cat gulps it greedily. Good old basic Nine Lives, I notice. Typical. Typical. No

Fancy Feast or Amore in this part of town. Even the cat is working class.

Out comes the Red Rose tea bags, the Domino sugar, and a container of milk. He sticks a candle in a Ring-Ding. "Go ahead. Make a wish. I'll spare you my singing."

I close my eyes and wish I knew what to do with my life. And I blow out the candle.

"Well, I'm still standing here. That's good news." Minnew jumps on Tommy's lap and rubs up against his shirt. "Hey Minnew, this is my friend, Jo."

I extend my hand and rub the white spot under her chin. Her four paws find my lap and I feel the vibration of her purr.

"Don't worship her, Minnew. And don't ever try to protect her. She's a real modern woman. She wants to see your true colors, so go ahead and show her what a miserable bastard you can be."

I look at Tommy and I look down at Minnew. I stroke Minnew's silky fur.

"Can I kiss you? Is that allowed under the new friendship treaty?"

Minnew jumps off my lap. I offer Tommy my cheek and his lips slide down my throat. I push him away after a while.

"What? What did I do wrong now?"

"Friends mean friends. That's it."

"You mean to say, we can't . . . ? Jesus Christ. I don't believe this. I'll join up with the La Salle Christian Brothers. At least they got sacramental wine to get them through the night. And how long do we have to wait, in your estimation?"

"There's no magic formula. I want to see a change in you."

"I'll be turning blue down there. How's that for change?"

I get up from the table. "Thank you for the tea and the Ring-Ding."

"All right. All right. I'll work on it, okay? I'll give it

my best shot. We'll be open and honest and communicate about everything under the sun. I'll try my absolute best not to put you up on a pedestal. I'll stop myself cold from ever trying to protect you from that shitty world out there. I'll try. That's all I can do."

"If it's no trouble, can you drive me home?"

"Trouble, sweetie? Trouble's my middle name. Come on, Minnew. Let's get you upstairs before O'Brien raises my rent. Pets cost extra. Even his pets, the stupid mick."

On the ride home I second-guess myself. For God's sake, this time I should have made a clean break. This will never work, not in a million years. Leopards don't shed their spots. Tigers don't lose their stripes. And McClellans don't suddenly become modern thinkers. Some birthday. Some confusing birthday.

"Can I walk you up? See, I'm being good. I'm asking."

I nod. "Okay."

At my door he grins and extends his hand for me to shake. "See ya 'round there, pally. Shoot some hoops tomorrow?"

I bite my tongue to stop the smile.

Twelve

As November takes over October, Tommy starts to feel himself slipping off the economic Good Ship Lollipop. Put it on the credit cards, I tell him. Take a loan and learn to work the mirror trick. It has kept many a holiday festive for families all over the United States. He refuses. I realize he is hopelessly unsophisticated about money matters. His solution is to moonlight for a few months as a security guard in a beef warehouse. I tease him, tell him he's a protector of dead cows.

But now when we are together, he either sleeps or we shop. That third "s" becomes a distant, pleasurable memory like summer vacation after three weeks back at school. It's all right, though, because I think we're making progress on the communication front. Oh, can't you tell? I'm all smiles now. The black ghost has flown away for now and I never know just how long I have. And I have to make the most of the time I do have because I never know just how much of Tommy will remain. So once again Tommy McClellan gets another chance. So, I guess I'm in deeper than I thought. I'm allowing myself to get involved. Just like he says, we're all jammed up for now. I'm starting to be part of his life and he's inching his way back into mine.

A future with the likes of him? I don't think so. Imagine one minute up, next minute down. One day he's my best friend and the next day he might be wearing the mask of a stranger. Ha! I need to work on my own future first. What is Joanna Barron going to do with her life?

I make trips to the bookstore near work. More quick glimpses into ten Quick Steps to a Better Me. More memorized parables from inspirational women. I also get more career advice from Vivien and more educational advice from Lisa Profeta. A course bulletin arrives from Pace University. Another arrives from Baruch. Nothing interests me. I will look at them later.

For my mother and father, I buy his and hers matching monogrammed blue velveteen bathrobes, the gift that offers warmth and whimsy. Warmth to combat our ten P.M. heat cut-off, and whimsy because matching, monogrammed blue velveteen just screams Queen Elizabeth and her hubby sitting before the fire sipping Earl Grey. The tea that has to be brewed and steeped and never, no never, shoved into a little permeable boiling bag. I buy a tin of tea and a silver-plated tea service. And to think at one time Hanukkah meant songs and dreidels. Oy, we've come a long way, bubee.

My coworkers opted for a Kris Kringle this year. We all picked names out of an empty coffee can and have to buy an item of at least fifteen dollars. I do, however, want to buy something special for the two bosses, as they always make a big deal out of presenting the staff with their bonus checks. One by one we are called in and are held captive for the speech about team spirit, our particular performance in relation to the team, la di da di da. Bonus. Thank you and here's a little something for you. Don't mention it. It's just a token. I could be tacky and buy them one gift for the house. After all, they do live together. Wrong, Joanna, they might take offense. It is common but unspoken knowledge.

As for Arlene and Gary, what concerns me now is shopping. What is the perfect holiday gift for dear sister Arlene? Tell me, how can I possibly buy something for a person who knows both the retail and the discount price of every brand name item offered for over-the-counter sale in the continental United States? I remember her saying something about exhibiting Lenox in the family room, Or was it the living room? So she'll know the price. What am I to do?

Tommy—I buy his gift early on, a VCR for his television. I come up with this while he's working two jobs and our dates consist of me listening to his breathing pattern. If he had a VCR I could rent a tape and be entertained while I stroke his hair.

My mother and I decided a few months back to take a vacation week between Christmas and New Year. We plan on waiting on line to get discounted theater tickets, go out to lunch, check out the shop windows, and possibly get a glimpse of the tree in Rockefeller Center.

When I tell Tommy about our plans, he is incredulous. I'm told the City is going to be packed with tourists. No, I'm paraphrasing. The actual quote was, "Are the two of youse outta your minds? Every friggin' hayseed from Kansas is in that week screwing traffic up for miles."

I don't really care. My mother looks like she could use a little Broadway to cheer her up. She looks so worn-out, so haggard. Schwab's Uniform put all the embroiderers on overtime this past month to catch up with some back orders. My poor mother is now working a twelve-hour day. She is dead on her feet, one of the walking wounded.

And Matty happened to be right about her not sleeping. I begin to take notice of the pat-pat of her Dearfoams on our flattened carpet at three and four in the morning. After twenty years she has stopped coloring her hair, and now she's half brown and half tabby yellow-gray. I'm told Daddy likes gray hair, but I think he's just being polite.

I think what's really nibbling at her must be that sapphire necklace Aunt Naomi received from Uncle Marc on their thirty-fifth anniversary. Sapphires, we are told, because diamonds come from a country whose ethical framework is still on faulty ground no matter what the newspapers say. I'm sure my mother will toss away her gloomies once she gets her annual dose of culture in Manhattan. Anyway, she's not that bad off. She hasn't found it necessary to repaint the bathroom. That's her one sure sign of being extra blue.

By the time Thanksgiving rolls around I decide to give Dahlia a two-pound box of Perugina chocolates, and for Ms. Reeves I buy a bottle of Cuorvoisier. I envision them stuffing bacci after bacci into their self-satisfied mouths and feeling all flushed and giggly from the cognac. Christmas at Home with Bloated Lesbian Market Researchers, a scene stolen right out of the Currier and Ives collection.

The big news is that Trudy invites me for Christmas dinner along with Teresa Ann and Jordan, Jordan's parents, the Arbrewsters (of Ardsley), and my parents (of Sunnyside). I get the feeling that Trudy wants me to become a McClellan. She does not know that our future is the one subject that never comes up. After all, we are friends now, just good friends. Our future means his next day off. It's just as well, like I said, I am still without any direction, and a real relationship with her son would offer no solution. And I'm positive that was one of my better decisions. We're learning how to talk to each other. We spend time with each other's families. And before Tommy's second job, we actually made it to the movies. We went bowling. We went out to eat and talked about our day. He did, however, absolutely draw the line at a coffee bar.

One day, he really opened up to me. He opened up to me more than I ever expected. We were sitting in his apartment after we had finished up a very nice dinner with the Profetas. It was one of those pleasant evenings where the subject of college didn't come up and place its uneasy wedge between Lisa and Eddie. So the Profetas went home happy and I went back to Tommy's apartment for a cup of tea. And out of the blue, when his back was turned to me, he said: "I found my father, you know. Teresa Ann asked me to track him down, the time we went over there."

"You what?"

"You heard me. I dug up my old man. I did it for Teresa Ann. Now I wish I hadn't done it."

"Oh my God. Where is he living?"

"San Antonio."

"Oh my God, Tommy. Does your mother know? Does Matty?"

He placed two mugs of tea on the table. "No. Just me and Teresa Ann."

"What are you going to do? Are you going to visit him?"

"Hell no. Not a chance. You see, I'd feel this pressing obligation to kill him after all he done to us. Premeditated murder wouldn't look too good for my career. But my sister's going down there right before Christmas. She wants to surprise him. Her and Jordy."

"Why does your sister want to see him after all these years?"

"She said she wanted closure. You know what that means?"

"She wants to end the wondering. She wants answers to all her questions."

He nodded his head. "Yeah, she said something like that. I tell you, she just about got down on her knees and begged me that day we were over there and the two of us were in her kitchen. I tried like hell talking her out of it. I told her it would bring nothing but trouble. I told her Ma would just about go crazy, if she found out what we did. And who could blame her? Digging up deadbeat Daddy after all these years.

"Think about it, the bastard never even sent us so much as a postcard. And my mother, who took all the trouble and raised us, Teresa Ann just about ignores. If my sister picks up a phone once every six months to call home, it's a lot. I think she's holding my mother responsible for him taking off. She was real little when he split. And she was Daddy's little angel. But all this time she's blaming my mother for her whole messy childhood. And she hates Billy with a passion. The sick part of it is, it was Billy who helped put her through school. Our real father didn't do shit. But my sister knows how to get what she wants. She always did. So I tracked him down for her. It wasn't too hard. Truth is, I was kind of hoping he was good and dead. But just my luck, the son of a bitch is alive and kicking."

I put my hand into his. "This must be very painful for you. All of this coming to the surface, after such a long time."

"Yeah, it stings real good. And it's a real no win situation too. I'm being disloyal to my mother in order to help out my sister. And I'm not really helping my sister. Not really. Because she's gonna end up good and hurt. She's gonna show up at his doorstep and he's gonna give her one of his big smiles, apologize for running away, and tell her he had no choice. He was going through some tough times, you see. He couldn't handle all that responsibility that our mother loaded onto him. He'll tell her Ma practically drove him out the door, she was so demanding. And then the bastard's gonna take one look at Teresa Ann's fancy clothes and Jordy's extra fat wallet and then the prick's gonna hit her up for money. Mark my words."

"Come on. Your sister isn't stupid."

"Yeah? Well, I wonder sometimes. With all them brains, there's times she can add up two and two and come up with five."

"Boy, she really put you in a bad spot."

"It's no good, Jo, what she made me do. I sold my mother down the river just to help my sister chase her rainbow. This can't end up good. Not for none of us."

"Your mother doesn't have to find out. Teresa Ann can make a quick visit, say what she has to say, and leave. No harm done."

"I'm praying that's what will go down. I'm praying hard. But I ain't exactly counting on it. Want some more tea, Sunshine?"

"No thanks. I wish I could help you in some way."

"Just you sitting here is helping me. It's helping me

more than you know. And I'm hoping one day I can help you."

"You do," I told him. "Every time we see each other, you make me feel so important. You really listen to me when I talk. Like I actually matter for what I am instead of what I can be. Everyone else just sees potential. You see what's there." And it was true. He had become more than a friend. He had become my best friend. But with his track record, how long could that last? In a flash he could disappear again. He could get nasty. He could shut me out. And he could play me for a fool if I let my guard slip down. Still, we are getting closer. He is playing by my rules, after all. What else can I ask of him?

"It's late. You better get on home, sweetie. See, I got this real sudden, powerful urge to be more than friends. I'm sitting here wanting desperately to crawl into bed with you and hold you real tight and slip far away with you, the way it used to be. But I also know I can't have you, 'cause of what I said and what I done. So put your coat on and let me drive you home, Sunshine, before I start something you're not ready for me to start and I screw everything up for us."

We didn't say one word to each other on the ride home, and I couldn't even hold onto his chest and brush a good-night kiss on him when he delivered me at my doorstep. I couldn't bear to feel his sorrow and stand there, not prepared to offer him any comfort. I could not be a true friend to him that night.

Not too long after that, I buy Tommy a gold pocket watch. I have the inside engraved: *For my best friend, Love, Jo.* Most men hate these pocket watches; they're so impractical. Too bad. I wanted to engrave my feelings. I wanted to let him know just how I feel. And what would his reaction be? Would he back away, retreat? Did I say too much? Too little? Would he laugh it off? I couldn't know. I'd have to take the chance. Anyway, I'm planning to let him know in the near future he's off probation. Why am I easing up? Because he tried. He really made an all out effort to climb out of the cave. Trust. He earned my trust for now.

Christmas and Hanukkah fall during the same week this year, which squares things away rather nicely for the retailers. Five days before Christmas, I ask him about decorating his apartment. He looks blankly at me and I assume he's fallen asleep with his eyes open. A few seconds later he tells me it's a kid's holiday and there's no reason to go to all the trouble. I yell at him, tell him I never got to do this before. I want to decorate. No, I am dying to decorate. He tells me to do whatever the hell I want, too tired to argue.

From fatigue he comes down with a terrible cold that doesn't let go of him. I beg him to quit the security job and he does. He listens to reason once a year. All his gifts have been bought and paid for in cash, just like people did during the Middle Ages.

I buy a four-foot fake Christmas tree, tinsel, ornaments, garland, lights, and a star. I even hang a wreath on his door. It's my first Christmas and I want to indulge. I put everything up myself. Tommy helps a little by introducing a winter motif with his white, crumpled tissues. And he spreads the fragrant, holiday aroma of fast-acting Vicks vapor rub all through the house. One night he runs out to buy cough syrup and comes back with what he calls a Jewish candelabra.

"Go ahead, stick it in the window."

"Come on, this is your house."

"Not when you're here, Sunshine."

I stand tiptoe on a chair to reach a narrow window right below the ceiling but the menorah wouldn't clear. He places it on the floor next to the tree. Eddie and Lisa Profeta stop by around nine-thirty and tell us we're equal opportunity celebrators. We exchange gifts and Tommy promises them we wouldn't open them until Christmas.

"No," Lisa says. "I want Jo to open hers now."

I start tearing at the green wrapping paper. "Oh, Lisa. Thank you. Look Tommy, it's a day planner." I hold up the smooth leather book.

"Excuse me there, Mrs. Profeta, but what the hell is a day planner?"

"It's a book that helps schedule your day and organize your time. Since Joanna is thinking about going to college at night, I thought this might help keep her life together."

"Thank you. I still haven't decided yet, but I'm sure when I do, it will come in handy."

"What are you waiting for, Jo?" Lisa asks. "Spring session starts in February."

"I don't know. I'm still undecided."

"Why don't you audit a class? Just to see if it's for you."

"I guess. I don't have any one area that interests me."

"A bachelor's will offer a variety of courses. It's meant to broaden you out as a person."

"Why don't you get off the soapbox, Lisa? Give it a rest," Eddie warns. "If Jo wants to go to college, she'll pick herself up and go. It's not for everyone, you know. My wife forgets this sometimes."

I look at Lisa but I don't say anything. Over time I had gathered that her educational pursuits had put some distance between them. Eddie must be feeling a little insecure. It's only natural when one person has the degree and the other person doesn't. I look over at Tommy, who is taking it all in. "Who wants a beer?" he asks with a smile.

The rest of the night goes smoothly. The subject of college doesn't surface again. And when the Profetas leave, I ask Tommy if Eddie is resentful that Lisa's furthering her education.

"I don't know. It never comes up. We don't have too many of them soul-searching conversations when we're out hunting perps."

"Would it bother you if I went to school?"

"No. I ain't Eddie Profeta, if that's what you're worried about."

I get my coat out of the closet. "It's late. I better go. You know your cold is sounding worse, not better. You might have to break down and go see a doctor."

"Jo, I just got this cough medicine from Ellen's boss, Philly. I don't need no doctor. What I do need is some loving. This abstinence business has thrown my whole system way out of whack."

"Feel better."

On December twenty-fourth I am called into the adjoining offices of Ms. Reeves and Ms. Barnett. Since they summon the employees in order of corporate importance, it is late afternoon before I am ushered in to be received.

"Ms. Reeves and myself would like to take the time. La di la di da. Excellent job. Our profits weren't as high. La di da. Organized. La di da. For someone without a college degree. La di da. Learned so much. La di da di da. A token of our appreciation."

And the envelope please. "Thank you, and here's a little something for you two. . . . Same to you. See you after the New Year."

Quick, run into the cubicle and pivot the chair to the file cabinet. Three hundred and fifty dollars. That's $400 less than last year. The hell with your increasing overhead. I have a mind to swipe my cognac and chocolates back, you ungrateful pigs.

I leave the building with two voices bouncing around inside me. Tommy tells me, "Fuck 'em. You'll get another job." Then my mother chimes in and interrupts Tommy. "Be happy you have a good job. You work with refined people in a pretty office. Next year the firm will do better and you'll do better too. You'll see. Stay with it, but get your credentials at night." In what? "In anything, Joanna. Get the piece of paper."

Oh, leave me alone, the both of you. I'm getting a headache.

Christmas Eve is also the first night of Hanukkah. Arlene and Gary come to dinner to exchange gifts. We're all off from work the following day so it is an unhurried visit. Tommy is working tonight but at least he's off for

Christmas. I have yet to comprehend his schedule and I've given up trying. He's home when he's home.

Arlene walks in two steps ahead of Gary and scans the room. Give it up, Arlene. Nothing has changed. "You've bought a new dustpan set," she says to my mother after the round of hello kisses are out of the way. "Rubbermaid?"

"Are you for real?"

"You're no better. You found fault with our toilet paper."

"I didn't find fault. All I did was ask you if No Frills was available in ecru yet."

My mother serves baked chicken cutlets tonight, a tossed salad, candied carrots, and potato latkes with applesauce. She has not yet come under the spell of her two Born Again Vegetarian sisters.

"Your aunt Adele and uncle Jack are coming down for dessert," my father says.

"I'm in no mood tonight for her idiotic rambling and his boring speeches about World War Two," Arlene lets us know.

"You could show a little compassion for the people who took good care of you when you were little."

"Face it, they're losers, both of them. I love them but they're losers. They depress me. I can't help it."

"You'll put up with them for an hour." My father loses patience with Aunt Adele too now and then, but then he's allowed, sibling privilege.

"Gary's in a good mood," Arlene declares. "The partners just handed him a seven thousand dollar bonus. Next year he'll be a partner too."

"Arlene!" Gary shouts. I never heard him raise his voice before. "Why don't you call up Eyewitness News?"

"Wonderful!" my parents and I say with pride, admiration, and a touch of envy on my part.

"And you, Arlene? What do they give to a comptroller of a real estate firm?" my mother inquires.

"Aggravation. And $2,500."

"Mazel tov, both of you."

Mom, I plead silently. Do not make me announce my $350. Please. I'll be good. I'll eat an extra latke. Please.

But now Arlene is distributing her gifts. My mother and I both receive tailored, silky, Diane von Furstenberg blouses. Mine is pale beige and size eight. My mother's is a deep rose and size fourteen. Otherwise, they're identical. "Stunning," we say. Must have been buy one/get one.

My father is handed a gray Shetland wool sweater. He'll have to wear a shirt underneath or he'll itch.

Arlene says, "Isn't everything beautiful? And I didn't overpay either. You have to know how to shop. It's a skill."

Gary invites me to shop with Arlene at one of their New Jersey malls. He almost hooks me with the no-sales-tax-on-clothing bait.

I distribute my gifts.

"Lenox. Always appropriate," Arlene says. Ssh! Keep it down. She's calculating now.

My parents model the velveteen robes. They could pass for a shorter, chubbier model of the queen and her prince regent. My mother starts setting up for tea. Over the clanging of the tea service and the whistling of the kettle on the stove, my father announces from the dining room, "May, I've been keeping a little secret from you." He has that look of concealed boyish mischief, but he's smiling so I assume he wasn't laid off. We've had a few of those announcements over the years.

My mother stops fiddling with the tea service. "What is it? Something happened at work, right?"

"Yep, something good. Rainbow Cars had a very good year, Mr. Milstein told me. He likes the job I do for him. He trusts me more than the other drivers. Most of the other drivers are just kids. They don't know how to talk to people. They're only interested in the tip, and that does nothing for repeat business. Mr. Milstein knows everything that goes on. He's a real smart cookie. Yesterday, after I finished up, he calls me over and hands your husband a bonus. Wait, let me finish. And a bonus for Sol Barron means a bonus for May Barron. So here May, after all these years, here is your bonus." Still wearing his royal robe, he walks self-consciously to the hall closet and presents my mother with a huge white box that had been resting up against the extra boards from the dining room table. We watch and wait as my mother cuts the cord and thrashes through the tissue paper.

"Oh my God, a mink jacket. A mink jacket. Sol! Sol!" She caresses the jacket delicately, like she's stroking a newborn. "Oh Sol, it's exquisite. Feel it. Feel it." She models it over the bathrobe. Even Arlene is impressed, pleased into a beaming quiet. She'll borrow it soon enough. Gary, on the other hand, fusses and fidgets uncomfortably in his chair, an unusual distraction in one so easygoing.

And then I start to think. And this thought wanders in uninvited, this thought that says mink jackets cost in the thousands, and even if Mr. Milstein loved my father's driving, he wouldn't have handed over that much money. I want this thought to leave right away. It's spoiling everything. Yet it stays and stays, loitering, lingering about, unwelcome as it is. My father took out another loan, had to be.

Aunt Adele and Uncle Jack enter during the commotion. Poor Aunt Adele. She is confused by a mink jacket that goes over a bathrobe. "Separate? Wear it in good health. Jack, it's separate."

Uncle Jack promises Aunt Adele that one day she will have such riches. Who's to say? He's playing the lottery on Wednesdays and Saturdays now to increase their odds.

We daintily sip our brewed English tea between the forklifts of Carvel ice cream cake. Get a load of Arlene scraping all of the chocolate crunchies onto her plate. She's so considerate of others.

"Sol," my mother calls across the table, "we forgot to light the menorah. Go, it's not too late. Jo, help your father. The matches are in the junk drawer. I'm too excited to be near fire tonight!"

Thirteen

It's the Barron family's Christmas Debut. "Why are we invited?" my mother asks with more than a tinge of suspicion in her voice. "Does this mean we're going to be family? Has Tommy said something? I thought you two were just friends now. Joanna, I'm telling you, whatever you do, don't sign any paper. That is my advice."

"What paper?"

"The paper that signs your children away to the Catholic Church. Did he ever mention a paper?"

"As it just so happens, yes, he did mention a paper once. We were out one Saturday night and he asked me about a paper. He said, Jo, you want a paper? And I said, yes, the *New York Times*, please."

"You think you're very clever, don't you? Everything's a joke with you. You're your father's daughter."

The only crimp in our first Christmas dinner is the weather. It's 21 degrees outside, and with the wind chill it's 2 degrees. Have I mentioned that we have no heat inside? Yes, two or three times a winter Mr. Santini neglects to buy oil for the furnace. We use space heaters, electric blankets. The oven stays on for warmth. Sometimes we do the relative hop.

I call Tommy at noon to advise him to dress extra

warm today. Trudy is busy cooking and she's apt to forget her eldest, who still has that terrible cold.

"Hello?" he answers sleepily. "Yeah, I was sleeping. Got in at nine. Yes in the morning. Don't worry about it. No heat? Fuck that man. Fuck 'em where he breathes. Long johns? Jo, let me get some sleep, will you? Merry Christmas to you too, sweetie."

My mother parades around the apartment in a wool skirt, boots, a deep rose marked-down Diane von Furstenberg blouse, and a mink jacket. She's chopping tuna fish for our lunch. I have not seen her this ecstatic since Arlene's march down the aisle. "Wait until Naomi and Rose see this coat. Sol, I can't wait to see their faces! They'll be so proud of you."

"Isn't Marc against minks?" my father asks. "Didn't he mention a mink philosophy one time?"

"No, Sol. You're mistaken. It was seals. I'm sure it was seals. He published a paper. Here, I kept a copy on top of the refrigerator. 'The Social and Economic Ramifications of the Fur Industry's Policy on Seal Clubbing in the Arctic vis á vis Anomie Amongst Native Peoples.' We breathe a collective sigh of relief. Uncle Marc is neutral on mink jackets.

"I bought Trudy and Billy a very pretty ceramic cake plate. I hope they like it."

"I'm sure they will."

"How she ended up with that man . . . I mean I don't blame her. She had three kids to raise. She was alone for a long time. She needed someone."

"He's all right once you get used to him."

"I know he's good to Trudy. I suppose that's the main thing. Anyway, I bought Tommy something too."

"That wasn't necessary."

"No, not necessary but we wanted to. I know you think I don't like him, but you're wrong. I do like him very much, and so does your father. We bought him a cashmere sweater. It's a very soft light brown."

"Cashmere is very expensive."

"Well, I bought the red one for you, the blue for Gary,

and the gray one for Daddy, and that crazy color Arlene likes, seafone. No, seafoam-green, that's it. You must have seen it last night. Don't you think Tommy deserves one? Granted, he's not family, but we still feel for him. He cares for you, I can see that. I watch his eyes following you around the room, like he can't believe you really exist. I'm surprised you haven't noticed that."

"That was very nice of both of you."

"We're not as bad as you think. We only want what's best for you. For your future."

And where does my future lie? Way out my window, in Manhattan? All the plays I haven't seen, all the museums I've never explored, all the concerts I haven't heard, call out to me. Wait, I must say. I am not ready for you. I am not yet comfortable in the looming shadows of your steely towers.

I dress for my first Christmas with great anticipation. Am I shivering with excitement or with cold? A few steps away from the space heater it's 43 degrees. My new red cashmere sweater is very warm. I had planned on a black wool skirt but my legs will freeze. Boots, boots, boots. Yes, I'll wear a pair of black boots. Sometimes I dazzle myself with my own brilliance. And don't forget the strand of faux pearls. Imitation elegance, the next best thing, right?

Tommy rings the bell at two-thirty carrying one gift and a box of tissues. "Nice weather we got in here. Keep hugging me. I'm freezing."

"Do you have your long johns on? Let me check." I slide my hand under a white fisherman's knit sweater and reach down below his belt. No long johns, but I am greeted by a gun under the waistband. The unexpected welcome nearly sends me into cardiac arrest.

"May! Sol! Save me. Your daughter's about to shoot off the family jewels!" They don't hear. They're in the bedroom, door closed. My father must be getting dressed. He requires my mother's constant supervision.

"You're wearing jeans and work boots on a holiday? On your most important holiday?"

"Don't hassle me on my most important holiday. Hug me. No, don't kiss me. I'm still sick. All right, just a little one. Mmmm. Jeez, how long has it been? Two and a half months? Get outta here. Some friend you turned out to be. No wonder I'm so—"

"Hello, Tommy. Merry Christmas." My mother has sprung out of the bedroom.

"Hey May. Whatcha got on there, a fur coat?"

"Courtesy of my father's Christmas bonus from Rainbow Cars."

Tommy looks at me for half a second. That look, it says it all. "Oh May. That's one classy coat you got on. Sure will come in handy today."

"Put your hand on it. Soft isn't the word. It's heaven. Heaven on earth."

My father emerges from the bedroom in gray beltless slacks and his new gray cashmere sweater. The XL is a tight squeeze across his middle but it works. "Merry Christmas, Tommy," my father chants. We love saying this. We've repressed these Merry Christmases for too long.

"Thanks. I see you got a lot to celebrate. That's some bonus your wife is strutting around in."

"Yep." My father grins. "Isn't that something?"

Oh yeah, it's something all right.

"What do you have there?" I ask Tommy. "You have something for me?"

"One for you and one for your folks. Hope I done good for youse. I'm new at this Hanukkah stuff."

I laugh a little when he transforms Hanukkah to Hanukkar, but it makes perfect sense for him. Soda is sodar. Vodka is vodkar. His pronunciations do follow a pattern. True enough, I'm not one to tawk.

"For Sol and May, a bottle of champagne, and not that imitation dago swill."

"Oh, you didn't have to. Thank you. Wait, we have

something for you. Sol, it's in the hall closet, next to the
electric broom."

My father extracts the box with the brown cashmere
sweater. Tommy's eyes widen. He didn't expect anything
from them. "Thank you." He rubs the sweater slowly
across his cheek to feel its softness. "Hey, this is something special. You shouldn't throw good money away on
the likes of me." He stoops to kiss my mother and extends
his hand into my father's.

"Well? Where's for Joanna?" I ask.

"Forget it, Franklin. I want to see what I got first."

"It's in my room. Mom, we'll be just a minute, okay?"

I hand him the wrapped carton with the VCR. He
looks pleased. "Thanks, Sunshine. Now we can rent dirty
movies. Come closer. I want to hold you again. I'm freezing. Yeah, everything's freezing. No, don't start. Not with
your parents right outside the door. Jo! Cut it out, huh?
And you used to be so shy. You'll come back with me
tonight. Tell them you're going to hook up my new VCR.
This friendship stuff must be wearing you down too."

"I have something else for you."

"My turn next." He reaches into a pocket and pulls
out a small package wrapped in red foil paper. "For you,
sweetie. This was supposed to be your birthday present
but I screwed that up royally."

Underneath the paper, a white velvet box hatches
open. Oooh, a necklace, a gold anchor studded with ru-
bies. "Oh Tommy."

"Well, I got no boat yet, but when I do you're coming
with me 'cause let me tell you, there's no one in this
world I want to take sailing more than you. I never said
this to you 'cause I'm not real good with words. And
maybe it took almost losing you to wake me up, but I
love you, Jo. I love you bad."

I take my faux pearls off and put my new necklace
on. It catches a patch of sun and twinkles a thousand red
dots onto the wall. "Oh Tommy, it's beautiful."

"Not as beautiful as you are, Sunshine. You crying
again? Here, I got a whole box of Kleenex to share with

you. And don't let me forget, I got something else for you
at home."

"Open this." I hand him the box with the pocket
watch.

"You're spending too much money." He peeks into
the small box. "Oh Jeez, a gold watch. I remember my
grandfather used to wear one. Before he died. He used to
work over at Silver Top, when they were still a bakery.
The bosses gave it to him when he retired."

"Open it up."

He eyes the inscription and I lean in to receive his kiss.

At three o'clock Tommy escorts us the one flight up
to Trudy and Billy's place. If our building had been archi-
tecturally designed rather than built in postwar haste, it
would follow that 5B would be a replica of 4B, two bedrooms, large rectangular living room/dining room, small
eat-in kitchen. No. Trudy and Billy have three bedrooms,
a small square living room, and a kitchen/dinette. They
gained a bedroom but sacrificed half a living room. As a
result, Trudy has to serve large crowds in Matty's bedroom. They had moved Matty's furniture out into their
room and set up an aluminum table all decked out in
holiday red. Eight folding chairs and Matty's high riser
provide the seating.

Understandably, we are the first to arrive. At the last
minute my mother leaves the mink jacket in our hall
closet, choosing a pink cardigan instead. More than anything, she is afraid to spill dinner on her new baby.

We exchange gifts. Everyone is merry, merry, chat-
tering on about everything and nothing. I hear Billy ask
my father, "Do people ever screw in the backseat while
you're driving? No? Oh Sal, you gotta make the switch
to limos."

Sal, Billy calls my father. Salvatore Barron.

Tommy's eyes patrol Forty-third Avenue, searching
for Teresa Ann out the bedroom window. He has his
doubts about the Arbrewster side of his family, but I remind him they treated us very nicely in the summer, and

besides, they wouldn't go back on their word. He laughs at me and tells me they're lawyers. I guess that's supposed to explain everything.

"Get over here, Matty. Hustle up. There's Jordy's car." Tommy wrenches up the window and gathers a handful of four-day-old sooty snow that had accumulated on the ledge. "Look, they just dropped the princess off at the curb. The rest of them are looking for a spot. Come on. Come on. Keep 'em coming, bro."

"Teresa Ann!" he yells out the window. "Treeesa Ann! Yo Treeesa Ann!" Tommy fires a barrage of snowballs at his defenseless sister. He raises a clenched fist. "Yes!" he shouts with glee. Then he leans farther out and yells, "Hey listen up. Don't nobody touch Teresa Ann's shiny new black BMW parked out by the school."

"Thomas, shut that window. Matthew, you're no better." They're both laughing so hard they pay no heed to Trudy.

Teresa Ann arrives at the door unruffled for her ordeal. She wouldn't give Tommy the satisfaction. Under her tailored blue coat she's wearing a white knitted dress with a pair of white and tan hand-tooled boots. Her blond ponytail is shackled with a silver clasp today. Class. Lower upper class. You can't beat it.

"Hey, Little Sister. Merry Christmas. You're back in the 'hood. Wait just a sec. Let me introduce you to your mother, in case you don't recognize her. Trudy, this is your daughter, Teresa Ann. Teresa Ann, this is your mother."

She gives Tommy a look. "I'm ignoring your snide comments today."

"Come in Ma's room for a second. Me and you, we got some talking to do about your recent trip to San Antonio. I'm dying to hear about it. But you know me, always one for educational travel."

I notice how much Matty and Teresa Ann favor their mother. Teresa Ann's features are Trudy's chiseled by a fine sculptor. Matty's features are Trudy's blunted by a kindergartner's rolling pin. Tommy appears unrelated to

his short, fair-haired mother and siblings. He's his father's child.

Jordan and his parents enter moments later. Mr. Arbrewster—or Everett, as he insists—is taller, thinner, and
more bald than Jordan. He has a bumpy red-splotched
nose and extra thin, smiling lips. He wears an out-of-date
navy suit and a red plaid vest looped with an ancient
gold pocket watch. Even the chain has seen better days.
You would think with all his money, he could make it
out to a mall once in a while. I know, I know, old money.
Never mind.

Mrs. Arbrewster—Olive, to her friends—is also tall,
but not thin. She has short, white hair that contrasts nicely
with her cornflower-blue eyes. Cornflower-blue, right out
of my prized sixty-four Crayolas. She's wearing—oh, who
cares what she's wearing? Trudy covers her up with a
sweater anyhow. Tommy borrows an orange down-filled
vest from Matty. With his jeans and work boots, he looks
like he's on a fifteen minute break from the road crew.

Billy certainly pours his liquor with a carefree hand.
My parents and myself are high on screwdrivers. Mr. and
Mrs. Arbrewster are steady with their vodka neat. Tommy,
Billy, and Trudy drink scotch over ice. Matty pours his own
Heinekens. To mark the birth of his Lord, he's using a glass
today. Jordan and Teresa Ann ask for eggnog but settle for
plain tonic water. We're all so happy now, ha ha ha, that
I almost forget that white spirits are way ahead of brown
spirits according to market research; 5B threw out their
questionnaire. My God, how that job of mine has taken
over my life, even on my day off. Foxgloves blooming in
June. The gardener. The exterminator. I can't track the
conversation. Another screwdriver? No thanks. I better
have some chips. Great dip.

Mrs. Arbrewster approaches Trudy meekly and asks
if they may sit anywhere at the table or if there is assigned
seating. This woman is searching for place cards in Matty's bedroom.

"Oh we're very informal," Trudy tells her guest.

"Yeah, just sit on your ass," Billy adds.

The Arbrewsters laugh deeply. Very deeply. They are tourists in a foreign land but they are delighted, just delighted, with the natives. Teresa Ann could strangle Billy at this point.

My mother follows Trudy into the kitchen. I strain to hear their voices, muffled under the din from my buzzing head.

"We're so glad youse could all come."

"We're happy to be here. After all, we go back a long way."

"I never thought I'd be living here so long. We started with a one year lease and kept on renewing."

My mother chuckles. "Yes, I thought we'd be in our own home, somewhere nice like Long Island, but it never worked out for us. Four more years I have. Four more years if the job doesn't kill me. Sol and I are going to buy a condo in Florida and really start to live."

"Ah, that's wonderful, May. We gotta wait till Billy's kids are all twenty-one before we can think of retiring. He pays child support, you know. You'd think one of them rotten kids would call and wish him a Merry Christmas. Not one. Billy's ex turned them all against him. She's a real piece of work."

"A shame. Let's think of happier things. Here, let me help you with that. Your daughter looks beautiful. What a success story. She and my Arlene. They're the ones with ambition. Look what they did with their lives."

"Teresa Ann's my special princess, always was. I just wish she'd be a little closer. I wish she'd visit more than once a year. I wish she'd pick up the telephone and we'd have mother-to-daughter chats, just like you see on the TV."

"Wait, here's a trivet. That's it. At least your sons are close to you."

"Matty is the closest to me, I guess 'cause he's still living at home. He's a lot of fun but he still got plenty of growing up to do. Plenty. And Tommy, I really can't complain about him. He's my rock. I can always count on him. Like I says, he's very good to me and all, but I don't know. He broods a lot and I can't reach him. He frightens me sometimes, May. He turns into someone I don't know. Know what I mean? But your Jo, she's done him a world of good. I'm so glad they're getting along again. You think the soup needs more pepper?''

"No, it's good. It's good. They can always add. It's delicious.''

"May, why don't you come down to the beauty parlor Thursday night no more? Rose Petruzzi was asking about you. You shoulda seen what Louise did to her mother's hair, dyed it flame-red. She come in Thursday night to get the color back to brown.''

"I gave up trying to look beautiful. I'm fifty-eight years old. I feel it and I look it. Oh Trudy, I'm working a twelve-hour shift now. I don't want to get up in the morning. Every day is the same. My eyes hurt. My back is killing me. I don't have to tell you. Work and more work. Over and over again. And there's no end in sight.''

"Come down to the beauty parlor, May. You'll feel better, give you a lift.''

Billy scampers into the kitchen. "Trudy, get a move-on. Them Arbrewster people look hungry.''

Trudy and my mother march in with vegetable soup and dinner rolls. The soup is tasty and hot, initially. Five minutes on the table, however, it cools to room temperature, 38 degrees. I pretend it's gazpacho. Dahlia adores gazpacho. Ms. Reeves thinks it's passé.

"Perhaps if the plates were warmed,'' Mrs. Arbrewster suggests, "the heat would be retained longer.''

"There's no room in the oven to start warming plates,'' Billy says. "Maybe if we breathe real heavy.'' Matty and the Arbrewsters laugh.

When everyone is finished with the soup, my mother and Trudy get up to clear. I shuffle around Matty's bed to get out also. Tommy grabs my arm downward and squeezes until I'm in pain.

"What's the matter with you?'' I whisper.

"Don't you get up to serve these people. Let my sister get off her ass. This is her mother. Why can't she help

her own mother?" he snarls back under his breath. He
glares at Teresa Ann with fire in his eyes. She doesn't
respond. I wrench free to help. They'll be needing more
hands. I can feel Tommy seethe behind my back.

We pile soup bowls into the sink. Out comes a Virginia ham, sweet potato pie, and creamed corn. Oh, what
a delicious smell. I could embrace it for warmth but instead I help serve it. Billy carves, we pass and ladle. And
then everyone begins to eat, everyone except the Barron
family. We observe momentarily. Do you eat those cloves
or are they decoration? We only know boiled ham from
King Kullen.

"Sal, you like this ham?"

"Best I ever ate."

It all tastes great, except by the third mouthful it's
cold. Good but cold. Uh-oh, a cockroach is running across
the wall behind the high riser. I'm the only one who sees
it. He must have smelled Trudy's Christmas dinner. Trust
me, he's not visiting to warm up.

"That does it." Tommy suddenly slams his fist to the
table, causing the drinks to shimmy. "I'm going down to
Gurtz and she's going to get me Santini." He turns to his
mother. "Excuse me," he says as he flies out the door.

"Go with him, Jo. Please."

Matty follows me down to the Gurtzes' apartment.
Tommy's pounding on her door just as Matty and I get
off the elevator. His face is deranged with anger.

"Calm down. Maybe she's out today."

"She's always home, stoned on downers. Open up,
Mrs. Gurtz."

Mrs. Gurtz twists open her greasy doorknob. That
oily, perfumed odor shoots out at us. "Why you hollering
at me?"

Tommy pushes her aside and walks in. We follow single file. In my whole life I'd never been inside Mrs.
Gurtz's apartment before. It's filthy, layered thick with
dust balls. Stacks of newspapers clutter every flat surface.
Shredded streamers from a long forgotten birthday party
hang half suspended from the ceiling. Abandoned furni-

ture from vacated apartments crowd her foyer. Thick
brown drapes are drawn tightly across the windows, leaving her rooms in shadow. I swallow hard to hold my
dinner inside me.

Another tenant, old Mrs. Blake from the third floor,
limps in behind us, clutching a wet wooden spoon. She
ignores us and limps up to Mrs. Gurtz. Tommy lets her
talk first, age before rage.

"My oven's broken," Mrs. Blake states in a tiny, little voice.

Mrs. Gurtz scratches under her blond Afro wig. "Show
me on my oven what's wrong with yours."

Tommy's patience screeches to a halt. "I'll show you
what's wrong with her oven." He wrenches the oven door
down. It's rimmed in black grease and smells sour.
Tommy doesn't flinch. "The hinges are busted. It's held
together with toothpicks like every other fucking oven in
this building. Right, Mrs. Blake?"

Mrs. Blake nods her head.

"I'll send my husband upstairs tomorrow. He doesn't
feel well today."

Mrs. Blake agrees to the postponement begrudgingly.
Then she turns to Tommy and whacks his hand with her
spoon. "You are a very fresh boy, Thomas McClellan.
That mouth should be washed out with soap." She limps
out without looking back.

"Give me Santini's number," Tommy demands. "I
know you got it, and don't mess with me."

She shifts some papers around her kitchen and produces the number.

"Where's the phone? You got a phone in this pigsty?"

She moves more papers. A matted orange and yellow
cat springs onto the kitchen table and licks around the
rim of an unwashed cup. The telephone is on her counter.
It looks slippery. Matty and I, in fascinating disgust,
watch Tommy pick it up and dial.

"Hello, who's this? Carmella? Honey, is Grandpa Vin-
cent there? Yeah sweetheart, tell him it's police officer
McClellan."

"That should give the man a heart attack," Matty mumbles.

"Santini, this is Tommy, Trudy Emmet's son, 5B. You know, your luxury building on Fortieth Street in Sunnyside. Jesus Christ, she paid the fucking rent two weeks ago. I'm calling about the heat. Yeah, there's been no heat in here since this morning. You want to maybe call your friends the Lasorsa Brothers and get their oil truck through right about now?" Tommy is quiet for a minute. "Listen pal, let's get one thing straight. The Italians got Christmas Eve. The Irish got Christmas Day. Don't hand me that bullshit. If you pay those dagos double on a gallon they'd make their grandmothers come out—hold on there. That's a crock of shit too. They're so stuffed up with clams and shrimps from last night they don't want no macaroni today. You'd be doing them a favor. Forget it. Maybe we should talk in person." Tommy cups his hand over the phone. "What's his address?" he asks Mrs. Gurtz.

She shrugs and hands him a food-stained scrap of paper.

"I'm gonna get on that Guinea Gangplank and keep going all the way to Victory Boulevard. Believe me, you'll regret it. . . . Thank you. Two hours? Yeah, send my very best regards to Mrs. Santini. No, you know I don't mean nothing by it. We all go back a long way. Merry Christmas." He hangs up and says to his brother, "If Lasorsa ain't here in two hours we're gonna pay your landlord a visit."

We leave Mrs. Gurtz standing expressionless in the kitchen. We walk out into the hallway and I ring for the elevator but Tommy just sits down on the floor. His face, which had been flushed with anger, pales suddenly. His voice fades to a hoarse whisper. "People really shouldn't have to live like this. This ain't a welfare building, you know. We've all been paying him rent for years. Christ, them people from Ardsley looking at us like we're some kinda freaks. Why do they talk about their flowers in December, Jo? I don't get it, do you? And the sick part is, they're alcoholics. They drank up Billy's bottle of Stoly straight. And that's who my sister wants to be like, friggin' gardening alkies from Ardsley. After all I done for her." He leans his head back against the wall. The elevator comes but he doesn't get up. He rambles on and on. "Teresa Ann's never gonna come back. Is she? Is she, Jo? I miss my sister. We used to have such fun together. Don't she miss me even a little bit?"

"Matty, let's bring him up to my apartment. Then you'll go tell your mother Tommy needs some rest. Don't spoil it for everyone. They must be up to dessert by now."

We help him in and out of the elevator and into my parents' apartment. We lay him down on the couch. I wrap a blanket around him, turn up the space heater.

"Get me some aspirin, Sunshine," he pleads softly. "It even hurts to breathe."

I touch his forehead. "You're burning up. You belong in a hospital. I'm calling your mother."

"No Jo, no. Don't take me to no hospital at Christmas."

"Who's your doctor?"

"Listen to me. Call Ellen's boss Philly over at the drugstore. He'll give you something. He's better than the doctors."

"No. He's closed anyway. Shut up and let me think." I once picked up a card from a diner, twenty-four hours a day doctors on call. They make house calls. I tear through my pocketbook like a madwoman until I find the card, and then call. Tommy's breathing is shallow, noisy. He sleeps until the doorbell rings.

"I want someone who speaks English."

"You stupid, prejudiced, shanty Irish idiot. You'll take whoever comes through that door or like it or not, I'm driving you down to Wycoff Hospital and a big, fat Black nurse is going to stick you full of needles."

I run to the door, get a swarthy male Israeli in his mid-thirties. Dr. Ben Akim, he lets us know.

Tommy's temperature is 103 degrees.

"Take off your shirt. What is this scar?" he asks

Tommy in Hebrew-accented English devoid of any bed-
side manner whatsoever.

"He was attacked by an automatic staple gun a few
years back," I say.

"No, this is a bullet wound. Look. I have one too."
The doctor lifts up his white shirt to flaunt a similar scar
on his chest. "Trouble on West Bank," he tells Tommy.

"Armed robbery, South Jamaica," Tommy replies.
Macho one-upmanship on a sickbed. It makes me proud
to be a female.

The doctor listens intently to Tommy's chest. He
checks his ears, throat, all the while grunting and mum-
bling. Finally, we hear his esteemed opinion. "You're very
sick. How long you been sick like this?"

"He's had a cold for over a month," I tell him. "He
had a really bad cough but it went away about two weeks
ago. I thought he was getting better."

"You talk for him?"

"He's extremely ignorant today, more so than usual.
You talk to me."

The doctor ignores me totally, nothing too unusual for
these he-man sabra types. "What have you been taking
for this cough?"

"My friend works for the owner of a drugstore. He's
a regular guy, Doc, gave me some really strong cough
medicine, loaded up with codeine. That's the only thing
that works, right?"

"Yes. It worked nicely to cover up pneumonia. Left
lung worse than right. I recommend chest X ray but I
know you're not getting one so we won't waste time with
that. Also, you have infection in the right ear. Aside from
all, this you're fine. I'm calling two prescriptions in to a
twenty-four-hour pharmacy in my neighborhood, Briar-
wood, not too far. Have this girl who likes to talk pick it
up in half hour. One is an antibiotic. The other is a very
strong expectorant. Very important. You must cough. You
don't cough, go to hospital. And get out of this cold room.
Don't you get heat here? Israelis would not put up with
this. Believe it."

I pay Dr. Ben Akim while Tommy puts his shirt and sweater back on. His cigarettes fall out of his pocket and Tommy looks away like a guilty fourteen-year-old. The doctor grabs the pack and jams it into his own pocket. "Stay away for a while," he tells Tommy.

"A doctor that smokes? That's very inspiring," I say to the exiting Israeli.

"Soldier first, doctor second," he says after lighting up. "Have a nice holiday."

"You too, Doc," Tommy says, and quickly falls back to sleep.

I telephone his mother. Matty is sent to get the medicine. I hastily pack a suitcase. This moron can't care for himself. My parents don't even protest my going. One look at Tommy tells them their daughter's reputation is safe for a while.

The company now dispersed, Trudy and Billy drive us back to Tommy's place in the limo. Matty meets us there in the Celica. About as soon as Tommy hits his pillow he falls asleep, and then I want to kick myself because I should have held him out another minute for his medicine.

Trudy takes her son's illness in stride. "Always something during the holidays. It was my mother this past Ash Wednesday, right, Billy? God, she didn't even make it to Easter."

"Your mother sick on Ash Wednesday? What the hell are you talking about? Your mother didn't take sick on Ash Wednesday. She walked home from OTB with a foot of snow still on the ground, fell and broke her hip. Get your story straight."

Trudy pays no attention to her husband and comes over to hug me. "I'll come by tomorrow as soon as I finish at the luncheonette. Believe me, you'll need help. He's a lousy patient. My mother was the only one he'd listen to."

"Sorry your dinner was interrupted," I say. "I think the fever made him snap."

Trudy holds up her hands. "Who the hell knows with

him? I can't figure him out sometimes. I never know what's going on in that head of his."

"He said some disgusting things to Mr. Santini. It was embarrassing."

"Sorry I missed it," Billy answers.

Trudy gets her coat. "Come on, let's go home. We still got cleaning up to do. Joanna, I appreciate you caring for him, giving up your vacation. Wednesday, I'm gonna call in sick. That'll free you up to go to the play with your mother. She's looking forward to that."

"Oh, that would be great. She really wants to wear her new fur coat into the City. She tell you about it?"

"Uh-huh. I told Billy to sell his franchise with Sonny's Limos and go to work for Rainbow Cars. All Sonny gave Billy is a stinking bottle of vodka. Cheap bastard."

"Yeah, and your daughters-in-laws downed it between them," Billy says. "Nothing worse than rich drinkers. Notice they head straight for the good stuff."

After we bid our last good nights, I check on my patient. A staccato wheezing fills his bedroom. I touch his hot forehead. He stirs and his eyelids flicker for a moment.

"Nana, Good Humor's across the street. Thirty-five cents. Chocolate fudge cake. I'll watch the baby. Can't go out today." He turns his head face down on the pillow. "Nana, some water."

I sponge his forehead with cool water. He opens his eyes. "Jo," he whispers. He's half awake and half floating in the dreamy comfort of a lost summer day.

"Tommy. I have to get some medicine into you. Cool you off."

"Nana went downstairs to get some ice cream. Hot day, huh?"

"Sit up a little. Take the aspirin. Good. Now the capsule. Good, Tommy. Now swallow the medicine on the spoon."

"What's that shit? Bungalow Bar? That stuff's poison."

"Let me take off your sweater. Keep your undershirt on. Here, unzip your pants."

"Can't tonight, Sunshine. I'm sick."

"No, no. Here, put on your sweat pants. The ones you sleep in."

In a daze, he hands over his gun. "Put it away. Don't let the baby get it. I gotta put a lock on the drawer."

"Okay." I don't have a choice. I put the gun away. Maybe I'll stop shaking in an hour or two.

"Help me to the bathroom."

He's unsteady on his feet. He leans against me. I look away until he finishes and help him back to bed.

"Don't leave me alone in the dark."

"I'm right here. I won't leave you."

"Look out the window. Nana's bringing up the good stuff now."

Tommy drifts back to sleep. I call Eddie Profeta and tell him that his favorite partner will be out sick for a while. Lisa gets on the phone and asks if I need anything. "Not yet," I say.

I call my mother just to hear another lucid voice.

"Make sure he drinks tomorrow. Drinking is essential. Does he have orange juice in the house?"

"Some."

"You want me to make chicken soup?"

"He has tea. I'll buy some soup tomorrow. Don't bother cooking."

"Call us if you need help. Daddy can get us there any time. That's what we're here for."

"I love you."

I watch some TV, put on a long flannel nightgown and try to sleep. Tommy coughs sporadically in his sleep. The blanket gets tucked up around us and suddenly hurled off us. He moans and yells and whispers and sputters into his damp pillow.

I get out of bed, locate an extra blanket and curl up on the love seat. It's cramped but it's quiet. I awaken to shouts in the middle of the night. "George. Get down. George. Jesus. I got hit." I run in; 3:12 the faceless clock flashes in red. Tommy's soaked with sweat and shivering. I sponge him down, help him change his clothes, feed him two more aspirin and kiss the top of his head. We've come such a long way, the two of us. We certainly had our ups and downs these past nine months. And now he says he loves me. And maybe now I can admit that I love him. Then, the night looks over its vast shoulder and surrounds me with dark thoughts. What if he dies? Don't some people die from pneumonia?

"Don't die," I whisper to his sleeping face. "Not after all this."

He wakes early the next morning less feverish but still pale and shaky. He looks perplexed when I greet him and even more perplexed when he looks down at his bed-clothes. "You been here all night?"

"Yes, you don't remember?"

"I saw my grandmother. I mean she was here, Jo, in the room with me. She touched me. I felt her hand on my head. I swear to Christ."

"She must be looking out for you."

"Yeah, between the two of youse I'll be better in no time." Then he looks around. "Hey there pally, where's my piece?"

"Well, you couldn't very well sleep with it, so I stuck it in your drawer."

"You? You held a loaded gun? You're all right. You know that?" He coughs. "Did you see your other present in the hallway?"

"No. I had my mind on other things last night."

"Go, sweetie, and don't thank me because I did it just as much for me as I did for you."

I walk through the kitchen and out of his door into the hallway. A red ten-speed stands beside his black one. Arlene's old bike has evaporated. Tommy leans against his door. "I once got a red bike for Christmas," he says between coughs. "It was my best Christmas and I wanted you—Ah shit, I told you not to thank me. Don't you hear nothing? We'll go riding again when I'm better. I brought your sister's bike down to the Salvation Army store. Hope that's okay."

"Don't ever mention that to her or she'll make you go back and get a receipt for tax purposes."

Slowly, he steers himself into the bathroom for a hot shower. I busy myself hunting, gathering, and discarding cigarettes. I find three opened packs in three different coat pockets. For such a light smoker, he sure doesn't take any chances of going without. I fix us toast with jam and tea and watch Tommy sip and nibble.

I give him his medication and watch him swallow the expectorant as if it were liquid rat poison. I ask him if he wants anything while I'm out.

"A *Daily News* and a carton of Newports. I see you didn't waste much time cleaning me out."

"How about some cough drops?"

"Real heavy on the menthol, sweetie."

Tommy searches for his detergent, an intriguing subject for one so caught up in the world of market research. Tide. Ah ha! No surprise. His mother fits rather nicely into their demographic target, no? Detergent is marketed primarily to women. He must have picked up on her brand loyalty. See Dahlia, I'm learning.

Tommy notices me staring at his box of detergent and shakes his head. "Don't wet your pants. It was on sale," he says smugly.

"That's a lot of baloney. You don't shop sales. You're as brand loyal as they come. Look around. There's not one product in your house that wasn't around when you were ten years old. Frosted Flakes. Martinson coffee. Oreo cookies. Campbell's soup. Wonder bread. Right Guard. And good old Tide detergent. You grew up with Tide and you're going to stick with Tide for the rest of your life."

He raises his eyebrows ever so slightly and I know I'm right on the money. "Don't start with that marketing crap now. I don't want to hear what your two dyke bosses think about my soap suds. And like I told you, I bought it because it was on sale."

"Thomas McClellan, you lie like a rug."

He laughs and his laughter brings on a fit of coughing.

That's good. According to that arrogant Dr. Akim, coughing is the best medicine.

I drag the laundry bag a few blocks to the laundromat under the elevated train on Jamaica Avenue. The laundromat is warm and has a sweet, soothing smell. I check out everyone's detergent. Let me tell you, Dahlia, with the exception of one Wisk and two Fabs, we're in Tide country.

I sit and watch Tommy's wet clothes spin. Toward the end of the cycle my mother's voice spins around too. What do you have in common? He's common. Common. Common. Don't end up like me. Like me. He's a good boy. Good. He cares for you. Cares. Love him. Love him. What future? Sick. Sick. Rinse.

I stuff more quarters into the dryer, and between the heat and din from the machines, my mind again wanders. It wanders back to the Fourth of July, to that stranger that appeared at my door, the stranger I had been a little too quick to forget. Poppy with the mirrors on his eyes and the stubble on his face. The images float menacingly about the laundromat under the stare of the invisible black ghost. I see the empty eye sockets of Dr. Rock too.

He almost killed Tommy, nearly starved him to death. He almost finished us off for good. Would these figments materialize again? Was that him, crouching over in the corner, waiting to grab Tommy by the throat and squeeze until nothing decent was left?

Those words of warning my mother had for me also spring to life. Love is not enough. You'll learn the hard way. Would I end up as bitter and as disappointed as my mother?

And then I think back to yesterday when Tommy told me that he loved me. How his layers of past had made it so difficult for him to say the words, to take the risk. Could I really back out on him now? Could he bear to see another person cut and run out on him? No, I couldn't be responsible for that. I'd sooner live in fear of a hundred black ghosts—but I need more. I need something for me. Something that cannot be taken away.

When the clothes are dry, the laundry bag and I head out to buy cough drops, orange juice, milk, and a paltry *Daily News*. It's something the way the newspapers shrink the day after Christmas. I lug everything back to the apartment. If I could drive a car with a standard transmission, things would have been a little easier.

When I return I find Tommy spread out in front of the television watching a game show with Minnew curled in a ball on his lap. He has me hunt for his dark sunglasses. The glare from the TV is giving him a headache. I bring him his glasses, hand over the box of cough drops and dump the laundry onto his bed to fold.

"Hold on there. I gotta iron it."

He must be hallucinating again. "It's sheets, towels, sweats and underwear. There's nothing here that needs ironing." I begin to fold.

"No. Everything gets ironed. Sit down, will you? Takes me no time."

"You're completely crazy. Do you know that? You'd keep a psychiatrist busy for five years. You can hardly stand but you have to iron your towels. Where the hell is your ironing board?"

"Joanna. Such language in my house!"

I iron everything. If I only knew where he kept the can of starch, I could have myself a little revenge.

The rest of my first vacation day is spent feeding, medicating, and sponging. Tommy gives up on the TV and tries to read the paper. This bothers his eyes too. I read it to him. He leans against me and falls asleep. Minnew sleeps happily on his chest. I get the feeling Minnew feels more at home with Tommy than with Mr. O'Brien upstairs. I take mental note of the fifteen cans of assorted Nine Lives cat food in the cabinet and the litter box in the bathroom. Tomorrow, I'm going to buy a book for myself. Nursing is a dull business.

*   *   *

Trudy stops by at two. She hugs me and thanks me and tells me how wonderful I am. I blush. She hands me two containers of my mother's chicken soup and some foil-wrapped leftovers from Christmas.

She spots the ironing board in the kitchen. "Don't tell me he's got you ironing for him. Tommy!" she calls into the living room. "What's the matter with you? You forced Jo to iron everything?"

"You got it, held the thirty-eight right to her head. What do you think? I was all set to do it but Jo didn't think I was strong enough."

Trudy turns to me. "It's all my fault. Blame me. I must have smacked him on the head once too many. Jesus Christ, get that cat away from me."

Trudy kisses her son and sits down beside him. "Nice tree. You decorate this?"

"Nah, Jo did it. Not too bad for her first try."

"Your brother's stopping by after work."

"Oh yeah? Good. My sister too?"

Trudy pokes his ribs. "Your sister loves you more than you know. She's just more reserved than us since—"

"Since she married into a family of rich assholes and told us all to kiss off."

I bring Tommy's medication in and hand them over to Trudy. She derives immeasurable pleasure shoving the spoon deep into Tommy's mouth and watching his expression sour.

Tommy goes into the bedroom to lie down. Trudy washes the dishes and hugs me once again. "Me and Billy will come by tomorrow night and drive you home. Wednesday's your day to spend with your mother. She misses you. Tell me something, Jo, is she all right? Is she having some kind of depression? She looks like her mind is on a hundred things all at once. I never seen her like that. I'm worried about her."

I think for a moment. My mother always looks like that, doesn't she? "No, no more than usual. She's really happy with that new coat. You should see her running

around the apartment with it. It really cheered her up,
made everything better."

"Yeah, she showed it to me last night. It's beautiful.
Your father's a prize. I mean that. You're a very lucky
girl."

"Yes I am."

She goes into Tommy's room and kisses his forehead.
She grabs her pocketbook off the kitchen table and opens
the door. "Go lie down, too. You look exhausted."

I take her advice. I slide in beside Tommy, but this
time he doesn't notice. We sleep until his brother raps at
the door. I stay in bed and leave the two of them alone
in the kitchen. I hear Tommy whisper an urgent request
for Matty to go out for a pack of cigarettes. Actually, I
just make out the words "swear to Christ I won't inhale."
Matty would do anything for him, anything. He idolizes
his big brother. I sit up and listen for his reply.

"Fuck you Jack," he says lovingly.

Tuesday brings my patient some improvement. His
temperature upon waking is an even 101. He coughs in-
cessantly. He's weak, weaker than three cups of tea made
from one tea bag. And his eyes are still so sensitive to
light.

To break the monotony of our daily routine of nurse
and patient, I walk to Woodhaven Boulevard and pick up
a newspaper which I'll have to read to Tommy to prevent
him from getting a headache. I pass the drugstore and
buy more cough drops and realize with some guilt that
I'm in no rush to return to the apartment. I browse up
and down the aisles. I read the studio cards, check out
the makeup. Oh good, they have books too.

I rotate a heavy black carousel filled with Current
Bestsellers. Murder. Drugs. A celebrity autobiography.
Maybe I can do better. The self-improvement books sit on
an end cap. I've browsed through enough of those on my
lunch hour. Oh, there's the Romance Novels, Aunt
Adele's favorite section. And there's Literature. Literature? Aren't those the books I was supposed to but never

actually did get around to reading? Aren't those the books
my mother had told me would show the world I was
educated? They're the books with which I can so easily
fake familiarity because they're often alluded to in the
New York Times Book Review. Yes, I know them without
ever having to open one book, not a one. Joanna Barron
is a phony. Did you hear that, Uncle Marc? Did you hear
that, Arlene? Did you hear that all you trendy up-and-
comers at Reeves and Barnett? I've been faking it all along
and you never caught me.

Literature. I touch their stiff, shiny jackets. Literature
feels no different than Current Bestsellers and Romance
Novels. Dare I? Well, why not? I held a loaded gun, didn't
I? Well, maybe something skinny. It's between Henry
James's *Turn of the Screw* and other stories or James Joyce's
Portrait of the Artist as a Young Man. Go for Joyce, I tell
myself. I don't want to think about the word screw for
another few days. I buy a pocket dictionary too. Literature
intimidates me big-time.

I return to the apartment with my purchases in a
brown paper bag. I produce the cough drops and the
Daily News but keep the dictionary and James Joyce under
wraps on the kitchen table.

"Whatcha hiding in that bag, sweetie?"

See, sunglasses and all, this guy is going to make detective sooner than later. "I bought a book to read. It's by
James Joyce. He's Irish."

"Yeah? Good for him."

"Doesn't being Irish mean anything to you?" I call
into the living room.

"Yeah, Sunshine, it sure does. It means that once a
year I go into the city to catch the St. Paddy's Day parade
with a bunch of rich kids who take the ten-fifteen in from
Massapequa to throw up green beer and bagels all over
Fifth Avenue."

"That's not very funny." Well maybe it is, but I'm
busy being superior now.

"Quit testing me, because I'm gonna fail. You got all
the answers today, so why don't you tell me?"

I walk into the living room and shut the television. Popeye can wait. "I never said I had any answers. I don't even have the questions. Why don't we just read it? It'll give us something to do."

I get the book and then, I don't know, maybe this is a mistake. Truthfully, I'm not educationally prepared for the words of James Joyce. I've only gotten through high school, after all. Tommy rests his head against me and I open my mouth to start but nothing comes out.

"Well, what the hell are we waiting for?"

"This is not the *Daily News*. This is literature. This is James Joyce."

"Oh I see, we're supposed to pray first. Wait, I'll get down on my knees. Will you read the goddamn thing already? Five bucks says the man's as full of shit as I am."

He always makes me laugh when I don't want to. Deep breath. I begin. Oh, we are as new and innocent as the baby Stephen Dedalus. On and on. The rolls, the turns, the cadences of speech escape me, and I turn to Tommy. He looks less confused. Somewhere, somehow, he has heard these voices before. They ripple distantly deep inside him like a stone hurled into a faraway pond. I shut the book when his eyes close. He sleeps peacefully against my shoulder, his shallow breaths synchronized with the drips from the kitchen faucet.

He wakes with a start in half an hour. He kisses my neck in that spot he knows by now can radiate pleasure throughout and leave me helpless. "Jo, it's been a long time, huh?" he says softly.

"That's not completely my fault. I mean you were working two jobs, too tired, and too busy catching pneumonia." I wriggle free.

"I'm all rested now. Come, on, sweetie. Be the pal that you are. Please."

He pulls me inside his bedroom. He's so weak, so sick, but those male hormones pump him up with lies. And I am not exactly discouraging him either. I hate to say this but I really missed it. You know something, I'm not the virgin I used to be.

"Take it easy."

"Real easy. You'll see, I'll go slow, won't even work up a sweat. Ah, isn't that nice? Woah, that's nice. Mmmm Jo." His breath quickens, his heart ticks away, his lungs are about ready to burst.

"Slow down." But don't stop.

"No, no. I can't. Can't."

We speed away together and we crash together. He gulps noisily for air. It's the death rattle, I'm sure of it.

"Tommy, are you okay?"

No answer. He is either asleep or comatose. Between our exploration of James Joyce and our exploration of each other, the patient is getting his much needed rest.

My mother's soup simmers happily on the stove. Two ham sandwiches wait patiently for the smear of Hellman's mayonnaise. Before Tommy wakes for lunch I pack my suitcase. Trudy and Billy will be picking me up tonight, and I decided that Tommy is no longer in danger and would be able to care for himself after Wednesday. This live-in arrangement is getting way too cozy.

We eat in the living room and I tell him I'd be over for a visit on Thursday. He sees my suitcase near the door all zipped up and ready for departure. "You cutting out on me already? What's the rush?"

"You seem to be getting better. Your mother will be with you tomorrow. By Thursday you should be much improved. I'll come by to see you but I don't have to spend the night."

"You gonna read to me again?"

"Uh-huh. I'll even read to you some more today if you promise to behave."

"Not to worry, sweetie. I don't want to kill myself."

He seems saddened by my impending exit but he doesn't ask me to stay, not that I would. A temporary arrangement is out of the question. Years of steady brainwashing has me hoping for something more traditional.

"Do you feel we did something wrong here?" I ask.

"What? No. No way. Try and keep it in your head

that I love you. I know I only said it once and I've been a real prize along the way, but that still holds. Don't ever forget that."

"Then why do you look like your conscience is working time and a half?"

"A previous sin. Nothing to do with you."

"Louise, right?" I had never brought this up with him but now is as good a time as any. Get 'em when they're down, right?

"If that bothers you, it shouldn't. Me and Louise happened a long time ago. Whaddya want me to say, it meant nothing? I could say that easy but I ain't gonna lie to you. It meant something at the time. We had lots in common, her and me. Her dad split. My dad split. She liked getting laid. I liked getting laid. But you know something? There was more to it than that. We'd talk about things, get high together. We're still friends, and Hector's always been real cool about it. In fact it was me who introduced her to him, betcha didn't know that. So there's no cause to worry. None."

"So, it's someone else you've sinned with. You're feeling guilty about someone. Who is it?"

"I don't feel guilty about no one I took to bed. What's the big deal about two people making each other feel good? It's so damn ugly out there sometimes. I've seen things, too many things. Just forget it."

"What's making you so crazy, then?"

He gets off the love seat and moves down on the floor to his knees. His head rests in my lap. "Forgive me, Jo, for I have sinned. And I feel so shitty and it don't go away. I was tempted and I gave in and I'm so ashamed of myself. Crack, remember? I wanted it so bad, and I'm damned to hell for it. It's lonely in hell."

"You made a mistake, one mistake. Everyone makes mistakes." I bury my fingers in his smooth dark hair.

"Charlie Cruz is doing time now and I don't know why but that makes me feel lousy. The guys in Corona are going down because of me, and I'm no better than any of them. Worse because I'm a goddamn liar that hides behind a badge. If I had any balls I'd turn it in."

"That's a lot of garbage. You can't erase ten years of good. As far as that Poppy thing, you're never going to make that mistake again. I believe that."

He looks up and takes my hands into his. "Pray for me. I'm so dirty from the streets. So filthy dirty. And most of all, I don't want to make you dirty. Pray for me. And pray for that junkie kid and her junkie baby. Pray for all of us. God will hear that trusting, innocent voice and listen to you. Maybe we'll all find some peace."

I nod my head. I do not have the heart to tell him that God and I haven't been on speaking terms since I was eight and He took Grandpa Leo from me. "I love you, Tommy. I kept trying to convince myself that I didn't. I thought if we were just friends I didn't have to care so much. But I outsmarted myself. It only brought us closer."

He coughs. His chest rumbles and squeaks like the brakes on the number 7 train where it slows down at Vernon-Jackson. "God help us both, Jo."

"Hey, you never did tell me what happened with Teresa Ann and your father."

"Well, I called Mr. Wonderful up two days before Teresa Ann and Jordy were supposed to pop in."

"You actually spoke to him?"

"Had no choice. My sister was setting herself up to get good and hurt. She was looking for some knight in sparkling armor to come galloping out of the San Antonio dust to rescue the little princess from the crude, rude world of her childhood. So, I took a deep breath and I gave the man a call. I told him just who I was and I told him I didn't want no trouble. I told him his daughter and her husband were heading down to see him. I told him when he flung open the door, he would right away recognize the little angel all grown up. He would fuss over her for hours on end. He would apologize for the way he beat up on my mother and for not ever calling or writing or sending us a friggin' cent. He would tell her he always dreamed of a day like this, a day of repentance. And this

was better than he had ever expected. And then I says to
him in a real nice way, that if he started crying poverty
to my sister in any way, I would personally go down
there and break his legs."

"Keep drinking your tea. I can't believe how calm you
are about this."

"Calm? Hardly. I wasn't alone, you know. I had my
good friend Mr. Dewar's right there beside me. When I
heard my father's voice after twenty-five years, I had this
sudden urge to blow a bullet hole right through the receiver. But I kept my cool for Teresa Ann, 'cause I wasn't
gonna allow him to hurt her again."

"And what was his reaction to all that?"

"First he was speechless. Then when he saw I didn't
want no money off him, he got real chatty. The stupid
ass even asked me how the baby was. You believe that?
I told him the baby is two hundred pounds now, belches
Heineken, and owes his soul to the shys. That shut the
bastard up good."

"Did he ask about your mother?"

"Not one goddamn lousy word. He's sponging off
some woman anyways. He probably didn't want to piss
her off."

"So Teresa Ann is happy?"

"Oh yeah. He musta gave a performance of a lifetime."

"How did you know he'd go in for that?"

"Well, other than threatening to break his legs, I did
one more thing for insurance 'cause I couldn't chance it
going down wrong."

"What did you do?"

"While I was digging him up, I came across some
information that was very useful. I just happened to find
out that Daddy Wonderful is sick with leukemia. No, no,
no. I see that face. Don't you go feeling sorry for him, Jo.
I hate this man. He screwed me up in the head real good.
He did a number on all of us."

"So how did him being sick ensure that Teresa Ann
got treated well?"

"Deadbeat Daddy needed blood. He needed B positive blood. And I dangled that B positive blood right through the phone line. I says to him if he was on his best behavior with my sister, I'd spot him a couple of pints, AIDS-free."

"No, tell me you didn't. You promised him your blood?"

"They stuck me real good down at the lab. It musta been the technician's first day on the job. Jesus, how I hate them needles. And then they charged me an arm and a leg to ship it. But it's done, Jo. And it wasn't for my stinking shitheel of a father. It was for my little sister, the little five-year-old sister that sat by the window hugging her teddy bear, waiting and waiting for her daddy to come home."

"I don't know very many people who would have done that. In fact, I don't know anyone alive who would have done that. You are a very special person."

"That's just a nice way of saying I'm an idiot."

Fourteen

Trudy and Billy come by at seven. Trudy stays and Billy drives me home in the limousine. I sit up front with Billy because after all, I'm not a paying customer and he's not my chauffeur.

"Jo, tell me. Is it true that all Jews got money hidden away somewhere?"

"Of course. Don't say anything, but my family lives on Fortieth Street so no one suspects us of being millionaires. Keep it quiet, okay?"

Billy laughs gruffly. "Well your old man's on to something. He must have caught the boss plugging some bimbo at the cab company. That's how I figure his bonus. You gotta hand it to him for being at the right place at the right time."

If only that were true. Then he changes the subject.

"Don't mind if I get personal now. Tommy's got no father. I think of him as my own son. Why not? My own sons don't talk to me. So, what's with youse two?"

Trudy must have coached him beforehand. I think behind her happy-go-lucky exterior she does more worrying than she lets on when it comes to her eldest. What do I tell this man? "We have some good times together. That's enough for now."

He stops at a light and turns to me with an all-knowing

smile. "Uh-huh, so it's just great sex. That's what I told Trudy but she don't believe me. She thinks her son might possibly be in love. I tell her your son ain't interested in love. He thinks with his Johnson, always did and always will."

At least it's dark. I can turn as red as I want without Billy noticing.

He goes on. "Now, don't get me wrong, he's a good guy and all, always was right with me. Don't say nothing to nobody, but when I throw a little too much on the horses or when I'm a few dollars short on my support, he's the first one to slip a few bucks my way. I mean I pay him back as soon as I can, but he never asks. Never says nothing."

It's no wonder Tommy can't save for his sailboat. His family is sinking him fast on land. "He likes you too. He's grateful for what you did for his mother and Teresa Ann." We are almost home, almost. No, not another red light.

"Don't mention that stuck-up bitch Teresa Ann. After all I done for her, she treats me like dirt. That don't bother me so much, but her mother's another story. She treats Trudy like dirt too and that just ain't right. And those fancy in-laws of hers, did you see them down a bottle of Stoly at Christmas? Hogged the whole fucking thing. No class whatsoever."

"Where are you parking?" He passes Fortieth Street, Thirty-ninth Place, and turns right on Thirty-ninth Street, two blocks past our building.

"Matty got a key to Schwab's and he made me a copy, showed me how to bypass the alarm. Nothing to it. I park in there now. No one knows. Hell, I'm outta there before they open. Best deal going," he says with pride.

"Good old Schwab's Uniform. They've done so much for all of us."

"Yeah, and they don't even know it."

My mother greets me like I had just touched down at Edwards Air Force Base. "You're home! Oh, I missed you.

I missed your voice. How are you, darling? How's Tommy? Did he like the soup?"

All this in one breath. My father is in his usual position, wedged in the corner of the couch, in the corner of the room, snoring. "I'm fine. I missed you too. Tommy's coming along. Yes, he liked the soup. Are we all set for the show tomorrow?"

My mother drags my suitcase to my bedroom and starts unpacking. No, this is not a wise idea. That little white plastic case could not be mistaken for a hamburger press. I carry this case whenever I'm going to be a mile within Tommy McClellan. Friends or enemies, pneumonia or acid indigestion, it's regulation. "Mom, really. I'll unpack. Sit down. What are we going to see tomorrow?"

My mother sits down next to the suitcase. "We'll wait on the half-price line in Duffy Square. We'll go in early like last year. This time it's a drama."

Every year we switch off. Musical. Drama. Musical. Drama. Yes, this year we're due for Drama. We completely avoid farces and light comedies. Since we only get to a show once a year, we want our money's worth in either bouncy, musical extravaganzas or deep, thought-provoking soul twisters. So this is our year to do the soul twist.

I fill our bathroom hamper with the few stray items that didn't make it into the laundromat. The bathroom still basks under the glow of peach melba, and that can only mean my mother's not needing the extra perk-up. Good. I'm not up to dealing with another case of the blues. Even Sigmund Freud must have taken a night off now and then.

I tell her I had dinner, but she insists on feeding me something in order to fulfill her own maternal needs. Tea? An English muffin? Wonderful! Wonderful!

My father smells the muffins toasting and emerges from the couch with crushed velvet flowers imprinted on the left side of his face. "How's Florence Nightingale?" he asks sleepily.

"Good. How's Mr. Milstein's best driver?"

"They didn't make me for president yet," he says with a smile.

"Your father should have been a comedian. Everything's a joke with him. The ship could be going down, but your father would say, 'Don't worry, May, it's water under the bridge.' That's his sense of humor. I wish I could be like that. I wish I could laugh at troubles like that. It takes a real talent."

"So what have you been up to on your vacation week? You miss Schwab's?"

"You shouldn't know from it. It's you who I missed, but actually, I've been busy planning our retirement. I know more about southern Florida than a lot of people. I want to be prepared when the time comes."

My father smears butter and jelly on his muffin, clogging up the nooks and crannies. "Your mother is getting a little ahead of herself. You know we still have another four years to go before retirement."

"Listen to him, Joanna. Like I don't know I have four years left until retirement. He thinks I'm not counting the days when they'll unchain me from the embroidery table. What I think we should do is buy the condo at least two years in advance. We can always rent it out, Sol. That's what Naomi and Ruth are doing."

Bow your heads for Naomi and Ruth. My father lowers his head and addresses his muffin. "They're very smart women. And your Uncle Marc, he must have an IQ of two hundred. We'll look into it," he tells my mother. "What do I know?"

I know something. If I don't remove myself from this conversation, I will ignite. I stifle a deliberate yawn. It works like a charm.

"Go, Joanna. We're keeping you up. I know that taking care of a sick person is no picnic. And men are the worst patients. This play will be the highlight of my week. So get your rest and I'll see you in the morning."

"Good night," I call, but I don't go to sleep. I write down all the new words I've learned from Mr. Joyce and their meanings. I add it to Lisa Profeta's cop dictionary.

I retitle it "Jo's Dictionary," and *Webster's* has nothing to worry about.

I awake Wednesday morning wishing I were still asleep. A wind is roaring and biting through the windows. I dress in layers of cotton and wool, preparing myself for the two-hour Christmas week wait for half-price Broadway theater tickets.

After our ride in an unheated subway car, we stand in frigid Duffy Square along with the combined tourist populations of fifty states and twelve nations. When it's our turn to buy tickets, my mother's mouth, numb from the cold, is unable to form words. She has to repeat the name of the play three times before the clerk in the ticket booth comprehends.

"Are we meeting Aunt Ruthie and Aunt Naomi in Savannah Gardens?" It's our pre-theater tradition to meet in this particular restaurant down on Thirty-third Street. It is reasonable, clean, and beautifully noisy with the clatter of china plates and the chatter of lunching matrons.

"Yes, of course. Let's take the subway one stop. We'll have to walk two avenue blocks but it's better than walking the whole way."

I follow my mother down the subway steps. She walks very quickly for a middle-aged, stubby person.

Thirty-fourth Street hums with rushing, chilly, post-Christmas shoppers. Savannah Gardens. Savannah Gardens. Get me into Savannah Gardens. "Mom, forget the window display. I'm freezing."

We walk up a small flight of stairs to reach the restaurant. "The store next door is a very elegant store, Joanna. They have fine, elegant things here."

My mother's description tells me I cannot afford the merchandise unless it's either marked down fifty percent or if I charge it and pay it off over six months. Elegant and fine, I stay clear of those two.

Already on line are my two aunts. They must have been waiting for a while; they look warm. And they sure look elegant and fine in their geometric print skirts and solid blazers. Yes, they dress similarly, but not identically. My mother shares the family resemblance, but up until now she couldn't match them in regalia. It is different today. May wears mink. May is a full-fledged sister now, minus the bump on the nose.

We kiss and hug and nearly lose our place in line. "Any deuces?" the hostess calls out. Two women appear and are seated. We're up, the next party of four. We are led into the huge green, floral-plantation style dining room and sit down along with a few hundred other hungry New Yorkers seeking food and Carolina living.

"May, I can't get over that coat. It's gorgeous. Is it real?" Aunt Ruthie asks with her usual tact.

"Of course it's real," I answer. "Why wouldn't it be real?"

"A gift from Sol," my mother clarifies.

"Your menus," the waitress interrupts. "Coffee?"

"Please," my mother and I answer.

"Decaf," my aunts call, "and no half-and-half. Plain milk, low-fat if you have it." The waitress nods.

"So what show are you seeing today?" Aunt Naomi asks.

"That English drama with Jeremy Irons. Got very good reviews in the *New York Times*," my mother answers.

"Oh sure. We saw that when it opened a couple of years ago. You'll enjoy it."

"Waitress!" Aunt Ruthie shouts into the din. Amazingly, she's heard.

"Ma'am?"

"My saucer does not match my cup." That is true enough. The saucer is of white china. The cup is beige with a border of roses.

The waitress examines the cup. "Nothing's wrong with the cup. No cracks."

"No dear, you don't understand. It doesn't match. I don't dine that way at home and I surely will not dine that way when I'm out. Kindly bring me a matched set."

I stare at my mother in disbelief but she is in awe. In my mother's eyes, Aunt Ruthie is merely showing off her good taste. The waitress must be used to these complaints because she returns in a matter of seconds with a matched cup and saucer. "Ready to order?"

We order. Two vegetable platters and two tuna salads, on the special. They arrive on trays in five minutes.

"Full of mayonnaise," Aunt Naomi declares, "and that brownie. Just forget about it, loaded with egg yolks."

I hand the two carrot curls over to my aunts, eat my tuna, heap extra butter on the roll, and gobble my brownie in two bites. It is a weak, silent protest that only I hear.

"Jo, is that the necklace your mother told us about?" Aunt Ruthie asks me.

"Yes. Take a look. It's real. Fourteen karat."

"Beautiful. One day we'd like to meet your young man. Your mother has only good things to say about him."

I smile gratefully. "He's sick at the moment with pneumonia. You'll have to wait until he gets better."

"Yes, and don't forget your uncle Marc. He has to approve of any young man with designs on a member of our family."

"We're not all that serious, Aunt Naomi."

Shouldn't the father, rather than the uncle, have the right of first refusal? I guess Aunt Naomi doesn't feel my father is suitably qualified to approve or disapprove of anyone.

My mother changes the subject. The thought of me getting serious with Tommy is too much for her to deal with right now. "Girls," she calls her sisters, "I've worked it out. Sol and I are coming with you to Florida. We'll be able to swing it, no problem."

Not this again. Please.

"Oh! Oh!" her sisters squeal.

"We'll be together again. Just like when we were kids."

Aunt Naomi says, "Marc wants to give lectures when we get there. All these condos have clubhouses and they're always looking for lecturers."

"Sociology lecturers?"

Aunt Ruthie jumps in to explain her brother-in-law's plans. "Yes, Joanna darling. These people will pay to listen to your uncle. He's interesting, witty, intelligent. And his credentials are impressive. People look for that."

"Mom, we don't want to miss the show." I picture a room filled with defenseless elderly people, as defenseless against Uncle Marc as my own family. It is downright cruel.

The sisters squabble over the check, each one wanting to treat the others.

"My treat," I announce to end the debate.

"Save your hard-earned money," Aunt Naomi advises. "I'm sure they don't pay you nearly enough at your place. Private industry always takes advantage of the subordinates." She plucks the check from my hand with the condescending air of a benefactor at a soup kitchen.

My aunts disappear slowly into the Christmas crowd. We take the subway up a stop and depart hastily into the frigid streets.

The theater is dense, overstuffed with people, coats, and conversation. I see the actors walk on stage, hear the crackle and crescendo of applause, a gray hum, and my fourth grade teacher Mrs. Sherman ordering the class to line up for the fire drill.

"Joanna, wake up." Someone is patting my face.

"I'm sorry. What, are we in intermission now?"

"No. It's finished. I didn't have the heart to wake you. To tell you the truth, I was sure you'd wake up at intermission. People were practically climbing on top of you but you were out like a light."

"How was the show?"

"Excellent, you would have enjoyed it."

"I'm sorry. I slept away our one day together. Such a waste, spending thirty dollars to sleep in a theater."

"You're your father's daughter, that's why we only go to the movies. It's a much cheaper rest. And don't worry. There will be other days."

*   *   *

I drive out to Tommy's Thursday morning. Trudy had Billy pick her up before dawn in order to make the breakfast shift at the luncheonette. The patient looks more steady than he was on Tuesday. I notice he's out of his sunglasses and is back to his regular gray tints. His eyes must be better.

"Missed you yesterday," he says cheerfully. "My mother wouldn't iron a thing. Told me to bend over and go screw myself. Made me do it myself, that I wasn't so sick no more. Can you believe that?" he asks with a sassy grin. "Your mother talk that way to you?"

"No. But I don't ask her to iron my socks."

I kiss him on his cheek. He hugs me tightly. "I'm going back to the Job tomorrow."

"What? Are you crazy? Do you know how close you came to going into the hospital? You're still coughing. You need—"

"Whoa. Hold on there. I'm better. No fever. Anyway, Friday should be a good rest because I gotta appear in court. That'll kill a few hours easy. And Saturday I'll request clerical, health reasons and all. Take it real easy at the typewriter."

"You type?" See Mom, we do have things in common.

"Oh yeah, Sunshine. About three words a minute. The sergeant will be real pleased, but the hell with him. He's given me plenty of grief. And Saturday night I'm back with Eddie and Paul."

"New Year's Eve?"

"Yeah. Whaddya want? I got Christmas. But if it's quiet I could get you after midnight. Have a few drinks with Lisa and Eddie. Okay?"

"Okay. But I still think you're out of your mind to go back so soon. You'll have to bring your medication with you." I can see him now. He's in the car, taking swigs right from the bottle, no spoon, no—

"Don't worry so much. Hey, let's go out for a walk later, get the hell outta here for a while. I got this urge to see the sky and inhale the exhaust from the cars on

Jamaica Avenue. I'm about ready to bust. But first let's you and me finish up that goddamn book already. I was a good boy, waited for you and everything. Didn't even peek."

"You can read to me today."

"Sure, sweetie. Be my pleasure."

I rest my head on his chest. Minnew sits at my feet and washes her paws. Tommy reads and plays absent-mindedly with a stray curl. I hold the pocket dictionary for easy consultation. Strange words appear when I least expect them, words that I don't want to rush by and gloss over in context. It's time to stop lying to myself. Stop faking it. I've been doing that for too long now. Suffused. Interstices. Cerements. Go ahead, don't be lazy. Get off your couch and look them up.

When we finish the book, I feel far more ignorant than when I began. I know we're missing a great deal, certainly all of the Latin and most of the symbolism. Those book reviews always go on and on about symbolism, but the reviewers like to keep the stuff secret from the general public. "Well," I say to Tommy. "What do you think of Stephen Dedalus?"

"He's a class A shithead. Gives up on God, gives up on his family, his country. The man's got no sense of loyalty and he's selfish as all hell. He can't even get his girlfriend's name straight. What can I say?"

"Gee, I'm sorry you didn't like the book." James Joyce would probably sit better with a healthy person.

"Don't you be sorry for nothing. I liked reading with you, liked it a lot, even if half of it was in Latin, for God's sake. They don't even teach that in Catholic school no more. Even Teresa Ann don't know Latin. I gotta tell you, though, this Joyce was one mick who sure knew how to knock out a sentence. Too bad he wasted his time writing about an asshole."

Isn't it unfortunate that Tommy's synopsis will never make New and Noteworthy? "I liked reading with you too. I just wish we understood a little more."

Tommy just looks at me for a minute. "You'll get back

to school one day. And then you can explain it all to me."
He jumps up. "Jo, if I don't get the hell outta here, I'm
gonna eat my gun. Come on sweetie, lunchtime."

"You better dress nice and warm."

"Yeah, you're right. I might catch pneumonia." He
laughs his easy laugh.

Friday night I spend in Louise's apartment with Ellen,
Louise, and a sleeping Frankie. Ralph is obligated to
spend a night here and there with his wife, and Hector
is working a second job to help pay the Christmas bills.

"You look good, Jo," Ellen tells me while shoving a
fistful of popcorn into her mouth. "It's good to see you
happy again."

Louise taps a two-inch-long, silver-glazed fingernail
on her kitchen table. "Of course she's happy. She's finally
getting it more than once a year. Whaddya expect?"

Ellen replies, "Even I gotta admit there's more to life
than sex, Lou. There's bowling, softball, not to mention
miniature golf. Don't you and Hector do nothing else but
fool around all day long?"

"Very funny. We work, we argue, and we shop. That
about covers it. Oh, once in a while we take in a movie.
And don't forget there's Frankie. He takes up lots of
time."

"Are you happy?" I ask her.

"Oh yeah," she says without hesitation.

"And you, Ellen? Don't you ever want to settle down
like Louise and have a kid?"

"Are you crazy? What the hell could I give a kid?
Three rooms on Thirty-ninth Street, next door to an auto
body shop. That's worse than nothing."

Louise takes no offense, but she adds, "You can have
a happy home under a pile of garbage. It don't matter
where you live. It's who you're living with that counts.
It's sharing a future that counts."

"Don't you want Frankie to have some grass to run
around on and live in a house that's not falling down?"
Ellen persists.

"Sure I do. Me and Hector are trying to convince my mother to sell this dump, chip in and buy something better. But you know my mother, she's nuts for this house. It's been in her family, you know the rest. Anyway, I'm kinda used to it myself. My job's right next door. If we want grass we go to the park. What's the difference? It's no reason to waste your life with some married leftover."

Ellen shakes her head in disbelief. She rolls up the sleeves on her sweatshirt. "And you? You, with all these goddamn questions. What the hell do you want?"

"I want to go back to school," I hear myself saying, and it's me saying it, me, not my mother, me, "because I'm starting to find out I really don't know all that much, and it bothers me. All this time I knew something was missing and I sort of knew deep down it's college, but now I know what I want to study. It just hit me over the head right now. And it took me so long to figure it out too."

My two friends look quizzically at each other. Louise refills our soda glasses. "You wanna go back to school. Quit your job? How you gonna swing that?"

"No, I couldn't quit my job. I'll go to college at night. Start up in the spring." Things begin to sort themselves out in Louise's kitchen. And why not in Louise's kitchen? I feel so safe here, so comfortable. I'm with good friends, friends who would like me even if I was a second grade dropout. After all this time, I see a life beginning to form, my life.

"Study what? Business?"

"No, not business. English, that's what I'd like to study."

"I hate to shake you up, Jo, but you know English already."

"Cute. I want to be able to read books and really know what they mean."

Ellen dumps some vodka into her Coke. This must be some new drink. "You know how long it's gonna take you at night?"

"Years, but where am I going? I'm going to get old anyway. I might as well learn something too."

"Then you'll get so stuck up you won't hang around by us no more," Louise says. "I see what happens to people once they go off to better themselves. They walk around like they're better than everyone else. Look what happened to Arlene. Two weeks ago, I'm standing in front of your building with my mother and Trudy. Arlene waltzes by, waves her diamond around and walks inside. Like we weren't worth her time to actually stop and say hello."

"That's just Arlene. Believe me, she was like that way before college. She was like that in junior high. And you have my word, if I get to be as stuck up as my sister, sneak up behind me and hit me on the back of the head with a baseball bat."

Louise purposely blows cigarette smoke into my face. "Oh Jo, we're only teasing you. We don't want you to outgrow us, that's all."

Ellen pats her huge chest and smiles. "She'll never outgrow me, not in a hundred years."

"I'll never outgrow either of you. We go way back."

Tommy knocks softly on the door Saturday night. It's past midnight so it's technically New Year's day. My parents are sleeping over at Aunt Naomi's. It seems she and Uncle Marc are hosting a small de-alcoholized wine and low-fat cheese party.

He kisses me hungrily, his mouth tasting cold and smoky. "Happy New Year's, Sunshine. Is that black velvet and lace you're wearing?" He moves his hand across my back. "Ooh baby, I'm gonna call Eddie and Lisa, tell them I'm getting a relapse. Then we can spend the night doing what we do best."

I step back. "No, that wouldn't be right. Let's go. I bought them a bottle of champagne."

"Ah, you're no fun."

"I want to start the new year out right. I want us to be completely honest with each other. So I want to ask you something. Is it true you had the last rites administered to you when you were shot that time? Why didn't you ever tell me how serious it was? Your brother said you almost died."

"I almost died from the food at that hospital. And as far as last rites, my grandmother brought the priest in before my tonsillectomy. Just in case."

I tried.

We ride out to Glendale. Eddie and Lisa live in a walk-in apartment of a two-family house, four blocks off the M line. I had been there once before by myself. Tommy lights a cigarette and glances my way. "Leave me alone, Jo."

"I didn't say anything."

"Your big brown eyes are doing the talking, and I wish they'd lay off tonight because I'd like to take it easy. Okay?"

"Okay. But you're an idiot."

Lisa and Eddie's Christmas lights twinkle inside and out. Lisa greets us at the door with two hearty hugs. Eddie and Tommy pick up on a lively conversation they must have begun hours ago. I hear three terms I don't understand and Lisa enlightens me.

She pours four glasses of champagne. Eddie and Tommy douse their discussion momentarily in order to raise their glasses.

Eddie slides his arm around his wife's waist. "To Lisa," he says with his mustachioed grin, "and her Christmas present."

We all drink. "Guess she got you that CD player you haven't shut up about since Thanksgiving."

"Yeah, but this is even better than that. She's graduating magna cum laude in two weeks. Now she can stay home and start popping out babies."

"Magna cum laude. That's great," I say.

"Exactly what does that mean?" Tommy asks.

"It's like one of us coming out with a gold shield," Eddie explains.

"Way to go, Lisa."

Lisa shrugs. "Eddie doesn't understand. I can't drop

everything to take care of a baby. I still have a long way to go. Two more years of grad school, but at least I'll be on days. We're taking out a loan. You just can't get a degree in social work at night."

"Social work?" Tommy marvels. "You mean you actually want to help people? Are you crazy or what?"

"Yeah, as crazy as you and Eddie."

"No comparison," Tommy tells her with a smug smile. "We carry thirty-eights or nines just in case these people ain't keen on being helped. What are you gonna be carrying, baby?"

"Considering I'm specializing in the geriatric population, I could carry a supply of soft food. How's that, baby?"

I applaud. Eddie laughs at his wife's snappy answer. Thankfully it breaks the tension between them. Lisa turns to me and points to Tommy. "You know he thinks he's so, so cool, one cop who thinks he's God's gift to women."

"I am God's gift to women. Tell her, Jo."

I take another sip of my champagne. "Well, I don't know about all women. I just know about one woman. And this one woman has no cause to complain."

Tommy puts his arms around me. "See? What did I tell you?"

"Jo's just being polite," Lisa tells him. "One day she's going to find a sweet, sensitive, brainy guy and forget all about you, Mr. Cool."

"Nah, no one forgets Thomas Patrick McClellan."

"Lisa, bring out the nachos, hah? I've been driving around listening to his crap all night and now his face is in our living room. I'm finding it real difficult to cope," Eddie says, trying awfully hard to look serious. "Sometimes we're together twelve hours at a stretch in a confined space. Bryzinski is not much better neither, with his goddamn country music. Sick part is, I know this asshole on my right hates country music but he lets Bryzinski play it just to hassle me, you know, McClellan logic at work. But the worst, the absolute worst, is when they gang up on me. Like they won't let me listen to the Giant

games. I'm stuck with the Jets. Is anyone here feeling
sorry for me yet?" he asks, trying to stifle a laugh. "Jo,
give me a few pointers. I need something that's gonna
make him crack."

Tommy wrestles him to the floor. They roll around
and knock over a snack table. " 'Your cheatin' heart,' "
Tommy croons in Eddie's ear.

They get up flushed and laughing. "I'm real sorry,
Lisa," Tommy mock apologizes. "I can't help myself. Day
in day out right next to him. And your husband's got the
cutest, roundest ass I've ever seen."

"Thanks."

"Except for you, Sunshine," he qualifies.

We drink and eat nachos and chips until three A.M.
and then Tommy drives me home.

"That was fun," I tell him.

"Yeah, two great people. I hope they make it too. He
don't cut her a break on that school thing. Keeps shoving
it in her face. Big mistake."

At my door he says, "I gotta get some sleep."

"You didn't have your tea. Come in for two seconds."

"Just tea and don't even think about messing around.
My mother told me about Jewish girls like you. You don't
respect a guy in the morning. All you want is one thing,
and once you get it, you take off. Sometimes I feel so
used."

"Shut up, will you?"

He laughs. "All right, all right. Your parents out on
the town tonight?"

"Uh-huh, with my two aunts in Manhattan."

"The two savage sisters?"

"Yes. No. That's not a very nice thing to say."

"From what you tell me, they ain't very nice people."

"They are so nice."

"Yeah, but you don't stop hearing about it. And that,
sweetie, ain't very nice."

I move a kitchen chair right next to his and hold my
teacup in one hand and his hand in my other. "You still
don't look so hot."

"Thank you very much."

"No, you look tired. I know it's late and all but even when you picked me up you looked exhausted. You went back way too soon. Admit it."

"I couldn't have stayed in another day. Nah, has nothing to do with that. I didn't get to bed till six in the morning, and then I didn't sleep too good. My mother, bless her, calls me yesterday at ten. To her it's the middle of the day. To me, it's like the middle of the night. That phone rang and I hit the ceiling. And once I was up, that was that."

"What did she want?"

" 'Good news, Tommy,' she says. 'You're gonna be an uncle.'

" 'Christ,' I says to her. 'Matty knocked up another broad.'

" 'No, you fool,' she says. 'Teresa Ann's expecting, beginning of August.' "

"Jo, I can't even picture them two messing up their bed. Must have been all that chamber music. You know how that riles them up."

"Aren't you the least bit happy for them? You sure don't sound it."

"Sure I'm happy for them. Not that my sister will ever let me go near the kid, bad influence that I am. I'm happy because it means something to my mother. I just hope they bring the baby around to see her more than once a year."

I put my cup down and rub his shoulders, kiss the top of his head. "Why are you so down? You put on a nice show tonight but you didn't fool me."

"I can never fool you. That's the problem, you see right through me. And I'm a real prize, huh Jo? Thirty years old. I thought by now I'd be some hotshot detective. I thought I'd have that boat, some money in the bank, rooms above the fucking ground. I'm nowhere. I got nothing more than when I started ten years ago."

"You got me."

"No, Sunshine, you got me. You're one pretty girl with no damn luck."

He brings his cup to the sink, washes it out, and kisses me goodbye. "You have a good New Year's now."

Monday morning. Back to Reeves and Barnett. Back to the two women who shrank my bonus worse than a cheap cotton T-shirt in the hot water cycle. I hope Dahlia scalds that tongue of hers on the coffee I serve her. That would serve Ms. Reeves right also.

At nine-fifteen I am greeted once again by Dahlia. She is accompanied by a well-dressed woman no older than myself. "Joanna, we're so pleased you're back. The rest must have done you a world of good, recharge the battery, hmmm? I'd like you to meet Susan Orbach." She puts her arm around the redhead in the gray double-breasted wool suit. I shake Susan's hand.

Ms. Barnett continues. "Susan is a recent graduate of the Wharton School of Business. This is a very fine school, Joanna. Susan has earned her MBA with honors. She is a very capable young woman. I've read some of her marketing campaigns that she did in school. Fabulous. Fabulous work."

Susan smiles a little. I nod my head. Dahlia goes on. "Joanna dear, I have great plans for Susan, and for Reeves and Barnett as well. If all goes well we will be gradually expanding from research into a full service agency. I would like Susan to get a feel for our shop from the ground on up. Let her spend a week with you, learn from you. I want her to know every aspect of every department. I think we have found the perfect person for the field manager's slot that's opened now that Frank Pascoe is retiring. And that's only the beginning." Dahlia exits like a duchess, leaving me standing in my cubicle with Susan Orbach, Wharton MBA.

I get her a chair and a cup of coffee. That "ground on up" comment is still stinging, me being the ground, I guess. "Sit down," I tell her. "I surely don't know what a secretary can teach a graduate from Wharton."

Susan isn't quite sure what I can teach her either. "What are Ms. Barnett and Ms. Reeves really like?"

"They are phony two-faced bitches who screwed me over at Christmas." Oh my God almighty. I am blushing. This is what the expression sleeping with dogs and getting fleas is about.

Susan Orbach doesn't blink. "What kind of filing system do you have?"

At five o'clock, after Susan Orbach has completed her first day, I take a deep breath and walk into Dahlia Barnett's office.

"Isn't she marvelous?" Dahlia asks me.

"She seems very capable. To tell you the truth, I'm kind of surprised you looked outside to fill the manager's spot."

"Joanna, you know we love you, but you just weren't qualified for that position."

"Me? You think this is about me?"

"Well then, what is this about?"

"You have someone right here that could have done a terrific job. Why didn't you pick him? Why didn't you give him a chance?"

"Who are you talking about with such intensity? My my, Joanna, I don't think I've ever seen you so animated."

"Vivien Oliver. Wasn't he the obvious person to promote? He is a field supervisor, after all. He is experienced. He works harder than anyone else. He even has the same degree that Susan Orbach has."

"I know Ms. Reeves and I talk to you about many things in confidence, and as far as I know, you've always upheld that confidence. Still, that secretarial privilege does not entitle you to question our personnel decisions. But you seem hell-bent on an answer, so we'll make an exception this one time. Vivien Oliver is a lovely man. He is a charming man."

"He is one of the hardest working people you have."

"Let me finish, Joanna. Yes, I agree he is a very hard worker. But he has found his spot supervising the inter-

viewers in downtown Brooklyn. He is perfect for that particular site. I see no reason to uproot him."

"It's his color, isn't it?"

"Don't be ridiculous. We have plenty of minorities
working for us."

She will squirm. I will make her feel as uncomfortable
as she had made me feel. I will do that much for Vivien.
"Yes, you put the minorities in minority areas. Shirley
Wu is the field supervisor on Canal Street. Ben Fernandez
is the field supervisor at our site on East 122nd Street. I
get it now. You color coordinate the supervisor to the
survey applicants. Isn't that some subtle form of racism?"
There, I have her now. She will squirm.

"No Joanna," she says without so much as a flinch.
"In the business world, that's called good marketing strat-
egy. I suggest you go home now and cool off. Your loyalty
to Vivien Oliver is very admirable, but your quick temper
and your wild accusations aren't doing him or yourself
any good. Susan Orbach will work well with both the
client and the field supervisors. The agency is best served
that way. Can you really picture Vivien, sporting that
ridiculous-looking blazer emblem that he insists on wearing every day like some long lost Etonian, with some of
the top marketing directors of corporate America? Surely,
even you can see that is not in the interest of Reeves and
Barnett. And I adore Vivien. I love him. No one adores
Vivien more than I do. He just does not project the right
image. He's way too cosmopolitan for middle America."

I mumble an unapologetic good night, return to my
cubicle and leave a hushed message on Vivien's voice
mail, telling him to call me first thing in the morning.
Why shouldn't he know what's going on? Why shouldn't
he look for opportunities elsewhere? I can help him up-
date his résumé and type up his cover letters. I can finally
repay his kindness and his patience. So many people are
counting on him.

My year is not starting out smoothly, not personally,
not professionally. After inheriting that unwanted red-

headed MBA for a week, I am also obligated to spend a
Saturday shopping with Arlene. She is meeting me at
Macy's Thirty-fourth Street because she has already swept
through the New Jersey malls. I beg my mother to come
and act as a referee, but she refuses, telling me that my
sister wants to get to know me better. She wants to be
close. This must mean her Jersey friends were not at all
interested in shlepping into Manhattan and paying sales
tax.

Brand names aside, my sister is dressed no differently
from Ellen on a good day. A red jogging suit and a pair
of high-topped sneakers peek out from under a long,
down coat. Shopping is Arlene's form of fierce athletic
competition.

"Where do you want to start?" I ask after our hellos
are out of the way. Arlene has the floor plan of every
department store tucked neatly away in her head.

"Really, Joanna, it's January. We start at the white sale.
We're doing Ralph Lauren in the guest room." Arlene's
dark eyes dart around the store. Her shoulders stoop forward. She prowls up and down the aisles on the balls of
her feet, ready to bag any bargain that lurks stealthily
below the surface of the counter displays. "I hear you
spent a week playing nurse."

"Yeah, the patient recovered too. Must have missed
my calling."

"You wouldn't want to be a nurse. It's a lot of work
for so-so pay. Believe me, there are easier ways to meet
doctors." She slips her hand under a cellophane wrapper.
"Not percale. I don't care what's on the package."

"I don't want to meet doctors or lawyers or accountants, accountants in particular. Especially comptrollers."

"You're very amusing. What do you think of this
batik?" She holds up a maroon and yellow print.

"It would give us nightmares."

"Us? Us? Tell me you're sleeping with him. You're
sleeping with Tommy McClellan."

"Lower your voice, will you? Two people on the
Broadway side of the store didn't hear you."

"Jo, I'm not a prude. Gary and I, you know, slept together after we had some kind of commitment. Do you have a commitment?"

I don't answer. I busy myself with a pile of marked-down pillowcases.

"I didn't think so," she says with a smirk. "Those are irregs. I won't tolerate that." She leads me over to another display case. "I care about you," she says loudly. "Should I stand by and say nothing?"

Now, that would be a switch. "I know you do, but you're so prejudiced against him that you can't be fair. You haven't seen or spoken to him in over ten years."

"Laura Ashley!" she calls out to the sheets. "Pretty but soooo Victorian. Reminds me of Grandma Fanny's old cherrywood living room set. Remember those shredded lace doilies and the spindly table legs with those ugly eagle claws? And her carved mahogany dining room table that collected dust in every corner? Ugh! I hate that old stuff. I want to create a look that's contemporary and modular. Something clean."

"What about plain white?"

"White sheets? It's a guest room, not a hospital."

"You know we're looking at sheets for half an hour already? I can remember Daddy buying his car in less time."

Arlene laughs. "That doesn't surprise me. He keeps the household bills in an old Woolworth's shopping bag. That's his file, a crumpled-up bag that he hides from Mom. We're talking financial savvy here!" Arlene becomes likable and disagreeable in alternating flashes. "That's it! Ralph Lauren as planned. Why did I even look at the other brands? Stripes. Simple, clean stripes. Fifty percent off. I'm going to buy the whole ensemble. Comforter too."

I shake her hand. "Congratulations. You bagged a winner."

Fifteen

I begin to suspect Tommy is back doing undercover work again. He hands out plenty of his streetwise self but keeps the man I've come to know imprisoned below the pavement. I call Lisa Profeta. No, as far as she knows he's been with Eddie all month. Well, that theory dives out the window in a hurry.

Well, so much for the open lines of communication. So much for progress. Once a caveman, always a caveman. And once a fool, always a fool. I am the star of that book, *Smart Women, Foolish Choices,* or in my particular case, *Average Woman, Asinine Choice.*

Yes, once again, Mr. Cool, shut me out of your world the minute it gets a little messy. Just like you said you wouldn't. The hell with you. I got set up again, didn't I? Well, you had me fooled for a little while. For a couple of months you actually played by my rules, for the most part. So what happened? You got scared, didn't you? We were getting too close, weren't we? You let your guard down, told me you loved me. You took the risk. And now? You want out, don't you?

Oh, I'm so brave fighting the battles in my own head. But do I confront the beast? No, oh no. I'm too afraid to hear the answers, coward that I am.

One day I drop by the Corner Luncheonette to question his mother. "What's with Tommy?" I ask her. Trudy doesn't know a thing, not a thing. The bastard hasn't spoken to her in a week. I don't know. Nobody knows. I feel him slip away from me. And I wait helplessly for the black ghost to steal him away for good.

Then one night he calls me up all exited. "Jo, got off next Tuesday. We're going out big. Valentine's Day, remember? Wear your best dress. I'll come by at eight. Gotta run. See you, sweetie."

One minute down, next minute up. I don't even have a chance to scream at him. Valentine's Day. I better buy cards, gifts too. My father always buys me and Arlene little heart-shaped boxes of Russell Stover chocolates. Year after year, he never forgets his girls. My mother lands the deluxe box, a not so secret fantasy of mine.

And my mother's hanging on barely. Schwab's promised to cut her hours back to a straight eight-hour shift in another month or two. And still she walks around the apartment in a daze with that fancy mink coat on, day and night. I know it's ridiculous, but my mother has fallen in love with that coat. Touch it, Joanna. Touch it, she says. It's so soft. So soothing. It's her own small version of the good life. It's her one luxury item. I swear, the only time she takes it off is when she's cooking or showering.

As luck would have it, Valentine's Day is a very busy day at Reeves and Barnett. My fingers cramp by noon. My shoulders stiffen by two. Like a yesteryear yuppie, I skip lunch. I do not want to stay late tonight.

At 4:45 my phone rings, the direct line. My father. My father? He never calls me at work. He sounds like he's in another city. "Daddy, talk louder. I can hardly hear you."

"Come right home. I can't explain. Come home."

"Hello? Are you there?"

I feel the blood rush to my head. I tell Dahlia I'm needed at home. She doesn't look up from her desk. "Get in early tomorrow."

I'm off the subway at five-ten. It's a clear, cold dusky evening, gray on its way to black. Two police cars are parked in front of my building, their lights throwing yellow circling orbs onto the street. As cold as it is, I start to sweat. Neighbors are gathered around the courtyard. They stare at me in awkward silence.

Tommy materializes from I don't know where. "Jo," he says so quietly. He looks at me and I know something is very, very wrong.

"It's Aunt Adele, isn't it? She lost her mind again, right? That hasn't happened in such a long time. I really thought she was cured by now. Between the medication and the romance novels—"

"Let me get you inside. We'll talk inside."

I follow him into the lobby, past the groups of people who say nothing. We wait for the elevator and he just looks at me.

Mrs. Gurtz opens her door and Tommy puts his hand up for her to back away, but she doesn't. "I'm sorry about your mother, Jo."

"My mother? What did she say? Did she say my mother?"

The elevator comes and Tommy pulls me onto it.

"My mother. What's happened to her? Where is she? She's dead, isn't she? Answer me."

I follow him off the elevator. We stand in the hallway and he holds me tight. "I'm so sorry, sweetie."

"What are you talking about? Stop looking at me like that. What happened?"

"I don't know what to say to you that's gonna make this any easier. She jumped, Jo."

This cannot be. I did not hear this. "What are you talking about? There's been a misidentification. My mother wouldn't have done that. Jewish people don't kill themselves. It's against the law, or something."

"Go inside. Your father's waiting for you."

"No. Show me where she landed. I'm going downstairs. I don't believe you." I pull away from him, but he holds me even tighter.

"I'm so sorry, Sunshine."

And I start to shake and I can't stop. My teeth chatter

and I can't get them under control. The elevator rumbles open on my floor again but it's empty. Empty.

"You gotta go in and talk to your father. He's blaming himself. Your aunt and uncle are with him. Cops are there too. They're gonna be a while."

The door is unlocked. My father is slumped in the living room between Aunt Adele and Uncle Jack. Six policemen walk about, four in uniform, two plainclothes. Tommy motions for them to join him in the kitchen.

"Daddy. Daddy."

He starts to cry into his hands. "I killed her. Me and my big ideas sent her plunging five stories."

And shaky as I am I start to understand. "It was that coat, wasn't it? Oh my God. She found out about the loan. There never was a bonus. I knew it. Let me sit down a minute. The room is spinning."

"I wanted her to have something nice, like her sisters have. I wanted her to be proud of me too. That's all I wanted." I hug my father, and Aunt Adele starts to cry. I hug her too.

"How did she find out?"

"They must have called here today. I was a little behind in my payments. Someone made a mistake. It was supposed to be a confidential loan. I'm telling you that file was marked confidential. I saw it with my own eyes. Your mother found out about the loan and she starts crying and yelling, 'I'll never get to Florida now. I'll have to work at that stinking Schwab's for the rest of my life. And for the rest of my life I'll be stuck here with you in this lousy dump.' On and on she went. I tell her, 'May, I made a mistake. So shoot me, I wanted you to have something nice. We'll sell the coat, pay off the loan. I promise, we'll get to Florida somehow.'

" 'No,' she screamed. 'Don't take my coat. No one is taking this coat from me. No one.' And then she went into the bathroom, quiets down. I wanted to give her a little time to compose herself so I went downstairs to the candy store to buy a paper, have myself a cup of coffee. And then Mrs. Lee and I see a crowd gather. Mrs. Lee goes outside and starts screaming. And then I run out too. My God, I can't believe it. Her body crumpled on the sidewalk, bleeding. My whole life, I'll never forgive myself. I killed her. I killed her."

"No Daddy. She did it to herself. She was not a happy person."

Tommy comes out of the kitchen. His conference with the other cops must be over. He looks at my father for a second and then at me. "Jo, you're coming upstairs to my mother's. The cops are gonna be here for a few hours. Just routine. I want you out of here now. Let's go."

I follow Tommy because I can't think, and he's talking in his cop's voice, quiet but authoritative. It was the voice I should have listened to back on that summer night when that horrible greasy-haired man tried to shake down Matty. He is in charge. I am helpless. He takes my arm and leads me to his mother's apartment. "Look, I gotta go back downstairs to be with your father, just until the two detectives leave. Understand? Hang tight. I shouldn't be too long."

Trudy hugs me and offers me food and drink. "No," I say. "I want to be alone for a while. I have to think. All I need is a little time to think."

I go into Matty's bedroom. "My mother is dead. My mother is dead." The more I think it, the more ridiculous it sounds, like the punch line of a sick joke. By the way, Mom's dead.

I stare out into the night and down at the pavement below. So where did her body smack the pavement? Where did she end her miserable life? What am I going to do now? I have to think, only my mind is all clogged up with disjointed thoughts.

Tommy's voice, sometime later. Minutes? Hours? I don't know.

"She wanted to be alone," Trudy whispers.

"Give me a break," he hisses back at her.

I hear him come into Matty's room but I don't turn around. He puts his arms around my waist but I keep looking off into the darkness. He talks to me and I can hear him but the room is humming loudly and he's so far away. "Sweetie, you're scaring me, just standing in a dark room, just looking out into space, not saying nothing. It's no good. Don't let yourself get hard inside. Don't go looking for no eclipse." He keeps talking. His voice is soothing. "Do you hear me?" My lips can't move.

Then he leaves me for a long time, and then I hear him again. "Drink this," he says.

I shake my head. I hate scotch. He should know that by now.

"Come on. Be a good girl. It's gonna take the shakes away." He pours some down my throat. It burns a hole but the shakes disappear. He finishes what's left in my glass in one great gulp. "Jo, why didn't you tell me what was going on in your house? Are you aware that your father is near bankruptcy? He owes lots of money. Big money. He's deep in the hole. I could've helped. Why didn't you come to me? Why didn't you tell me?"

Tears. I'm crying now and he holds me even tighter. "Make it all go away."

He kisses me gently on the forehead and I push harder against him, against his body. He pulls back. "No, sweetie. Believe me, you'll only feel worse. Listen to me, I'm gonna give you some money. Your sister is downstairs now with her husband. Youse all got things to go over."

He pulls a bunch of bills from his pants pocket and gives them to me. I hold onto the money, keep it pressed in my hand. I don't put it away. It's good to hold onto something real. "Two thousand dollars. It should help some. Wish I could do better but it's all I got left."

"Why are you carrying all this cash around?"

"Long story. Another time. Come on, they're waiting for you. Cops are gone now."

"Except for you."

"Nah, you can't get rid of me that fast."

"Take your money back. I don't want your money."

"No, stick it in your pocket."

*   *   *

Arlene sits on the couch between Gary and my father.
Aunt Adele and Uncle Jack have left. Tommy pulls up a
bridge chair. I kiss my sister. My sister and I both have
wet faces and red eyes. We look alike now. Grief is the
great equalizer.

"I just can't believe this," Arlene sobs. "I don't know
why Daddy couldn't have come to us. We could have
paid for the coat. Why did he have to go into debt?"

"Don't go blaming him. He wanted to do something
on his own. Can't you see he feels bad enough?"

Arlene wipes her eyes on the sleeve of her suit. "I'm
not blaming him. I'm asking him."

"Girls. Girls," my father says. "Don't fight. Your
mother wouldn't—"

"It wasn't just the damn coat," I tell her. "There's
more to it than the coat. She was unhappy about lots of
things. She hated her life. She hated the apartment. She
hated her job. She hated my life too. She hid it, that's all."

"Look, we have to discuss the arrangements," my sister says. "The funeral has got to take place relatively soon.
Daddy, did you and Mom ever plan your estate?"

This question enrages me. It churns grief into anger,
heats up my face. "Estate planning? Jesus Christ, Arlene,
they were too busy paying for your goddamn nose job
and your tuition and your trips. You cleaned them out.
You and you alone. And you didn't even know it. And
now you come back here to ask if Mom has prepaid her
own funeral." I reach over to choke her with two hands
but Tommy holds me back. "Let go of me! Get her out
of here. She doesn't belong here. She's a stranger in this
house. She hasn't lived here in fifteen years."

"Jo, stop it," Tommy says. "Arlene, don't pay no attention, she don't know what she's saying."

"Don't you go apologizing for me. You, of all people,
Mr. Rant and Rave. You think you're the only one who's
allowed—"

"Shhh, come on now, huh?"

"We're not accomplishing anything here," Gary tells
us. "We have to plan this thing. People will have to be

called." Who will call Aunt Naomi and Aunt Ruthie? Who will tell them?

"Daddy," Arlene goes on, "did you have any life insurance on Mom?"

"No, we cashed everything in years ago. Wait. Wait a minute, she has something from her place, I think. Nothing big."

"I'll call Schwab's tomorrow. They'll have to know anyway that their star embroiderer checked out." I have stopped crying. Anger takes over. I mean, she didn't even leave a note, not a sentence. Nothing. And then I find I can't stay angry. I want to but I can't. I'm a puddle once again.

"What about the coat?" Arlene asks. "We can sell it now, pay for the funeral and keep paying off the loan."

"No, Arlene," Tommy tells us. "You can't. She was wearing it."

Oh, I'm going to be sick. No, I can't be sick. Fresh tears are forming. I picture the fall. Over and over she jumps. Over and over she lands. I get up to go the bathroom, locate a new box of tissues. "Arlene!"

We see on the floor, arranged neatly around the tub, an unopened can of paint, a folded dropcloth, a roller, an aluminum pan, a brush, and a stirring stick. They wait expectantly for a painter who will never show. I kneel down. Mojave Sand. Something bright, something fresh, give the place a lift. We hold each other. "I'm sorry for what I said before. I have a terrible temper."

"You were right, though. I am a stranger here. I haven't lived here since I was fourteen. Sometimes I feel more like Aunt Naomi's daughter."

"I didn't know what I was saying."

Out in the living room Tommy is talking quietly to my father and Gary. He stops in mid-sentence when he sees us. Details. He doesn't want me and Arlene to hear what he is saying. She jumped from my window. I know it. She went out onto the fire escape. That's why he had me leave before. My window. My father goes into the kitchen to dial Aunt Naomi. My aunt's scream carries into the living room.

"Arlene," Tommy addresses the organizer. "That Schwab policy's gonna do none of youse any good. Your mother's death was a suicide and no policy pays out on a suicide."

"Yes. Of course. You're right. Does anyone know how much this is going to cost?"

"You can't get away for less than seven grand, and I'm talking bare minimum," Tommy tells her.

"Split three ways, $2,500 a piece. Jo, do you and Daddy have it?"

Our mother has just killed herself and Arlene is able to do division in her head. "Forget Daddy. He'll be lucky if he doesn't have to declare bankruptcy."

She recalculates. "So we're talking $3,500, figure $4,500 apiece, ballpark."

"Arlene," Gary says. "For God's sake, stop it already. Do you hear what you're saying? We'll take care of the whole thing."

Arlene looks at me. "Yes. I'm not thinking. Of course we'll take care of everything."

"No," Tommy answers. "Jo will pay her share. It's her mother too."

Again there is a humming noise in the room. I hear everything, but stray sounds are bouncing off the walls. And the telephone keeps ringing. "Hello," my father keeps saying over and over again. Relatives, it's always the relatives.

"I have some money in the bank," I tell my sister. "Let's do this tomorrow. We'll make all the calls and visit the chapel. I can't deal with this now. Please go home." They hesitate but they leave after a while. My father still talks weakly into the receiver. I'm left with Tommy.

"Why the hell did you stop them from paying for this? Don't you understand they have a lot of money? They're both professionals. They have credentials, big-time god-damn fat credentials. Can't you see they can well afford it and I can't?"

"Your brother-in-law did a nice thing there. He's all right. But not for nothing, you let Arlene pay for this she's the kind to never let you forget it. And I don't want you being made to feel grateful the rest of your life. Understand?"

"All I have is around three thousand in the bank. I'm going to have to finance the rest." Where did all my pay-checks go? On clothes and gifts. There was rent money I'd force on my father when my mother wasn't looking. There was food money I'd force on my mother when my father wasn't looking. Where did it all go?

"No. You got the two grand I gave you. No more loans. No more friggin' cards. No more mirrors. That's why we're in this mess. Can't you see? This is what did your mother in."

"No. It wasn't just the loan. People don't jump out the window over a loan. It was everything, her job, this place. She was walking around exhausted from the over-time. She couldn't sleep nights. My father disappointed her. And I disappointed her. She always held her sisters up as the yardstick, and me and Daddy always fell short." My chin starts quivering and Tommy holds me closer and starts rocking me back and forth in his arms. "My mother wasn't strong, not like your mother. Not like you. And I'm not strong either. I want to be like you. Make me tough like you."

"Shhh. Easy, Jo. You're the one who's strong. You, sweetie. Shhh."

I'm not strong. I'm soft and mushy like a rotten old peach. "She jumped out of my window, didn't she? That's why you had me leave, didn't you?"

"No, not your window." He's lying. He's a great liar but I know he's lying. "Let me make you something to eat. Your aunt Adele made your father something before. You should have something too."

"I can't eat now."

Tommy gets up and boils water for tea, opens the refrigerator, closes it and hunts through the cabinets for a frying pan. Then he sets me down in the kitchen in

front of two slices of buttered toast and two well-done
scrambled eggs.

"You forgot the hash browns, Jimmy."

He smiles at me. "Whaddya want from me? I grew
up behind a counter."

My father hangs up the phone. "I'm gonna take this
off the hook. I gotta lay down."

"Daddy. We'll get through this somehow. You and
me. We'll be okay."

"You want something to put you out?" Tommy asks.
"I could go down to Mrs. Gurtz. She can spare a few
pills. She owes me."

"No, no. I want to thank you for—"

"No need."

"Good night," my father says, and leaves me and
Tommy alone.

The toast is like wet plywood. The eggs dry up in my
mouth. I put my dishes in the sink and look up at the
clock. Eleven twenty-five. It should be later. "Stay with
me tonight. Talk to me. Where were we supposed to go
tonight?"

"I had big plans, but that don't matter now. Let's sit
back down on the sofa here. Put your head on my lap
and try to sleep."

"Were you going to take me dancing? You're such a
good dancer. Let's dance now, something slow."

"No, Sunshine, another time. Why don't you close
your eyes?"

"If I sleep I'm only going to have nightmares. She'll
fall again and again. I don't want to sleep. Talk to me.
What were you doing here so early?"

"Not important. I had stuff to do. I'll explain it to you
some other time."

"Tell me now." I want to hear his voice. When he
speaks softly the words roll up and down, a spoken
lullaby.

"Wait a sec, let me lean back and shut the light. That's
better. I don't know where to start and I really don't want
to start. All right. Tuesday. I was over here last Tuesday

afternoon. My mother called me up and said she wanted
to talk to me. Alone. She said it was important, so I go.
She sits me down in the kitchen, makes me a cup of tea
and says to me, 'You know, I never butt into your personal life 'cause I screwed up my own life good enough,
but I'm gonna make an exception here. Tell me, what the
hell is going on with you and Jo? She comes into the
Corner the other day asking me what's the matter with
you. She said all of a sudden after New Year's, you don't
seem happy with her no more, that it ain't been the same
between youse. And I don't know what to say to her. I
don't get it. Answer me this, do you love her? Do you
love Jo?'

"And I tell her this; 'She gives and gives and never
asks for nothing in return. She laughs and cries and she
holds nothing back from me. She's more alive than the
two of us put together. What do you think? Of course I
love her. I love her so much it hurts.'

"Then my mother gets angry. 'You love her. Anyone
can see she loves you. You ain't kids no more. What the
hell are you waiting for? Is it the religion thing? Your
aunt Bertie is Jewish, betcha didn't know that. She and
your uncle John worked it out somehow. You'll work it
out too.'

" 'No,' I tell her. 'The religion thing don't bother me
and I don't think it bothers her.' Does it, sweetie?"

"No."

"And then my mother, she gets crazier and crazier. I
mean she freaks out in a big way, starts screaming. 'So
what the hell is it, then? You don't want to settle down?
You liked it better when you had a different girl each
week? That's what you want to go back to, a fast fuck
with a stranger?'

" 'Shut up already, huh?' I says to her. 'Calm yourself
down and shut up. Stop and think, will you? I can't marry
Jo. I got nothing to give her. She deserves some smart
guy with money, someone who can buy her a big house
somewhere, send her back to school, get her out of this
roach motel. I can't do that for her and I ain't about to

drag her down with me. For a month already I'm trying to break it off but it's way, way outta control. And every time I see her I can't get the words out. I just can't. She's all I got going for me. I don't want her to go and I got nothing to make her stay.'

"Then my mother starts shaking me and hitting me and screaming. 'So, you're gonna leave her? You're gonna walk out on that girl and break her heart? You think she'll ever let herself love again? Trust another man again? You bastard. Get outta my house. Get out. You're no better than that stinking lousy father of yours. The two of you, you steal love and then you throw it away. Go to hell, I hate you.' "

I sit up and turn the light back on. We squint at each other.

"Let me finish this, Jo. You got me started and I'm gonna finish."

"Are you leaving me? Please don't go, Tommy." I sob into his shirt. Trouble. Nothing but trouble. Trouble on all sides.

"Shhh. No. You're gonna be stuck with me for a long time. You're the one who wanted me to talk, so let me get this out already. My mother is freaking out. She throws her cup of tea at me, and good thing for me she got lousy aim. She's a wildwoman.

" 'Ma, what the hell's a matter with you?' I say. 'I can't take this no more. You're looking at me but you don't see me. You never see me. You see him, not me. I can't help it that I look like him. I just can't help it. And this ain't the first time I see that look, but it's sure as shit the last. Let me tell you something, I'm a better person than my father ever was. I'm no saint, we all know that, but I came through for every person in this family. Every one of 'em. I'm the one you all lean on, and you know it. And the next time you give me that look, I'm outta here. You'll never see me again, I swear to God.'

"And then she starts crying. And Jo, I never seen her cry. Never. I don't know what to do now. So I say something to her to make her laugh and it shuts her up. She quiets down. And two minutes later she starts up again. 'What are you gonna do about Jo?'

" 'I'm gonna marry her, okay?' I tell her. 'You convinced me. You nearly burned my face off but you convinced me. You know, I only wanted what was best for her. The girl deserves prime rib and she's gonna end up with corned beef hash. It just ain't right.'

"And then, sweetie, she starts hugging and kissing me. She goes into her room and brings me in Nana's engagement ring. 'Take it,' she says, 'clean it up, change the setting. Do whatever the hell you want with it. Give it to Jo on Valentine's Day. Take her out somewheres nice.'

" 'No, thank you, but no,' I tell her. 'I want Jo to have something new. She's getting a guy that's been around the block a few thousand times. The least I can do is get her a new ring.'

"So, that's why I was around so early. I was meeting my mother here after she finished up her shift. We were supposed to run down to Canal Street this afternoon to get you that ring. That's why I had all that money on me. Oh sweetie, I had it all planned. I wanted this to be the nicest night of your life. Made us a reservation at the Water's Edge, down on the Long Island City docks. Manhattan was ready to bow down to my Jo, lay her whole city right at your feet. And then I was gonna beg you to be my wife."

"Like you ever had to beg."

"You lean on me now. There you go. I'm gonna take real good care of you. And your father too. After we get married, we're all gonna live together. I'll bring Minnew. Right here. I'll take over the rent. We'll help your father pay off his loans. You'll see."

"You would do that?"

"We can't leave him alone now. That wouldn't be right. Besides, we're gonna have a blast here together. Me, you, and Sol. Ma, Billy, and Matty, upstairs. Your dingbat aunt running naked through the halls, downstairs. Man, this is gonna be one long party. See, you're laughing. You're laughing and crying. That's okay too."

"Tommy?"

"What, sweetie?"

"I wish my mother were here."

"Me too."

"Where is she?"

"Well, the way I see it, by now she's probably up there in heaven with my grandmother. Nana's busy showing her how to box her bets so when the angels go racing across the rainbow, she's all prepared. Nana's looking out for her real good so don't you worry."

My mother's funeral is on Thursday at noon. Everyone's been called. Arlene and I spend Wednesday putting it all together.

Arlene plans the buffet, or shiva party, as she calls it with her usual eye for detail, from the extra lean corned beef down to the miniature Danish. Lilac and gold flowers. Lilacs were Mom's favorite. Color-coordinated table linen. If it were possible, she'd have the casket liner coordinate too. I don't mind this strange behavior, though, because I realized something during this mad dash for the dead. I love my sister. I spent far too many years resenting her every move. She's not selfish, I'm discovering, just naturally insulated.

Wednesday was an okay day. We were busy, in control, making the arrangements. My mother's death was hidden, tucked away in the background. I called my boss. She tried nobly to cover her grief about me being out another week. "Oh I'm so sorry, I didn't know your mother was ill."

"Heart condition, suffered for years."

But that was yesterday. Today, death takes center stage. For a weekday, the chapel is packed. Ellen, Louise, Rose Petruzzi, Lisa Profeta, Vivien Oliver, people from the building, relatives, the two Indian embroiderers Narinda and Bupinda, Trudy, Billy, friends of Arlene's, Arlene's in-laws and Sandy, my mother's union rep. He refers to my mother as Sister May. Oh, look who's there, Marilyn Friedman the Bookkeeper, a bony, sour-faced relic left over from the reign of Mr. Schwab the elder. I see the boss is a no show. Embroiderers don't even rate the fat half-wit son-in-law. True, he did have his secretary send a lovely flower arrangement. Matty. I didn't expect him. He tells me my mother took good care of him, punched his card every Monday morning without fail.

I feel stares. People are looking at me. My entire building is looking at me, the observer. That's a hoot. Some observer I turned out to be, couldn't even see where my own mother was heading. Why is Roz Lefkowitz here? My mother couldn't stand her. Madeline Curry? When did she ever say boo to my mother? This must be an outing for them, class A entertainment. Go ahead, stare at me. What an unhappy home the Barrons must have had. Poor May. She must have suffered plenty. Can you imagine what went on in that apartment? They must have all given her heartache. The father went from job to job. The daughter's seeing that hooligan who used to live upstairs. Yeah, don't you remember the time he threw an M-80 into the washing machine? You don't remember? It shook the whole building. Poor May, she really suffered.

No, I want to say. We were happy. We had a nice home. We were as happy as any other family. She just didn't think. She was very emotional. She made a mistake. We would have sent her to Florida. We loved her. Stop looking at me. Don't you dare look at my father.

I sit up front between my father and Tommy. Arlene and Gary are on the aisle. My two aunts weep loudly in the row behind us. They lost more than a sister, they lost their audience. Uncle Jack sits alone. He won't let Aunt Adele come to funerals. It's really just as well. She shouldn't risk another episode.

I look up and down the rows and I smile a little before the service begins. Totally improper, I know, but if you could see some of these faces under yarmulkes.

My father supplied the eulogy material and the rabbi. He lists my mother's charitable donations. And it's quite a list. She gave something to everybody, a regular Rockefeller on a Sunnyside shoestring. I think back to all the gifts that came through the mail, purple and red neckties from the American Indians. Key chains. Greeting cards. Address labels. Luggage tags. The story of Father Flannigan. Notes from Appalachia. A bank from United Jewish Appeal. Diseases. She was big on finding cures for diseases.

It is a beautiful speech, not too heavy on the wife and mother stuff. And the rabbi manages to skirt around the life-taking issue with, shall I say, amazing grace?

The graveside service is the worst. Tommy has to hold me up. My father calls to my mother, "May. I'm sorry. Come back to me. May." Will this ever end? "Good-bye, Mommy," I whisper into the cold air. The casket goes so deep into the earth, so very deep. Each shovel full of dirt announces our loss, broadcasts our pain.

Trudy and Aunt Adele were good enough to set up the buffet before the mourners arrive. The house is tumultuous, almost festive. Hey, it's party time. The only one missing is the guest of honor. It's wrong, but I'm hungry, starving. The roast beef looks good. Leave it to Arlene, she knows her stuff. People dig in when they see me put together a sandwich. Jimmy from the Corner Luncheonette walks in, still in his long white apron.

"Who's minding the store?" I ask him.

"It's four o' clock. Nothing doing now. Manny and Felix can take care for a while. I wanted to pay my respects to you and your father. Your mother was a nice lady and I'm going to miss her. It's a tragedy. I don't know what else to say."

"She liked you too. She loved the way you sprinkled cinnamon on her matzoh brie during Passover. You told her it was Greek style. That always made her laugh."

Oh no, tears are dripping down Jimmy's cheeks. Tommy comes over and hands him a scotch. "You making my Greek brother cry, Jo? Shame on you. Were you telling him about the scrambled eggs I cooked up for you the other night?"

Louise and Ellen circle around us. They must think

I'm going to shatter or something, but I won't. I have to
hold on for Daddy. And for Tommy. They both need a
lot of love. I put my two best girlfriends in charge of the
drinks. They've always excelled at pouring.

Aunt Ruthie and Aunt Naomi come over, shaky and
teary-eyed. "Jo, darling. You'll be our girl now."

"You'll have two mothers."

I nod. It's easier.

My uncle Marc approaches. "I hate to bother you at
a time like this, but could you spare an apple?"

How could I have forgotten the three vegetarians?
"Sure, no problem." I fill a bowl with fruit for him and
my two aunts. Actually, it gives me something to do.
Thank you, Uncle Marc. What would I do without you?

I'm obligated to introduce Tommy to the relatives. My
friend, I will call him. This is certainly no occasion to
announce our engagement, not that we have a penny left
to get married. Weddings and funerals, very costly.

"This is my aunt Naomi and uncle Marc. And my
aunt Ruthie."

He shakes my uncle's hand. The aunts excuse themselves, too upset for small talk.

"I hear you're one of New York's finest," Uncle Marc
says with unexpected glee. "Tell me, don't you find that
justice is synonymous with nihility for the underclass?"

Tommy grins and pauses a second to light a cigarette.
"You sure are loose with them ten-dollar words. And you're
probably betting that I'm gonna make up some half-assed
answer too. No way," he offers with a challenge. "You ask
me in simple English, and cut the bullshit, huh?"

Now Uncle Marc is flustered, and I'm not a bit dis-
pleased. I'm just sorry I never had the nerve to say something similar, maybe a little less foul but similar. No,
that's not entirely true. It would have made my mother
angry. Oh, I don't know what to think anymore so I excuse myself. Tommy can fend for himself. Nihility? Nahi-
lity? Today it will wait.

Sixteen

In the months that follow my mother's death, I make some changes in the apartment. I tear down the massive, avocado drapes and buy miniblinds. You're absolutely right, Mom, we'll freeze in the winter. Just keep your spirit-to-human I told you so's to a minimum. My next change is in our bathroom. I donate two gallons of Mojave Sand semigloss to Mr. Gurtz. Matty and Tommy wallpaper in between swears and heated accusations of blindness and illegitimacy. I never want to smell paint in the bathroom again.

My dad asks me in a roundabout way if maybe Arlene and I could go through Mom's stuff and donate what we don't want to charity. You know, if it's not too much trouble. I ask Arlene to help me, but she declines, she just cannot. Understandable, but it has to be done sooner or later. I summon my two best girlfriends and together we go through the closets and drawers and fold everything into empty Schwab cartons, courtesy of Matty.

Louise and Ellen work diligently, drawer after drawer, hanger after hanger, not pausing to comment about any one particular garment. When it is all empty, I cry. They hold me until I stop and then they treat me to a White Castle dinner.

In May, with Lisa Profeta's encouragement, I apply

and I am accepted into a night program at Queens College. I owe a lot to her and to Vivien Oliver. As I said to Vivien, even though I am not following in his exact footsteps, I am still on the trail.

Within this century, I'm hoping for a B.A. in English. Maybe if I had done this sooner, my mother would still be around. God, that sounds ridiculous and self-important but at times I half believe it. You know, here and there I still find myself doing things just to please her, expecting at any moment I'll hear her key in the lock and she'll run over to me in a gush of all-forgiving gratitude.

So, Mom, one day I'll have those credentials whose importance you tried your best to impress upon me. Not wishing to be disrespectful in any way, I could care less about the credentials. I really want the education. The credentials just come with it. At least I have a plan now, not a career plan, but a life plan. I want to learn things just for the sake of knowing them. And I know I will never throw what I learn in anyone's face. That hurts too much.

I fill the fire escape with window boxes full of flowers. Pink, red, purple, and white tiny-faced flowers. I had wanted to grow lilacs as a living memorial, but the lady at the nursery advised against it when she heard the location of my garden. Lilacs are far too fragile for sooty fire escapes. These little flowers look so delicate, but boy are they thriving up here. They have a peculiar name; impatiens, I believe they're called. Those people from Ardsley would know for sure. At least I don't dread the window anymore. It's just fine as long as I don't look down.

And in July, I marry Tommy. Oh brother, we had some lively discussion beforehand over the ceremony. He wanted a priest and a rabbi, and I wanted a plain old neutral judge. I told Tommy that having two clergymen would be too circusy. Then Tommy made his usual cracks about judges not being able to make the life sentence stick.

"Whats the matter? God don't rate an invitation?"

To which I replied, "Which God, yours or mine?"

Well, this comment really sent his temper soaring. "I

don't like what I'm hearing out of you. And from what
you're saying, you don't want to believe in God. And if
you don't believe in God, you can't believe in miracles.
Don't you ever stop and think how we found each other
after ten years?"

"I'm not senile. We met up again at your grandmother's wake."

"You're real smart. Now, any moron could see that
Nana arranged the meeting. She brought you to me, Jo.
You were her parting gift to me. She sent you over to
love me because she knew with her gone, I'd be needing
someone. There's your miracle, and let me tell you, God
supervised the whole operation."

\ "Mmmm, sort of like the Bureau Chief?"

"I'll give you a two minute head start. You better start
running, Sunshine."

That's how we ended up in the U.N. Chapel with a
priest and rabbi. But don't for a minute think I let Tommy
get his way all the time. After all, I did make him come
into Manhattan for the ceremony. And he didn't moan all
that much.

Afterward we had a small reception at a catering hall
in Rego Park. Trudy and Billy helped pay for it, otherwise
we could just about afford the Corner Luncheonette. Everyone had a good time at that reception. Even my father
managed to tuck his depression away for the day. He and
Aunt Adele danced such a wild lindy, I thought we'd
have to call the paramedics. And Tommy, with all that
Dewar's sloshing around inside him, was still one guy
with the moves.

We forced some of our gift money over on Trudy and
Billy. What remained, we took a chunk of it and booked
a five-day Disney World honeymoon. It sure was great to
be six years old again. Even the airplane ride down to
Orlando was extra special because it was the first time for
both of us.

Right after the wedding, Tommy closed up his apartment and brought over some of his stuff. He and Matty
casually replaced the salmon-cushioned telephone table in

its old spot in the lobby. I could see Mrs. Gurtz watching them from her door, but she didn't say one word. Not one.

"Hey baby, your favorite table's back," Tommy shouted to her. "And I'm back too, hot stuff. Want to rub up against Minnew?"

Door slam.

I sold my mismatched bedroom furniture and put Nana's mahogany set into my—excuse me, our—room. Arlene suggested without the slightest bit of hesitation that the white Antionette spread be replaced with Laura Ashley, if we absolutely had to go Victorian, but I keep it as lovely as it has always been, same for Nana's engagement ring, although I had to size it down some.

My father, I'm happy to say, discovered a friend in his new son-in-law. Tommy's always dragging him out to the Mets game, or the candy store, the dry cleaners, anything, anywhere, just to get him off the damned couch. And he goes with Tommy, follows him like a lost dog that keeps sniffing around for the previous owner.

And me, I settled into a busy routine of work, school, housework, and caring for my two men. Then early in October I begin to notice a change in Tommy, a darkening of his mood.

"You're back in Narcotics, aren't you?" I ask him two nights later when I realize maybe I'm not crazy and he is acting peculiar.

"Didn't have a choice, not if I want a promotion one day."

"When were you going to let me know?"

He looks away. "I didn't want to worry you. You know, after what you'd been through and all."

"No. It's better that you sit and stare into space, and jump five feet into the air every time the phone rings. You're absolutely right. Don't worry me. You working with that girl Milagros? Are you Poppy again?"

"Yeah, something like that, but I'll be closer to home. Don't worry. Nothing like last time's gonna happen again. I promise. I made a full confession to Watkins before he got permission to hand my ass over to Narcotics. Me and him had a long talk and he still wants me to transfer out of Anticrime. 'Why?' I says to him. 'Why the hell are you pushing me into Narcotics?' Then he tells me it would be a good move for my career. I'm getting stale, wasting my talents, throws me a whole bunch of bullshit. Then I ask him why he's been looking out for me so much. Why is he so hot to be my friggin' rabbi?''

"The night you were shot you were with him, weren't you?" I ask. "He wasn't always a sergeant. He was your partner. And I would bet you did something really nice, like maybe save his life."

"Lisa Profeta tell you this? Christ, that lamebrain husband of hers got himself a big mouth."

"No, Lisa didn't tell me anything. I'm a smart girl, remember? Couldn't play outside till four-thirty, had to finish my homework. Besides, when you had that high fever you did a lot of talking. I just put two and two together."

"It's nothing like you think. It just—happened."

"Oh, what's the difference now? How long will you be?"

"Three weeks, a month, maybe more, maybe less. Depends."

I reach over to kiss him but he holds up his hands to block. "Don't get yourself dirty."

"Oh yes, excuse me. I have to hop back up on my pedestal."

"Jo, don't do this to me now. I tried to change. And I did change in a lot of ways. But this is real ugly and I don't want you to be a part of it. So cut me a little slack."

It can only get better. I tell myself that again and again. My worst fears are realized. Tommy's emotions, buried under layers of street filth on the job, are exposed raw and throbbing when he's home. The black ghost hovers over us once more and he's low to the ground this time. If my husband is not yelling at me, he sits and says nothing at all. Nothing.

And when he's not home, my imagination takes over. I can't get absorbed in my own day anymore. I'm typing and Tommy's being stabbed. He is shot while I toss the salad. He's in Milly's bed at two A.M. when I can't sleep. His key jingling in the lock at three A.M. terrifies me too. He heads straight to his Dewar's and takes a huge hit right from the bottle. I sit in darkness, waiting for the hinges to creak on the liquor cabinet door, waiting for the cap to slap on the shelf, waiting for the three deep gulps and the "Ah" that escapes like winter steam from the back of his throat. Last night I made the mistake of getting out of bed and handing him a glass. He grabbed it from me and smashed it hard against the living room wall. "Yeah, Trudy?" he shouted. "Next you'll be calling me a drunk. Right, Trudy?"

"I'm not your mother. And you're not your father."

"Go on back to sleep. I'm outta here."

He pulled his bicycle out of our bedroom and he looked at me with the coldest of blue eyes, eyes that had seen too much and didn't want to see any more. Old man's eyes. I held the door open as he wheeled the bike into the hall.

"Leave the fucking glass. I'll get it later. You shoulda known. An animal don't drink from a glass."

"You're not an animal. You're my husband." I forced a hug on him. He stiffened to my touch. I felt his heart pounding through his sweatshirt. He was frightened, scared to death, only he would never talk about it, not to me anyway, maybe not to anyone. "It's very late. Be careful."

"That's a real laugh, Joanna. You always had a great sense of humor." He slammed the door behind him.

Day after day I go on like this, saying the wrong things, doing what doesn't need doing. I'm just glad my father is out working most nights. He would not understand and I don't think I could offer an explanation, not being too sure about this myself. Impatiently, I wait for the end that cannot come too soon. Take me back where we were a few weeks ago. So much for happily ever after. I'm starting to believe that only occurs in Aunt Adele's books.

This Friday night in hell, all three of us are sitting in the living room and watching the eleven o'clock news. My father has a half an hour before he has to get down to Rainbow Cars. Tommy's jumpy as usual and can't find a place for himself.

"Rub my shoulders, huh?"

I rub his shoulders. At least he's civil.

"Get into my neck."

I rub his neck.

"Now my back. Come on, like you mean it. I had a real exciting day."

I picture Poppy and Milly in a crack house somewhere. Stop already, concentrate on the television. Better. Better. A woman gave birth to twins on the J train. Isn't that something?

"Let's go in our room. Then I can lay down and you can do it right."

"Wait a minute. I want to see the weather report." I don't want to be alone with him. We'll only fight. I don't want to fight. I'm so tired, worn-out by weeks of worry, weeks of tension.

As my father leaves for work he says, "Go on, Jo. Your husband's back needs rubbing."

"What's your problem?" I ask. " 'Don't touch me. Don't touch me. I'm dirty and filthy.' That's all I've been hearing from you. Now it's rub this, rub that. Go get your precious Milly to give you a massage and leave me alone."

"Shit. That's what you think's been going on? Let me tell you something. Milagros is living with someone now, a girl, Jo. She's as butch as your two bosses, so chill out, huh? Ain't that something now? Best undercover in New York is a little Puerto Rican dyke. Try and keep that one to yourself. Remember, you heard nothing from me. Besides, maybe you forget we're married now. We took vows before God, and I don't take vows lightly so you got nothing to worry about. Look, I know this hasn't been exactly easy for you but it ain't been a picnic for me neither. Those vows were for better or for worse. And believe me, Sunshine, it don't get much worse."

"I'm sorry. Okay, I'm sorry."

"Me too. For all of it." Then his eyes brighten and he grins. I hadn't seen that grin in weeks. "Hey, don't you notice the beard is gone? Took a haircut this morning too. Remember what that means?"

I nod. I smile too.

When I come out of the bathroom, he's in our room, talking on the telephone. Mrs. Gurtz. Does she call any other tenant at midnight?

"Call 911. It's my night off." Then he starts shouting. "I don't care if they kill each other. That's how hard I am now. . . . Yeah, 911." He hangs up.

"Jo, if you don't get us an unlisted number tomorrow, I'm packing up and moving back to Woodhaven."

"Can't you at least be civil to her?"

"She don't think twice about calling me up any time, day or night, and I'm supposed to be civil? The hell with her. Come here, I got a surprise for you. Check out my right pocket. A gift from Poppy."

"This is a trick, isn't it?" I dig my hand into his pocket.

"Easy there. Watch them jewels, sweetie."

"I feel some paper. How nice, you're giving me your dry cleaning ticket. How romantic."

"Come on, piece it together. We got evidence here. What did I get dry cleaned?"

I look at the ticket. "A suit."

"Good girl. Keep going. What's the date on the ticket?"

"Today's date."

"Good. Now why would I get my suit cleaned today?"

"I don't know."

"Friday morning. Took a haircut. Shaved. Wore a suit. Where did I go?"

"You went to court."

"You think I'd take a haircut for some suck-ass judge? You can do better than that."

"Tommy, please. You're leading me around like some detective."

"Ah, now we're cooking."

"You went to One Police Plaza today."

"Go for it."

"You had your interview to become a detective. Oh Tommy, why did you keep this a secret? How could you?"

"What if it didn't go good? You'd be all disappointed in me."

"I can't believe you live in this century. Haven't you heard of open lines of communication in a marriage? I feel like I'm always on a roller coaster with you. So, how did it go?"

"Just relax and I'll tell you. I sat before three bosses. They knew more about my time on the Job than I knew. They questioned me up and down for an hour. They even asked me about us. Does your wife want a big house? What do you owe on your cards? See, they wanted to make sure I'm not gonna sell what I confiscate. They don't want no dirty cops."

"So what did you tell them?"

"Tell them? Hell, I opened up my wallet. Alls they saw was cash. No credit cards. Not one. They loved that. They liked your picture too."

"So tell me already, what happened?"

"What, do you have a bus to catch? I'm in. Next week I got to report in to OCC. They basically handle narcotics investigations. And if I don't screw up, I'll be a detective third grade in around two years."

"Oh my God, you'll have a gold shield, just what you've always wanted." I hug him, pounce on him. It's so good to touch him again.

"Like I said, a gift to you from Poppy for putting up with all his crap."

"But if you're working OCC, you'll be Poppy all the time."

"No. You got nothing to worry about. From what I hear, they want me to use my brains for now, something entirely new for me."

"You said it, I didn't. Can I turn off the light now?"

"Hold on. Good investigators don't leave any loose ends. Aren't you gonna ask me about the dry cleaning ticket?"

"You wear me out. Do you know that? Since I met you, I must have aged twenty years. Okay, Mr. Detective, what's with the dry cleaning ticket?"

"Oh, that's easy. After the interview, I stopped by Teresa Ann's office. I wanted to see what she looked like in her pregnant state. So I take one look at her and I start to laugh. I couldn't help it. Jesus, she's due in three weeks and she's as fat as a house. Jo, she got so pissed at me for laughing at her, she threw a buttered bagel across her office. I'm telling you, her hormones are busting loose at the seams. Anyways, the bagel got me right on the jacket so I brought the suit in. Can you pick it up for me on Monday?"

I just look at him. He is so exasperating.

"Hey Sunshine, want to be screwed by one extremely horny future detective?"

The next morning I discover my diaphragm has a hole in it. I wake up my partner in crime and show him the damage.

"Nice," he says. "A bullseye. Perfect shot every time. Am I a stud, or what?"

"Don't flatter yourself. It was long overdue for its five-thousand-mile check-up. I just hope we don't get caught."

Marriage, my two aunts keep telling me, is a learning experience. And with this experience I learn a new rule. Never take gynecological advice from a policeman. The little ring turned pink. Pink is positive. Positive is pregnant. I check this brochure over five times and each time it says pink is positive. And Tommy wasn't worried at all. Married people have to try for kids. They have to try for years on end. Only single broads with deadbeat boyfriends get caught. No, nothing to worry about. Elation and terror wrestle each other inside my guts. Look, Dahlia, my ambivalence is showing again. Wait a second, elation is winning the match. Terror is down for the count. One, two, three . . . Who am I kidding? Tommy is going to throw a fit because we have just started to put a little money away. Very little.

I wait up for him until one in the morning. Impatiently I watch him take off his jacket, and then right before the closet door closes, I hit him with the news. Oh am I ever grateful when that look of shock gradually thaws into a grin.

My father too is pleased when I tell him toward the end of my first trimester. Grandfatherhood is very appealing to him.

Trudy is overjoyed. She doesn't get to see her little grandson Darcy too often, and our baby will be right downstairs. Everyone is happy, come to think of it, although Arlene is rather bewildered. She thinks we're very irresponsible. "Just where do you intend to put a baby?" she asks on one of her Sunday visits.

"In our room temporarily. We're next on the list for a three-bedroom. Come take a look. Matty got us the crib already."

Arlene walks into our room. Tommy's about to leave for work. I must say he has to be the best dressed cop on the force. Of course he chooses this particular moment to stick his gun into the shoulder holster, just to bring the white into Arlene's cheeks. "Sister Arlene," he drawls preacher style, "check out this crib. Jenny Lind. Matches the bedroom perfect." Then he lowers his voice and loses the preacher. "See, my brother Matty has this in at Toys 'Я' Us."

"He gets it wholesale?" Arlene leans forward. She is very interested.

"Better than wholesale," he tells her. His eyes twinkle merrily as he continues. "His friend Raymond got himself a job working nights in their warehouse. Them two lifted it right off the goddamn truck. This price can't be beat, not even in Jersey."

"You don't want to be late for work, Tommy."

I can hear him heh-heh-hehing all the way out to the elevator. And Arlene thinks he's joking.

"What about a name? Did you pick names? You're due in two months, Joanna. What are you waiting for?"

I do believe that Arlene and Gary have already chosen names for their as-of-yet conceived child. Plan ahead. The names. The room. The nursery school. Med school. Prepare. It can't hurt.

Then her next question, the question my mother would have asked had she stuck around. "What about the religion?"

"I don't know. We don't discuss it. I'd really like to celebrate all the holidays, every single one of them. Our child will have a great time here, the best of both."

"I see you have a crucifix on your dresser. What does this mean?"

"It means something to Tommy." Oh, leave me alone, Arlene.

"I wonder if our great-grandparents escaped the pogroms, crossed the ocean, and struggled in the sweatshops just for you to end up with a crucifix on your dresser."

"I wonder if our great-grandparents escaped the pogroms, crossed the ocean, and struggled in the sweatshops just for you to celebrate the sabbath with a Chinese roast pork dinner and an extra shopping day at Nordstrom. Oh, I get it now, Arlene. I marry someone out of the faith, and all of a sudden you're Jew-of-the-year."

"You take everything I say the wrong way. I just don't want the chain to end with you. We have that responsibility to preserve our heritage."

"In case you forgot, my husband has a heritage too. Should we throw that out the window?"

"No, of course not. But you really should have discussed all of these issues before the wedding. All of this should have been settled beforehand. What's with you two?"

"You have a point. Next time we'll try to do better. We'll try not to fall in love with each other. We'll try not to build a life together. You're right. It's just too confusing, Arlene. I should have done it your way. I should have gone to the same college as you. I should have majored in accounting like you. I should have gotten your job and I should have married your husband. Then and only then you would have approved of me."

"I'm not your enemy, Joanna. I'm your big sister. I want what's best for you."

"You want me to look up to you the way Mom looked up to Aunt Naomi and Aunt Ruth. You want me to hang on your every brilliant word. What is the right food to eat, Arlene? What is the right outfit to wear, Arlene? And what is your opinion on the furniture, Arlene? What temple should we join? Let's face it. You want me to bow down to you the way Mom did to her sisters. So maybe I should sign the baby away to you now so you can raise him or her in the proper Kent environment. We certainly don't want the kid associating with the wrong people. That's what Mom did, didn't she? She saved you from Sunnyside."

"What are you talking about? Don't you think I want what Mom would have wanted for you? Well, Mom isn't here anymore. Someone has to step in. My intentions are her intentions. Her good intentions."

"Well, you can take your wonderful intentions and shove them where the sun doesn't shine. It took me almost twenty-nine years, but I finally like my life. And I don't want to be saved by you or by anyone, Arlene."

"I'm sorry. I'm sorry. You're right. You're a big girl now. You want to do things your own way. I respect that. But I just want you to have everything I have. There's nothing wrong with that, is there? Really and truly, you could do worse in a sister." Then Arlene gives her extra large, Arlene sigh. "My God, I can't for the life of me figure us out. How is it that we always end up fighting?"

"Because it feels so good when we stop."

Arlene laughs. "You know if you weren't pregnant, I would've smacked you for what you said to me before."

"Oh, you would not. You might have broken a nail."

"I can still pull your hair."

"Ow. Let go. I'm in a delicate condition, you know."

"Tell that to your big mouth."

Seventeen

It amazes me to see just how far human flesh can stretch without tearing. Women are more elasticized than bra straps. My stomach, usually flat, looks pumped up to the bursting point, and I still have one more month to go. I'm a lady of leisure now, on maternity leave from Reeves and Barnett. Only Vivien Oliver knows it's going to be a permanent arrangement. And only I know he has a third interview for a manager's spot at a full-service marketing firm over on Third Avenue.

I finished my last class the end of May and decided to take the summer off. So I'll be fifty when I graduate. What's the rush? I'm still reading, still learning, and that's all that counts. I'm due in mid-July, only a year after our wedding. Irresponsible, that's us.

When the time comes, my father drives me to the hospital. Tommy meets me in Labor and Delivery. Contractions without dilation. Hours and hours of pain with no gain. Why bother? Demerol drips into my IV along with Pitocin and I sleep between the jolts of pain. Tommy holds my hand and feeds me ice chips. Ice chips minus the strawberry daiquiri. It's awful. "Shoot me, Tommy. I can't take it. Then you can shoot Dr. Adair. He promised me a spinal. I wasn't supposed to feel a thing. Owwwwww. I want to be numb. Make the hurt go away."

"Push. Push. One more push," Dr. Adair orders. "Good. Good. Hey. What do we have here? A girl. You have a girl! Congratulations."

I don't care if it's a goddamn puppy as long as it's out. Have we been here twenty hours already? Now look. This is charming. Scissors, needles, and thread. Snip. Snip. Let's see you embroider me a perfect bullion star and anchor down there, Dr. Adair, you liar. She's crying. My baby is crying. What a soft, little cry. "Tommy, we have a baby."

Finally, after the washing, measuring, weighing, and whatever else, the whole medical crew clears out to give the new family a few minutes together. I peer down at this small pink blanketed person. She has a tiny pixie face and a head full of light, wispy hair. I hold her close and listen to her breathe. My mother must have held me like this too.

Tommy sits beside us and his burned-up, Cajun-blackened heart must have done some healing today because he is choking back waves of tears. I wipe his eyes with my free hand. "Oh, go ahead. Even a tough guy like you is allowed to let go once every twenty-five years. Tommy, it's okay."

"She's so beautiful," he sobs. "Jo—Jo . . . I . . ."

"I know, I love you too. Here, take her from me. I have no strength in my arms. I feel her slipping."

He sits on my bed with our daughter held close to his chest, wiping tears away with the back of his sleeve, rocking back and forth. "Listen up," he tells her. "I'm always gonna be there for you, no matter how tough times get. I'm not ever gonna get shit faced drunk and beat up on your mother. You're never gonna come home from school and find my closet empty and my razor off the edge of the sink. I'm gonna do better by you, Little Sunshine. I swear. I'm gonna be a good father. This job I'm not gonna screw up. You have my word."

"And I'll try to do better too," I say. "I'll try not to

blame your father for everything that goes wrong in my life. Because your father may not believe it, but he is the best thing that ever happened to my life. And I promise, I'll try to let you find your own way, no matter where it takes you and how long it takes you to get there."

"She's so little, Jo. And it's so ugly out there. I'll have to protect her from the outside."

"It's beautiful outside too."

A nurse comes in and puts the baby in an isolet. "Come on, miss. We're taking a ride to the nursery. We'll introduce you around to the other babies. Ooh, this one's a keeper. You hungry, hon?" she turns to me. "Labor is hard work and there's no fifteen-minute coffee break."

"Yeah, that would be nice. I am kind of hungry. Could I get some breakfast cereal?"

"Breakfast cereal? Sure, why not? Frosted Flakes okay?"

"Make it two," Tommy tells her, the serious look gone from his face.

"Oh, so the daddy wants a bowl of cereal too? Isn't that cute? Tell me, Mr. McClellan, what was it that you did all these hours?"

"I watched."

We name her Agnes May, after the two women who gave us so much and left us with such a void after their departure. Aggie, we call her most of the time, the Little Mope, when she's being wicked.

MOTHER'S DAY,
NINETEEN MONTHS LATER

Dear Mom,

I'm writing this letter one day after our cemetery visit. I know you didn't feel any need to leave us a note but I would like to get these few thoughts down on paper.

As I've mentioned to you in our daily conscience-to-conscience dialogue, I married Tommy McClellan and you have a beautiful granddaughter, Aggie May.

There's not a day that goes by that I don't think about you and wonder Why? I know it's kind of late, but tell me, could I have done anything to prevent it? Tell me. I don't know. One bolt of lightning for no, two for yes. Sunny outside? All right, maybe next time. I try so hard to make myself tough. It would be much easier, you know, but your daughter is still a mush, much to her husband's relief. Sometimes I swell up with anger. What a stupid, selfish thing you did. Admit it. Can't you at least admit it? Well thank you. Thank you so much. Now, we're getting somewhere.

Let me be the very first to tell you that Arlene is expecting in October. It must have been pressure from the neighbors. You see, Mom, Arlene and Gary weren't meeting their Fisher Price quota. Yes, it's a joke. You got it, just like my father.

I do want you to know I'm very happy with Tommy. You didn't think I would be but I am. How's that for an I-told-you-so. He's a wonderful father. He and Aggie are wild for each other. We bought this little seat that attaches to the back of his bike and we go flying down Skillman Avenue together. She has a helmet, so don't worry.

And don't go fretting about his language either. He's very good about covering her ears when he lets loose with his mouth. In fact whenever Aggie sees her daddy, she covers her own ears.

He's a super husband too. You'll have to take my word for it but we do have a lot in common, now more than ever. Most importantly we have our love and our dreams and nothing will ever take them away. Can you believe it? We're sailing under the two bridges on a preowned fourteen-foot Laser sloop. I've convinced Tommy to take the $2,500 loan for an anniversary present to ourselves. It's taken a lot of persistent convincing but I've worn the man down. I told him it would be good therapy for me, and for me he did it. True, it was devious on my part and it did go against Tommy's absolutely no-loan mentality, but I didn't want him going through life disappointed, so here we are. Can you see us, Mom? We took sailing lessons and we actually own a boat. We are just like those lower-upper-class people in the New York Times *magazine section, only we're not wearing poly cotton knit shirts with little animals embroidered on them.*

I hope you are proud of me too. I'm going to college at night, and one of these years I'll have a bachelor's in English. Credentials yes, but like I told you before, it's not the degree that I'm after. It's all those books out there just hanging around waiting for me to open them. And I'm not afraid of them anymore, not even afraid of missing the symbolism. Professor Sterne told the whole class that a book has to work on more than one level, anyway. And whatever I read for school, I share with Tommy. He has been very supportive of me. I invite Daddy to read with us too, but he always makes up some excuse. It's too late, he tells us. Go on without him.

Why did you lock him out all those years? He could have taken part in all that cultural stuff you claimed to hold so dear. He would have done anything for you, anything for a tiny smidgen of your respect. But that's it, right, Mom? In your eyes he was a failure as a provider and that meant he was a failure period. He just wasn't Uncle Marc, was he? He couldn't buy you your sisters' fancy clothes and send you off on pricey trips, but he worshiped you. That pile of bills and papers he kept hidden in the shopping bag proved it. He was dangling over the edge of bankruptcy and he kept it all to himself, didn't want you to worry.

And look how you repaid him—you ruined the rest of his life. He's not the same, believe me, none of us are. You've made failures of all of us. Are you aware of the guilt I'm carrying around? I was so busy worrying about Tommy and the dangers he was facing, I neglected you. There you were, self-destructing within the walls of our own apartment, and I missed it, missed it completely. I missed your black ghost, Mom. Forgive me.

I hear your voice all the time. Your words sail around in my head. Look at you, you say. Just like I told you. You'll end up in the building for the rest of your life. Look at you, making the same mistakes I made. But, can you hear my voice, Mom? No, I say.

They may carry me out of the building in a pine box, but I will not make your mistakes. I will not hold my husband

responsible for my own shortcomings. I will not be intimi-
dated by the wealth and credentials of others, the way you
were. I have learned from your mistakes. And when I dream,
you are with me. We're in Sunnyside, together, all of us.
What I wouldn't give to wake up and hear your footsteps on
the carpet.

Yes, yes, I hear your cries of protest. You say, Joanna, you
can't understand. You're young yet. You haven't worked a lifetime and ended up with nothing.

You're right, I'll never understand. You had two daughters
who loved you. Don't you think we would have seen you down
to Florida? And let me tell you something, aside from Disney
World, you can keep it. You know what our kitchen was like
that day in August when you got it in your head to bake the
chicken with the cornflake crumbs when it was 93 degrees outside? That's Florida in the summer.

Look, can you blame me for being angry once in a while?
Aggie May will always be one grandma shy. And she gives us
all such joy, Mom. She adores Aunt Adele and Uncle Jack.
They babysit for her sometimes when I'm at school or at work.

Uh huh, I'm still a secretary, but on a part-time basis over
on Northern Boulevard. I like it. I like being a secretary. Don't
ever tell me it's nothing to be ashamed of. God, do you say that
to Arlene too? Do you say, "Arlene, being a comptroller is
nothing to be ashamed of?" Okay. Apology accepted.

I'm finally proud of the way I earn a living, proud of what
I am, proud of where I'm from. I AM A SECRETARY, a lower-
lower-middle class super secretary from Sunnyside, Queens. We
may step into the City now and then to visit a museum or
see a concert, but it's not where we belong. We belong in the
neighborhood. We are safe amongst our friends.

It's funny, but it all came together on a trip to the supermarket, of all places. Between aisles five and seven Tommy got
me to admit that I really liked Stove Top stuffing and Ritz
crackers with Cheez Whiz, Pop-Tarts, and Twinkies. You'd better believe I'd take a Twinkie over some fancy fruit sorbet any
day of the week.

Aside from the pearls, my faux days are over for good. True,
I'm still peeking into people's cabinets, but now I'm relieved

when I see that smiling package of Kool Aid. It means I'm with my own people.

The hell with that social class pyramid. Why does one class have to sit smugly on the backs of the class they left not too long ago? If it were up to me, I'd redesign the whole thing. I'd stick each class next to the other, no top, no bottom. That's right. No, you're not listening. Can't you listen for once? I do not want to teach. Never, never, never.

Oh, before I forget, we all moved across the hall to 4G into the three-bedroom. Tommy finagled a three-year lease out of Mr. Santini, unheard of these days. Do yourself a real big favor, try not to imagine that conversation. Trust me, you'll rest easier.

Oh, did I tell you that Arlene went all out and gave her niece some present? She accessorized her room in a Raggedy Ann and Andy theme. She even had the wallpaper custom-painted so Raggedy Ann's shirt coordinates with Aggie's carpet. Daddy thought she should be committed when he got wind of that, but Arlene said that this is commonplace in Kent. It makes me glad I'm still in Sunnyside. She'll be out to see you one of these days. The leader of her survivor's group recommends the confrontation, so prepare yourself. You're in for a good whine.

Before I forget, Sandy Sussman is engaged to be married. He met this lovely Filipino nurse in the hospital emergency room when he broke his ankle playing tennis. She has a seven-year-old daughter from a previous marriage, which didn't please the senior Sussmans too much at first. They came around, though, after a while, and I'm glad for Sandy's sake.

Sometimes what looks so wrong can end up so right. I'm learning that life doesn't come in a neatly wrapped package. Life can be messy sometimes, as well you know. It's crumbs on the floor and stains in the sink. But it's all we got, Mom. It's all we got.

Well, I'm about to sign off. Sailing is really a two-person operation. Tommy sends you his regards. He wants to know if his Nana's tips are any better on the angels than they were on the horses. Gabriel in the fifth? Cute, Mom, very cute.

Oh, you'll never believe it. Aunt Adele and Uncle Jack hit the lottery. No, not the big prize, but they did win enough to take a suite last weekend at the Sheraton Center. We drove them into the City Friday night. A bellhop took their bags but Tommy and I followed them in anyway. We sat down near the front desk and just watched as the two of them checked in. Oh, they were so excited. Uh-huh, and when they were about ready to go up to their room, we rushed over and requested their autographs.

A group of people gathered around them, wondering just who these two were. "They're big-time English royalty," Tommy said loudly. "He's absolutely right," I said. "They spend most of their days as guests in one of the queen's castles, you know, the white one. I'll bet they just popped in for a fund-raiser." I winked at Tommy and he bowed and I curtsied and we all went on our merry way. It was great because this one time Aunt Adele thought we were nuts and—oh forget it, you just had to be there.

Hey, did I tell you? They closed Savannah Gardens. Your sisters cried buckets.

So Mom, before I cast these pages into the sea, I want you to really look at us. So give me your undivided attention, will you? Look at us! We are so happy together, in spite of all our differences. Oh Mom, take a moment. It's such a glorious day. Can you feel the wind tease the sails of the Sweet A.M? Isn't it beautiful out here, the sun flirting openly with the water? We're drifting now, just me and Tommy, drifting out to the Sound like two carefree Gypsies. No, no—Aggie May is keeping her grandpa Sol company this afternoon.

Lost? Not us. Our tiller is strong and we know where we're headed. When the sun stretches west in the sky, we will follow it. West we will travel, coaxing the sails toward our piece of this earth. Uh-huh, don't worry. You know we're always back by supper. We'll never let the tide take us too far from home.

All my love,
Joanna

THE BEST IN FICTION
BY PULITZER PRIZE-WINNING AUTHOR

ALISON LURIE

THE TRUTH ABOUT LORIN JONES
70807-8/ $11.00 US
"Funny, intelligent...entertaining...
confirms Ms. Lurie's stature as our leading comic novelist"
The New York Times

FOREIGN AFFAIRS
70990-2/ $12.00 US/ $16.00 Can
"Wildly funny and genuinely moving"
Chicago Sun-Times

WOMEN AND GHOSTS
72501-0/ $9.00 US/ $12.00 Can
"Superb...enchanting...provocative"
Cleveland Plain Dealer